D0396512

PRAISE FOR *NEW YORK TIMES* BESTSELLING AUTHOR MARY McNEAR AND HER AMAZING BUTTERNUT LAKE BOOKS. Her peers agree . . . BUTTERNUT LAKE is a special place!

"*Butternut Lake* is so beautifully rendered, you'll wish it was real. McNear takes the reader on an emotional journey with this story of second chances, starting over, and the healing power of love. A book to relax, enjoy, and savor any time of year, but especially during the long, lazy days of summer."

—#1 *New York Times* bestselling author
Susan Wiggs

"A great, emotional read for every woman who must face the past before moving forward."

—#1 *New York Times* bestselling author
Sherryl Woods on *Up at Butternut Lake*

"A delicious setting and a heroine to cheer for, *Moonlight on Butternut Lake* is my favorite kind of book, one that treads that pleasurable line between romance and women's fiction. Enjoy!"

—*New York Times* bestselling author
Susan Elizabeth Phillips

"*The Space Between Sisters* explores the complex relationship between sisters, their differences, their mirrored history, their love and support of one another. This triumphant story had me reading until the wee hours of the morning."

—#1 *New York Times* bestselling author
Debbie Macomber

The Secrets We Carried

Also by Mary McNear

The
Secrets We Carried

A Butternut Lake Novel

Mary McNear

WILLIAM MORROW

An Imprint of HarperCollins*Publishers*

FIRST EDITION

Designed by Diahann Sturge

Library of Congress Cataloging-in-Publication Data has been applied for.

ISBN 978-0-06-269927-5 (paperback)
ISBN 978-0-06-284610-5 (library edition)

18 19 20 21 22 LSC 10 9 8 7 6 5 4 3 2 1

To Andrew Aldrich and Fabienne Blanc. For keeping me sane and, more important, making me laugh.

The Secrets We Carried

PROLOGUE

Hiding behind Gabriel's closet door, she heard them talking. She heard it all. Dazed, she sank down on her knees, somehow managing to gather up the rest of her things. Before Gabriel returned, she'd pushed open the window and climbed out, falling the few feet to the yard below. She started running, struggling for traction in the slushy snow. She heard Gabriel, concerned, calling after her—"Quinn. Quinn!"—but his voice was far away, as though it were coming from inside a tunnel.

She ran like she'd never run before, her long hair streaming behind her, the wind—her wind— whistling past her. She ran through backyards still dreary in the morning light, past the parked cars on Glover Street, past a woman walking her dog, past a pickup truck rumbling to life in a driveway. Panic rose in her. She pushed herself harder. She had to get to her house. By the time she turned onto Main Street, her lungs were burning, and she could hear the blood pounding in her ears. She ran past the drugstore, where Mr. Coates was opening the awning, and past Pearl's, where the smell of coffee drifted out onto the sidewalk. By the time she reached Webber Street and the yellow split-level house where she lived with her dad, she'd slowed down. She stopped, doubled over, on the lawn, under the beech tree whose branches spread in all directions, beside the birdbath her late mother had put there, years ago. She could hardly draw in a breath. Nothing would ever be the same again . . .

CHAPTER 1

Why am I here? Quinn thought, sitting in her idling car in the parking lot of the Butternut Motel in a cold, bluish twilight in late March. *Here* was the town of Butternut, Minnesota, her home for the first eighteen years of her life, and by all accounts an idyllic and lovely place, with quaint shops, small houses, and a beautiful lake surrounded by great northern pines. It was her home, if home was the place you were born and grew up. But for Quinn it was also the place she'd avoided for the last ten years.

Who was it who wrote "you can't go home again"? she wondered now. Thomas Wolfe, she decided, and, for a moment, she wasn't in a motel parking lot but was back in her AP English class in the fall of her senior year, Mrs. McKinley droning on about autobiographical fiction while the boy at the desk next to Quinn doodled an image from *World of Warcraft* in the margin of his notebook. *No*, she thought, *Thomas Wolfe was wrong*. At least in her case. You *could* go home again, but maybe you *shouldn't* go home again. Maybe you should listen to the same voice that, a decade earlier, had said, as you packed your suitcases after graduation, *Leave, leave now, and don't come back*.

She wanted to put her car in reverse, but she didn't. She wouldn't go. Not yet. She'd do what she'd come here to do. She'd promised herself she wouldn't run this time. She'd stay for the weekend. Probably longer. She turned off the car's ignition. The engine stilled, and the heating vents, which had been piping warm air into the car, went cool. But she didn't get out yet. She cocked her head and looked at the view through the windshield. It wasn't encouraging. The Butternut Motel, a single-story building whose twelve rooms faced the parking lot, had struck Quinn, when she'd last lived in town, as charming and retro, with emerald-green paint, bright white trim, and an emerald-and-white-striped canopy that shaded the front office and had *Butternut Motel* printed on it in a jaunty cursive. Now, well . . . now the whole thing looked a little worse for wear, though in fairness that might have been the season. Mounds of tired snow separated the parking lot from the sidewalk that fronted the motel, and the bare shrubs that stood in for landscaping between the rooms shook, disconsolately, in the wind. Saddest of all was the plastic table and chair that stood sentry outside of each room. Who was sitting outdoors when the nights were still below freezing, and the days barely edging into the forties?

When the car started to get cold, Quinn got out. She lifted

her suitcase from the trunk and wheeled it over to the office, where, through the windows, she could see a woman sitting at a reception counter. As Quinn pushed open the swinging glass door, though, her eyes slid past the woman and settled instead behind her where, on a table, there was a wire cage with a ferret inside of it. She flinched. She *hated* ferrets. Her neighbor had raised them when she was growing up, and she'd always found there to be something faintly repulsive about them.

"That's Hank Williams," the woman said, turning around to look at the ferret too. "Believe it or not," she went on, "last year, one of our guests checked out of their room and left him behind."

"I believe it," Quinn said, though she smiled as she said it.

The woman smiled back. She was young—early twenties, Quinn guessed—and the general impression she gave was one of paleness. Pale hair, pale eyes, pale skin. Even her lips, when she smiled at Quinn, were pale. "Fortunately for Hank," she confided to Quinn now, "—the Hank's for Hank Williams, 'cause he just goes crazy when he hears country music—the owner, Mr. Tremblay, took a real shine to him. So, he put his cage in here, where he'd always have someone to keep him company." She added, without a trace of humor, "It's a selling point for some people, I think. Especially when we put his little leash on and let him walk around. You know, let him have the run of the place." She paused. "You don't remember me, do you?" she asked Quinn.

"Do we know each other?" Quinn said, realizing that she did indeed look familiar.

"Well," the woman said, brushing pale bangs off a pale forehead. "I grew up in Winton. You went to high school with my brother, though. Liam Schultz. I think he was a couple of years behind you. I was in middle school when you graduated. I'm Carla Schultz."

"Riiight," Quinn said. The Schultzes. She remembered them now. They'd lived in Winton, the next town over, but their school had emptied into the same high school as Quinn's. There'd been several children in that family, as she recalled, and they'd all been equally pallid.

"I couldn't believe it when I saw your name on the reservations for today," Carla continued. "And then I was, like, 'oh, yeah, she's here for—'" Something stopped her, though. "Here for the thing," she said.

"The thing." Quinn nodded, hoping Carla wouldn't say any more. She didn't want to talk about it. An awkward silence followed, interrupted by a gnawing sound emanating from Hank Williams's cage. Quinn took her wallet out of her handbag, extracted a credit card from it, and slid it across the counter. "It's for two nights," she said. Carla nodded and ran the card.

"There's free Wi-Fi," she said to Quinn. "And a free continental breakfast in here every morning. Have you had dinner yet?" she asked, handing the card back to Quinn.

"Not yet, no," Quinn said. "But I'm not that hungry."

"No? Well, there's the Corner Bar, three blocks down. You remember that, of course." Quinn nodded. What she *really* wanted now was a drink. A glass of pinot grigio would be nice.

"How late is it open?" Quinn asked.

"Until ten tonight," Carla said. "And if you'd prefer to eat in your room, you can call in a take-out order. Otherwise, we've got vending machines around the corner from room twelve. One of them has a chicken-flavored noodle soup in it that's not too bad."

"Oh, well, chicken *flavored*," Quinn said. "I don't know if I can pass that up." But Carla stared back at her, a serious expression on her face. No, Quinn didn't think she'd be eating chicken-flavored soup when the Corner Bar was down the street. She'd always loved that place; the atmosphere was casual and friendly and the bartender, Marty, was a local institution, as was the Corner Burger, the only thing on the menu that anyone ever ordered. She wanted to stop there at least once before she left Butternut.

"You're in room six," Carla said, taking a key out of a drawer and handing it to her. It was a real key, not a key card. When had she last seen one of these at a motel? Never, she decided, but Hank Williams had stopped chewing on whatever he'd been chewing on and was standing up on his hind feet and looking at her challengingly, as if he knew how much she disliked him and his kind, so Quinn thanked Carla and headed to room 6.

When she let herself in, her morale sank a little lower. It wasn't the *worst* motel room she'd ever stayed in, and maybe, when this place had opened—in the '50s?—it had had a kind of charm. But it had been redecorated since then, redecorated during a decade that favored heavy faux-walnut furniture, cheap brass light fixtures, and aggressively ugly bedspreads and curtains that were neither fabric nor plastic but some shiny compromise between the two. Quinn towed her suitcase inside, placed it on the luggage rack, and hung up her coat in the closet. She checked the bathroom—small but serviceable—and the bedside table drawer. Yep, there was the Gideon Bible. She reached to turn on the bedside lamp—more brass—and was amused to find it bolted down to the table. Who would *ever* consider taking it, unless, of course, they also decided to take the artificial potted fern standing in the corner? There were framed photographs on the walls, too, photographs of what appeared to be the local lakes, but the colors in them were so bright and garish—autumn leaves! blue water!—that they somehow made the scenery look as fake as the room.

She sat down on the bed, pulled her cell phone out of her pocket, and made a call. "Quinny?" she heard a moment later. She smiled. Her dad was the only person who'd ever been allowed to call her that. "Are you there?" he asked.

"I'm here," she said. A big part of her, though, wanted to be back in Evanston, Illinois, in her safe, sunny second-floor apartment, not far from Lake Michigan, but *plenty* far from Butternut.

"And how is it?" he asked. He sounded casual, but Quinn could hear the undercurrent of concern in his voice.

"I don't know, Dad. I just got here. I'm going to get through it, though," she added, as much for his benefit as for hers. "I'm only committed to this weekend. Then, we'll see." What she didn't say was that she felt as if a kind of darkness was encroaching, right on the edge of her consciousness. But she couldn't explain this to her dad. "Oh, and by the way," she said, wanting to change the subject, "there's a pet ferret in the lobby of the Butternut Motel."

"Oh, God," he said. "You hate ferrets. I still don't understand, though, why you're staying at that motel. The Johnsons would have loved to have had you." Like her, Quinn's father had left Butternut ten years ago. Unlike her, he'd stayed in touch with his friends from there.

"I know that, Dad. And it's true, this place is a little depressing, but"—she glanced around the room—"it suits my mood. Besides, I don't think I'd be very good company at someone's house."

"You're always good company," he said.

"How's Johanna?" Quinn asked. Johanna was her stepmother, of whom she was very fond. Quinn's mother had died when she was too young to remember her, and her father hadn't remarried until he'd met Johanna, seventeen years later. Since this was after Quinn had left for college, the three of them had been spared the challenge of building a life together. What they'd gotten, instead, when Quinn visited them, was a comfortable family of three. Comfortable because Quinn liked Johanna—who was approachable, warm, and down to earth—but also because the two of them shared something in common: they both adored Gene, Quinn's father.

"Johanna's fine," Gene said. "She's right here. She sends her love."

"How was the show today?" Quinn asked. "Did Johanna sell any quilts?" Johanna's quilts were beautiful, and because of them, she and Gene had embraced a nomadic lifestyle, spending part of the year at their house in Winona, in southern Minnesota, and the other part of it on the road, in their Airstream trailer, attending quilting shows all over the country.

"The show went well," Gene said. "Johanna sold three of the cathedral windows quilts," he added, mentioning one of the more difficult patterns Johanna did.

"Oh, I love those," Quinn said, lying back on the bed. And she imagined her dad and Johanna in their cozy trailer, surrounded by quilts, a pot of Johanna's beef stew—or something comparably delicious—bubbling on the stove, a loaf of bread baking in the oven. *I miss you two*, she almost said, but she caught herself. She wanted to visit them, but this was the busiest time of year for them. They spent most of their spring and summer on the craft fair circuit and wouldn't be home again until September.

"Did I tell you that Theo suggested I write about this?" she said, changing the subject. "You know, the dedication ceremony tomorrow. Write about it for myself, at least. Not necessarily for publication." Theo Grayson was Quinn's editor at *Great Lakes Living*, the online magazine she freelanced for. She'd written so many articles for him, in fact, that she was practically a staff writer.

"Really?" he said. "Just the dedication, or the accident, too?"

"All of it," Quinn said, running a hand over the bedspread. It felt more like plastic than fabric.

Her father was quiet. "Would you be in it?" he asked. "I mean, would you be a part of the story?"

Quinn hesitated. "I think that's the idea. To write a personal essay. He thinks the harder it is to write about something that's happened to you, the more important it is to write about it. He also thinks I should take a couple of weeks off. He says I work too hard. Imagine that," she added in a joking tone. But it was more than that. Theo was worried about her. And the truth, however uncomfortable for Quinn, was that she was worried about herself too. Since winter she'd been struggling through even the simplest routines in her life. And the dreams, the dreams had begun again. The last time this had happened, back in college . . . But she pushed the memory of that time in her life away now. It couldn't happen again. She wouldn't fall apart. She wouldn't let it happen. That's why she was here. For reasons she didn't entirely understand, she felt that returning to Butternut—which had long seemed to be the problem—was part of the solution.

"I think taking a little time off is a good idea, Quinn," her dad said. "I don't even remember the last time you took a real vacation." He paused. "What did you say to Theo, though? About the personal essay?"

"I told him . . . I told him I didn't know. I mean, that's not my specialty. And I'm not sure I want it to be." She rolled onto her stomach. It was true. *Personal* wasn't her specialty. *Writing*, on the other hand, was. And since she *wanted* to write, *needed* to write, *must* write in order to feel complete, she knew she would write something during this trip to Butternut. And she couldn't imagine how, in doing this, she could avoid the personal.

"Well, whatever you write, I'd love to read it," her dad said. "And by the way—stop me if I'm being too personal—is this thing with Theo an editor-writer thing or something more?"

"It's not clear yet," Quinn said. "I'll let you know before Thanksgiving, though." She smiled. It was a standing joke in their family of three that Quinn never brought the same man twice to Johanna and Gene's Thanksgiving dinners. Although for the last two years, she'd come alone.

He chuckled. "Well, you have lots of time to figure that out." Then, after a moment of silence between them, he said, "Quinn, I wasn't sure, at first, about your going back to Butternut. I didn't know if it was a good idea. But I'm behind you now. This whole thing, though, this facing the past, it might be harder than you think."

"I know, Dad," she said, thinking to herself that even though she'd told him this was her plan—to return to Butternut and "face" the past—she wasn't entirely sure what facing the past entailed.

"I'll let you go, Quinny," he said.

"I love you. And tell Johanna I love her, too."

"I will. And it goes without saying we love you."

After she put her phone down, she remained, for several minutes, lying on the bed, staring at the hideous pattern on the bedspread. She wanted to fold it up and hide it in the closet, but she didn't have the energy. She'd only stopped twice during her ten-hour drive from Evanston, once for coffee and gas and another time for fast food. When she finally stirred now, it was to get an envelope out of her handbag. She sat down on the edge of the bed and examined it. The postmark on the envelope was from Butternut, but there was no return address and the handwriting—a neat cursive—was unfamiliar. The sender had addressed it to Quinn LaPointe at *Great Lakes Living*, and the magazine had forwarded it to her Evanston apartment. When she'd opened this envelope the first time, several weeks ago, standing at the kitchen counter of her apartment, her earbuds still plugged in from her evening run, she'd tipped the contents out and discovered there was no letter inside, no note, no explanation, just a clipping about a dedication ceremony from the *Butternut Express*. She'd felt, for a moment, while reading the clipping, the kitchen floor soften beneath her, as if her running shoes had sunk a few inches into the linoleum. It was a form of emotional vertigo, she knew. Now she took the clipping out again, unfolded it, and read the first few lines:

A Dedication for Three Young Men
Who Died Ten Years Ago

A special ceremony is scheduled for Saturday, March 25, 11:00 A.M., at the Shell Lake Beach and Picnic Area off Birch Road. A dedication stone will be unveiled and Jack Mulvaney, the Northern Superior High School principal; Jane Steadman, the Butternut mayor; and Jeffrey Dobbs, Dominic Dobbs's father, will all speak.

A short article followed this, but Quinn didn't read it now. She folded the clipping and put it back in the envelope. *Who sent this to me?* she wondered, not for the first time. Someone who wanted her to know about the dedication, obviously.

Someone who wanted her to come back to Butternut for it. But who? It was getting dark outside now, and she considered turning on some lights but instead lay back down on the bed. She wanted to rest for a minute. Then she'd get up and find some dinner.

It must have been more than an hour later when she woke with a start. The room was dark now and the light from the motel's parking lot cast a yellow band onto the floor beside the window. She sat up. She felt feverish. She'd had one of the dreams.

Jake sat in the front seat of his old blue Ford truck. It was nighttime, and the truck's headlights illuminated the leafless birch trees and the frozen expanse of Shell Lake before it. Smoke from the truck's exhaust pipe drifted into the starry sky and mixed with burning filaments of ash from the nearby bonfire. Jake's window was rolled down and music from the radio sounded tinny in the cold night air. Quinn stood a short distance away. Someone, a shadowy presence, stood somewhere behind her. Jake leaned out of the truck window and called to her, "Quinn. Quinn! Don't let me die."

But she had. She shivered now, violently. She already knew how that night had ended.

CHAPTER 2

The next morning, after a restless night's sleep, Quinn picked up the "continental breakfast"—a Styrofoam cup of coffee and a plastic-wrapped Danish—from the motel's office and drove the few blocks into town. With one hand holding her too-hot coffee and the other hand on the steering wheel of her Subaru, she cruised down Butternut's Main Street. It had changed since her senior year in high school. Or, more likely, *she* had changed. Back then, it had still held all the small-town attractions of childhood; the rubber ball vending machine outside the variety store; the spinning red leather stools at the counter at the local coffee shop, Pearl's; the always fascinating collection of glass animals at Butternut Drugs.

But now she noticed, as if for the first time, how pretty it was, with its candy-colored striped awnings, cheerful window boxes, and painted wooden benches. In another couple of

months or so, when the piles of old snow had melted and the
window box flowers were in bloom, it would be even prettier.
And that would go for Butternut Lake, too. Less than a mile
from town, it was a spring-fed, twelve-mile-long lake that Butternut residents firmly believed was the most beautiful lake in
a state that had thousands of them. And the tourists and the
summer people who flocked there between Memorial Day and
Labor Day agreed.

Stopped at the only stoplight in town, Quinn checked her
reflection in the rearview mirror. Her long, honey-brown hair
was pulled back in a ponytail, and her hazel eyes were green
in the morning light. Well, at least she didn't *look* as if she'd
barely slept last night, she thought, as the light changed and
she turned left on Glover Street, heading in the opposite direction of Shell Lake. The dedication ceremony wouldn't start for
another hour, and there was something she wanted to do first.

As she drove out of town, the businesses and then the
houses thinned out and then Glover Street turned into Route
89, and she saw the TOWN OF BUTTERNUT, POPULATION 1,200
sign receding in her rearview mirror. Then the countryside
opened onto fields patchy with almost melted snow that were
edged by pine trees and punctuated by the occasional farmhouse. As promised, the day was cold, and while the weather
report was calling for sunshine later, it was overcast now, and
the light that fell on the fields and trees had a muted, gray
quality to it.

Quinn knew this road by heart. There was the tepee-shaped
school bus shelter at the end of a farmhouse's long driveway,

there was the funny crooked oak tree in the middle of an otherwise empty field, looking as if someone had been in a hurry and had left it behind, by accident, and there was the hand-painted billboard for a snowmobile dealership that had closed before she could even remember it being open. She'd driven this route every day from the time she'd gotten her license at sixteen to the time she'd graduated from high school.

Quinn slowed as she drove past the TOWN OF WINTON sign and the high school came into view. It wasn't an imposing building, but in a landscape this flat, with so little else to compete with it, it nonetheless had that effect. Northern Superior High School had been built in 1930, when Americans still had a reverence for public education, and the two-story brick building, with a white stone arch over the entranceway and two white stone columns flanking it, spoke to the seriousness of the work to be done inside. A less visible, modern addition, consisting of a cafeteria, a gymnasium, and science labs, had been added in the 1970s. The nearby towns of Butternut, Auburn, Baldwin, and Red Rock all fed into the high school, bringing the student body to almost six hundred.

Quinn had intended to drive by the high school, but once she saw the building she wanted, suddenly, to go inside. She turned into the driveway, hoping there would be someone there who could let her in, but when she pulled up in front she saw that one of the front doors was propped open. She parked and hurried up a front walkway lined with bronze-based light posts with white globelike lamps and up the wide, stone steps.

"Hello?" she called inside. Her voice echoed in the empty

front hall, but, a moment later, a maintenance man came into view down one of the hallways, wheeling a garbage can ahead of him.

"Yes?" he called back.

"Mr. . . ." Quinn ransacked her memory. "Watts?" she asked, as he came closer.

"Uh-huh," he said, rolling up to her. He looked slightly more gray, and grizzled, than he had a decade ago.

"My name is Quinn LaPointe," she said. "I was in the class of 2007. I'm back in town and I wanted to take a look around." She smiled. "You know, old time's sake, that kind of thing."

He stared at her, inscrutably. "Yeah. Okay," he said. "But just for a few minutes. I'm about to lock up."

"I'll hurry," she promised, coming into the front hall, a high-ceilinged room with pale pink marble walls, and a red-and-brown-tiled floor shiny with wear. Mr. Watts disappeared down another hallway, and Quinn walked, her high-heeled boots clicking on the tiles, past the administrative offices on her left, and the entrance to the auditorium on her right, to the far wall, where there was a series of glass display cases.

The first of these featured the high school's "Wall of Fame," and Quinn paused to look at the photos and bios of several illustrious alumni. More recently, these had included: a graduate of the class of '97 who was now a state senator; a woman, class of '04, who was now one of the hosts of a local morning show in the Twin Cities; and a member of the class of '06 who'd played baseball, briefly, in the major leagues. Quinn smiled. At Northern Superior High School, you had to take your heroes where you could find them. The rest of the cases were devoted to the school's athletic glories, and while Quinn hadn't bothered to pay attention to them while she was there, now she moved down the row of them, trailing her fingers over the polished glass. "Go Bobcats," she whispered to the photographs of championship teams, and to the pennants, the plaques, the trophies, and the two or three retired jerseys on display in them. The 1950s were obviously the heyday for the Bobcats, but every subsequent decade had brought some honors with it, however fleeting. When she got to the '90s—the boy's wrestling team had held sway—she felt a heaviness settling into her limbs. *Coward*, she scolded herself, pushing on.

She stopped in front of the second-to-last case, where, on the fourth shelf, right at eye level, in a silver frame leaning against the back of the cabinet, there was a color photograph of the 2006–2007 cross-country team. Twenty-four boys, in three rows of eight, each of them exuding youth and health from every pore, and, in the middle of the middle row, team captain Jake Lightman. She leaned closer, her breath clouding the glass in front of her. Jake must have just taken a shower; the habitual cowlick to the right of his part, the cowlick that Quinn had loved, was still combed down. Otherwise, the picture was pure Jake, so vital, so full of life. His head tilted back, his dark gold eyes staring straight into the camera as if he had nothing to hide, and his smile, his smile as natural, and as easy, as his running form had been. She wanted to slide the glass door open and get a closer look at the photograph. Years ago, she'd put away her photographs of Jake—most of them were in a storage box in her father's garage—and seeing this one now made her wish she could look at all of them again.

"I'm sorry," Quinn whispered to Jake's photograph. "Can you forgive me?" She felt a tightness, a pain, building in her chest, a feeling that, most of the time, she had learned to breathe through. She looked to the right of the photograph, where a trophy announced the team as *State Champions, Boys Cross-Country, 2006*, and a plaque next to it read *Jake Lightman, 2006, Runner of the Year.*

Then she forced herself to keep moving, and she walked down the long corridor to the left, her heels click, click, clicking on the tiled floors as she passed rows of pea-green lockers, several bulletin boards, and classroom doors. There was something else she wanted to see. She stopped in front of a door labeled *Communications Room* and tried the handle. It was unlocked. Once again, she'd gotten lucky, if luck was in fact what it was. She turned on the lights and scanned the room. It looked totally different. Updated, reordered, and rearranged. She went inside anyway, to the back of the room, where she and Gabriel Shipp had had their newspaper "office." This had consisted of a blue couch with the stuffing leaking out, a scuffed coffee table to put your feet up on, a poster on the wall from the movie *The Shawshank Redemption*, with the quote "Get Busy Living or Get Busy Dying" on it, and a uniquely ugly ficus tree that had been watered mainly with Diet 7UP.

These were gone now, though why wouldn't they have been? How could any of them have meant as much to anyone as they'd meant to Quinn and Gabriel? She went over to the one familiar-looking piece of furniture left in the room, an old walnut cabinet pushed back between two sets of windows. She reached down and ran her fingers under the edge of one of its shelves. *That* at least was still there. She knelt to see it. G-A-B-R-I-E-L was carved into the wood, the letters pale against the walnut's exterior. She smiled in spite of herself, remembering the winter afternoon Gabriel had carved this with his geometry compass. It had been a very un-Gabriel-like thing to do. He hadn't had a shred of sentimentality, or so she'd thought at the time. She wondered if he would be at the dedication today. She rose, slowly. Better get going. She didn't want to be late.

She checked her watch as she got into her car. That had taken longer than she'd expected. Instead of returning the way she'd come, she could take the Scuttle Hole Road shortcut. But the thought of taking this route to the dedication filled her with dread. It was on this very road that she'd seen Jake's truck parked outside a run-down house, ten years ago, on the day of the accident, and even now the memory of it troubled her. She was pretty sure he'd lied to her about why his truck had been parked there, but she'd never found out why. *No, I'm not going to take that shortcut,* Quinn thought. *I'll take the long way. If I'm careful, I'll get to the dedication with a couple of minutes to spare.* She started the car, pulled out of the driveway, and headed toward Route 89.

CHAPTER 3

When Quinn took the turnoff for Shell Lake Beach and Picnic Area, she was surprised to discover that the parking lot was full. She parked behind a dirt-coated pickup truck on the rutted shoulder of the road and followed a stream of people down a paved trail to the picnic area. There was an unmistakable solemnity in their progression. The other guests hardly spoke to one another, and, when they did, their voices were low and serious, as though they were already practicing the gravity they felt the occasion required. When Quinn reached the clearing, it was more of the same. The group assembled there—at least a hundred strong—had a formality to it, a weightiness, that provided an odd juxtaposition to the picnic tables, barbecue grills, and fire pits in its midst. Indeed, she couldn't imagine a typical summer afternoon unfolding here, an afternoon of fluttering gingham tablecloths, burnt hot dogs, and half-gnawed watermelon rinds. The only thing that could have made this scene feel any more portentous, Quinn decided, would be a funeral dirge playing in the background.

She moved through the crowd, searching for a place to stand so that her back would be to Shell Lake. This would be easier if she didn't have to look at the water, she thought. The problem was that other than the dry pine needles carpeting the ground, the slender birch trees that ringed the clearing— some with snow clumped at their bases—and the overcast sky above, the slate-gray lake was one of the few things *to* see from here. And it was a pretty enough lake, too, on a nice day. But in a part of the country with so many lakes to choose from, Shell Lake was considered something of a poor cousin to Butternut Lake, which, at its closest point, was a little less than a mile away. Shell Lake was smaller, shallower, and, as part of a national forest, less developed than Butternut Lake. There were no houses or resorts on its shores, only the rustic picnic area. And, unlike Butternut Lake, there were no businesses, either, no places to rent kayaks, or buy bait, or order an ice cream cone. What Shell Lake *did not* have to offer, though, was also what it *did* have to offer. Its lack of amenities guaranteed the visitors who did come here—mainly locals—a degree of privacy they wouldn't find on the busier lakes in the area. And so it had become something of a refuge for families in the summertime, ice fishermen in the wintertime, and high school students year-round. The last group was most prevalent here, at least on weekend nights. After all, if you wanted to have a party at a lake with a beach, a fire pit, and no one nearby to complain about the noise, then Shell Lake was the lake for you.

Quinn found a place to stand. From here she could see a few local dignitaries who, facing the crowd, had gathered on an incline that put them slightly above everyone else. Her eyes rested, for a moment, on the memorial stone. It was covered with a drop cloth, which was secured against the wind with a series of large rocks around its base. She saw then, to one side of the stone, Jake's parents, Maggie and Paul Lightman. Maggie, she thought, looked a little thinner, and Paul a little grayer, but both still looked basically the same as they had ten years ago. This surprised her. *Well, what did you expect, Quinn? That after the loss of their son they'd become . . . unrecognizable?* But, in truth, a part of her *had* thought that. She felt a surge of affection for them; she'd always liked them and she'd known from the first time she'd met them, the summer she and Jake had started dating, that they'd liked her, too. A man standing next to them caught Quinn's eye. He gave her a nod of recognition, and then smiled at her, a smile of unmistakable encouragement. *We'll get through this*, it seemed to say, and Quinn felt a jolt of recognition. *Tanner.* Tanner Lightman. Jake's older brother. He reminded her so much of Jake that she felt a little disoriented. She pulled her coat more tightly around herself and smiled back at him. She thought that ten years had done nothing to diminish his good looks, though, under the circumstances, it occurred to her that this thought might not be entirely appropriate.

She concentrated instead on the other people standing around the memorial stone. There was Mr. Mulvaney, Northern Superior's longtime principal, who had even less hair now than he had had when she was in high school, but who wore the same wire-rimmed glasses, which still had a tendency to slip down his nose. And there was Mr. Drossel, who had been the high school's cross-country coach, and, for all Quinn knew, still was. And Pastor Hanson, of course, the minister at Butternut's Lake of the Isles Lutheran Church.

She scanned the rest of the crowd for familiar faces. There were more than a few. Some of them Quinn had known well. She gave a small wave to Veronica Malley. She'd had six siblings and when Quinn was in second grade she'd told her dad she wanted to "borrow" some of them for their family, which had made him laugh. She'd been Quinn's chemistry lab partner in eleventh grade, and Quinn could see her as she had been then, her eyes squinting with concentration behind safety goggles as she bent over the Bunsen burner. Now, she held a chubby baby, dressed in a light blue snowsuit. He babbled, loudly, blissfully unaware of the somber mood around him. Quinn also smiled at Joe Gardella. She'd had a major crush on him in middle school. They'd grown up on the same street and had waited at the same school bus stop, and Quinn remembered the almost drunken pleasure with which the two of them, on rainy days in grade school, had stomped violently in the puddles that had formed on the sidewalk.

Not everyone in the crowd looked familiar. There were a couple dozen teenagers—high school students, obviously—shuffling in the cold. *Why are they here?* she wondered. They were too young to have been friends with the three boys who'd died. One, a girl with heavy blue eye shadow, stood to the left of Quinn, scrolling down her iPhone screen with rapt attention. Quinn, annoyed, looked away from her and swept her eyes around the assembled guests once more. She was looking for just one person now. No, she decided finally. He wasn't here. Gabriel, once her closest friend, was nowhere to be found in this crowd.

Part of her was relieved. In all likelihood, he no longer lived here. He'd gone on to do the things he'd always wanted to. Even at sixteen, when he and Quinn had first become friends, Butternut could barely contain his ambition, talent, and energy. She could remember him so clearly now: his longish, light brown hair, his pale skin, and his intense blue-gray eyes that seemed almost to be lit from within. At the time, she had perhaps underestimated his charm. The way he'd brushed his hair out of his eyes, the way he'd smiled that uneven, slightly crooked smile, the way he'd lounge on anything as though it was the most comfortable piece of furniture on the planet. Most of all, though, she remembered the way he listened to her in a way that was thoughtful, intense, and without judgment. It would be years before Quinn realized what a rare quality that was in someone. But it wasn't just his physical presence she remembered. He'd been a dreamer whose dreams had never seemed beyond his grasp. He'd wanted to take a road trip with

Quinn through the American West, taking photographs of the landscape and of people. And he'd wanted to go to college, to study photography, and then to travel the world, working for *National Geographic*. Quinn figured, now, they'd be lucky to have him. He was probably photographing the Namibian sand dunes even as she stood here.

But she frowned, slightly. Thinking about him always brought with it a familiar uneasiness. Because as close as they'd once been, they'd lost touch with each other since then. Not gradually, either, the way you do with some old friends, but suddenly, almost overnight, during Quinn's freshman year of college. And it wasn't just losing touch that made Quinn uneasy. It was her memory of what she and Gabriel had done on the night of the accident, after they'd left the bonfire, that troubled her too. She rubbed her gloved hands together for warmth. She missed him, though. If he hadn't returned for the dedication, it meant she wouldn't see him during this, her one and, she hoped, only visit to Butternut.

"If you could please give us a minute," Mr. Mulvaney, the principal, said, his voice sailing over the heads of the crowd and interrupting Quinn's thoughts. "We're waiting for one of the speakers to find a parking spot." Quinn puffed out a breath and squinted at the sky. The weather report was right. The sun was beginning to burn through the clouds, though its light carried little warmth. She shuffled her feet, wishing she'd chosen her boots for warmth instead of for appearance.

"*Quinn!*" someone standing to her right said in a low, throaty voice. Quinn turned to see a woman in a pink paisley scarf.

"You don't remember me, do you?" she asked her, with a deep chuckle. "It's okay. I haven't seen you since you graduated from high school."

"Mrs. Fast?" Quinn said, because the woman standing beside her was both heavier and blonder than her seventh-grade social studies teacher had been.

She nodded, pleased. "Yes, but you can call me Kathy."

"Kathy," Quinn corrected herself.

"Do you remember the extra-credit project you did on the Lewis and Clark expedition?" Mrs. Fast whispered, since there was now an expectant stir of movement that suggested the dedication was about to begin. "You wrote a wonderful monologue about Sacagawea."

"I do," Quinn said, with a smile. In Mrs. Fast's presence, she was remembering other things, too, from that social studies class: the Louisiana Purchase, Manifest Destiny, and the Industrial Revolution.

"Are you still writing?" Mrs. Fast asked her.

Quinn nodded. "I'm a journalist."

"Good for you," Mrs. Fast said, or rumbled rather, her deep voice resonant. She placed a pink gloved hand on Quinn's arm. "You're one of those students of mine who got away. You left here and never looked back." She gave Quinn's arm a final squeeze and released it, then worked her way back to where she'd been standing in the crowd. *Got away?* Quinn thought. That was an odd choice of words. She was pretty sure, though, that Mrs. Fast meant this as praise. So why did Quinn feel this might also be a kind of indictment? And was that what Gabriel had done too? *Gotten away?*

"We're almost ready to begin," Mr. Mulvaney said, and Quinn saw that he had been joined by a petite woman in her fifties or sixties whose wispy red hair refused to stay in the bun she had fashioned it into. *That must be Butternut's mayor, Jane Steadman*, Quinn guessed. She'd read in the newspaper that the mayor was going to speak here today, and for some reason, Quinn felt sorry for her. She looked ill at ease, handing the piece of paper she'd brought with her to Mr. Mulvaney and trying to do something complicated, and unworkable, with her hair. Quinn glanced at the teenage girl to her left. She was still on her iPhone. Quinn wanted to ask her to put it away, but the girl, as if sensing Quinn's disapproval, looked up and shrugged. "He made us come," she said to Quinn, cutting her eyes to Mr. Mulvaney. "The whole junior class."

"He did?"

"Well, I mean, he 'strongly encouraged' us to come," she said, putting those two words in air quotes. She stuffed her iPhone into her down jacket pocket. Quinn wondered why Mr. Mulvaney had wanted them to come. Perhaps it was simply as representatives of the high school, or perhaps it was more than that. Had he seen this as a life lesson for students? A teachable moment? In any case, though, that lesson might have difficulty taking hold. Alone among the crowd, the students appeared unimpressed by the seriousness of the occasion. Quinn watched as one boy knocked the baseball cap off another one in a mocking gesture, and the other one picked it up with a dramatic flourish and put it back on his head. It would take a lot more to impress them than the deaths of three young men. Quinn remembered that age, with its almost unshakable belief in your own immortality. Death was something that happened to other people, *older people*, not to your peers, and least of all to you. She'd thought that then, too, thought it until the spring of her senior year.

"Welcome, everyone, and thank you for coming," Mr. Mulvaney began. "We're going to begin with an invocation from Pastor Hanson." Quinn and everyone else—even the girl with the blue eye shadow—bent their heads for the opening prayer. When it was over, Mr. Mulvaney spoke again. "No parent, principal, or politician ever wants to give a dedication like the one I am giving today," he began. "It was here, on Shell Lake, ten years ago, that three remarkable young men—Jake Lightman, Dominic Dobbs, and Griffin Hoyer—died." He halted. And hearing their names, Quinn felt emotion well up in her. She fought the impulse to cry. *This isn't a good place to fall apart*, she told herself, standing up a little straighter and tightening her scarf. Mr. Mulvaney continued, "Many of you know what happened that night. But for those of you who don't, these three young men drove a truck out onto this lake, which they believed was still frozen through. But it wasn't. And all three young men drowned . . ." Quinn stopped listening to Mr. Mulvaney. She was remembering the newspaper clipping about the dedication she'd brought with her and looked at last night before she went to bed. The clipping she'd read only twice but remembered verbatim:

The driver, Jake Lightman, 18, along with his two passengers, Dominic Dobbs and Griffin Hoyer, both 18, drove a 1980s Ford truck out onto Shell Lake, a little after midnight on March 24, 2007. And although many people drive their trucks and snowmobiles out onto area lakes in the winter, this was late in the season when the ice is notoriously unstable due to fluctuations in temperature. Mr. Lightman and his friends had been attending a high school bonfire at the Shell Lake picnic area. According to witnesses who'd been at the bonfire that night, it appeared that Mr. Lightman stopped the truck in the middle of the lake for several minutes, before the truck broke through and was submerged in the water. The police report said that stopping on the ice may have increased the load beyond the ice's breaking point, causing it to give way beneath them . . .

". . . all three of these young men were seniors at our high school," Quinn heard Mr. Mulvaney say now. "They had their whole lives in front of them: college, jobs, and family. We have all been deeply saddened by this tragedy, and each of their families has suffered an unfathomable loss. But today, as we unveil this dedication stone in their names, we choose to remember them and to honor them." Mr. Mulvaney looked at the crowd through his half-lowered glasses. Quinn felt suddenly unsteady. She was afraid she was going to faint. She loosened her scarf, unbuttoned the top button of her coat, and hoped that the cold air would prove bracing. It did. She took a deep breath, and her vision cleared. But she couldn't follow the rest of what Mr. Mulvaney said. Couldn't or wouldn't. She had known this service would be difficult. Standing here, though, she understood that knowing this wasn't the same thing as being prepared for it.

To steady herself she focused on the people near the memorial stone. She noticed Dominic Dobbs's parents, Jeffrey and Theresa, standing off to the side. She hadn't seen them earlier, but she knew from the newspaper article that Jeffrey was going to speak today. Dominic had been Jake's best friend since elementary school. He had been different from Jake, quieter and more serious. But theirs was a bond forged in early childhood. Quinn had liked him. She hadn't known him before her senior year, but once she'd started dating Jake, Dominic went out of his way to make her feel comfortable. Griffin, on the other hand, had only been friends with Jake since high school. He'd moved to Winton from Wisconsin in ninth grade, but when he'd joined the cross-country team, he'd fallen in with Dominic and Jake. And she'd liked him, too, but he was much harder to get to know. Quinn's father had told her that Griffin Hoyer's parents and siblings weren't coming to the dedication. The family had moved back to their hometown in Wisconsin, where they'd lived before the accident, and they weren't making the trip back for this event.

Mr. Mulvaney finished speaking and introduced Mrs. Steadman, the mayor. Whatever credentials she'd brought to office with her, public speaking wasn't one of them. Her voice was much quieter than Mr. Mulvaney's and Quinn could make out little of what she said. As she talked on, Quinn saw something out of the corner of her eye. A black bird had alighted from a nearby tree branch, and she followed it as it flew into the sky above. The clouds were breaking up, and in between them were patches of blue. Medium blue. The same color as Jake's Ford truck. Jake had loved that truck. She had loved that truck too. They'd spent a lot of time in it together. But whatever good memories she'd had of it had long since been wiped clean. And, suddenly, she imagined the truck the night of the accident: Jake and Dominic and Griffin crowded together in the front seat as Jake drove out onto the middle of frozen Shell Lake. The truck's windows rolled up, the cab filling with the smoke from Dominic's cigarette, the radio pulsing on the hard rock station Griffin had liked. And then, before they had time to register it, the ice groaning and then cracking beneath them, and the truck plunging into the water. Coldness. And then blackness. Quinn felt a wave of nausea roll over her, and then a hot, prickly faintness. She wanted to sit down at one of the picnic tables, but instead she squeezed her eyes tightly shut and then opened them. *Focus, Quinn. Focus on the present.*

The mayor finished, and Jeffrey Dobbs came to stand next to Pastor Hanson, while his wife, Theresa, who looked much older to Quinn than she had ten years ago, held back on the edge of the crowd, an unreadable expression on her face. Like the mayor, Mr. Dobbs lacked Mr. Mulvaney's ease in front of a crowd, but unlike the mayor, he was loud enough, and he spoke, too, with an unfiltered emotion it was impossible to ignore. "We miss our son every minute of every day," he said, pushing gloved hands into the pockets of his parka. "Theresa and I would do anything to turn back time and change the outcome of that night. But we can't. Our Dominic and Jake and Griffin are with God now. And I hope that by dedicating this memorial stone here, today, it will remind other young men and young women not to take the same kind of risk," he added, his voice cracking. He stopped speaking, and, moving with an awkward heaviness, he pushed away the rocks that had secured the drop cloth and pulled it back to reveal a large granite stone with a brass plaque embedded in it. The rock glinted in the sun and Mr. Dobbs, looking around at the crowd, said in a steadier voice, "Thank you for coming today, and please come back to the Butternut Recreation Center for the reception." There was silence, a silence that felt almost loud to Quinn, and then, as if in unison, the gathered crowd began to loosen and the guests, talking quietly, began to drift toward the parking lot.

Quinn didn't move. She was replaying Mr. Dobbs's words. "I would do anything to turn back time and change the outcome of that night." Mr. Dobbs, she thought, couldn't have altered the course of that night. Quinn, on the other hand, *could* have, but didn't. How many times had she wanted to go back and change what she had done? Change what she had said. Many, many times. Too many times to count.

CHAPTER 4

Quinn?" She felt a hand on her shoulder and turned to see Tanner standing beside her.

"Tanner," she said, and though the last time she had seen him had been at his brother's memorial service, ten years ago, he pulled her into a surprisingly natural hug now.

"I was hoping you'd be here," he said. "I asked someone about you, a couple of weeks ago, and they said, 'Quinn LaPointe? She left. She's gone. As in, completely dropped off the map.' And I said, 'That sounds about right. She was always very . . . *enigmatic.*'"

"I don't know about *enigmatic*," she said. "*Busy* is probably a better word." But as soon as she said this, she regretted it. It was a callous excuse for not coming back even once, especially when you considered the tragedy she'd left behind. The truth was, she hadn't *wanted* to come back. She'd been afraid,

afraid that if she did, her memories of her senior year would overwhelm her. And yet, avoiding Butternut hadn't protected her from the past. Far from it. So she'd changed tack. Perhaps she didn't need to be protected from it. She needed to confront it.

Tanner, who had been stopped by an older couple, turned back to Quinn now. "That's good," Tanner said. "Good that you're busy. Not good that we haven't seen more of you. Where are you living these days?"

"I'm living in Chicago. Evanston, actually. I'm writing there. Freelance," she added, disarmed by how much he resembled his brother. Same dark hair, prone to cowlicks. Same gold eyes. Same square jaw. Why hadn't she noticed before how alike they were? Or had she known this but forgotten? It was hard to say. She and Jake hadn't spent a lot of time with Tanner. By their senior year, he was already a junior at the University of Wisconsin at Madison, and when he came home over vacations, he was more interested in spending time with his friends than with his family. Still, their lives had intersected, a handful of times, like when Tanner was back for Christmas and paid too much attention to Quinn at a family dinner. *She'd* thought Tanner was trying to make her feel comfortable. *Jake* had believed he was flirting with her.

"Jake told me once you wanted to be a writer," Tanner said, bringing her back to the moment. "Good for you. You're doing what you wanted to do. And, by the way, you look beautiful. You haven't aged a day."

"Neither have you," Quinn said. Tanner paused then to say

good-bye to a middle-aged woman who was leaving the dedication. Quinn took a steadying breath and realized that he and his
brother were not, after all, carbon copies of each other. There
was plenty to separate the two of them, starting with the fact
that Tanner didn't have a scar on his right cheek. (The small scar
Jake had had there, two parallel lines that looked like an equals
sign, was the result of running into a tree branch when he was
six years old.) Even to the untrained eye, though, there were
other, bigger differences. Tanner was several inches taller than
Jake had been, and he had the build of a conventional athlete—
he'd been a double letterman in high school—broad through
the shoulders and chest, whereas his brother had had the leaner
build of a distance runner. And Tanner's features were a little
heavier than Jake's, his voice a few notes deeper, though that
might have had to do with the fact that Tanner, at thirty-one
or thirty-two, was a man now, whereas Jake . . . Jake would
be forever caught somewhere between boyhood and manhood,
balanced on a threshold he'd never cross.

"How long are you here for?" Tanner asked, turning back to
Quinn.

"Until tomorrow, definitely. But I'll probably stay longer," she
said. An older man now stopped by to greet Tanner. This was
true, she thought, she might stay longer. That didn't mean she
wanted to stay longer. And she couldn't help but think of her
small but perfect apartment in Evanston, which was where she
had gone to college at Northwestern University. She rented it
from a professor of hers and his wife. It was a one-bedroom
unit over their garage and, in the winter, when there were no

leaves on the trees, Quinn could see Lake Michigan if she stood on her kitchen counter. (She actually had done this once or twice.)

"I'm sorry," Tanner said, turning to Quinn as the older man walked away from them. "Looks like everyone I know is here. I hope we can grab a cup of coffee before you leave town, though."

"Sure, a coffee would be great," Quinn said. She realized that despite all the people milling around them, Tanner was looking at her intently as if the two of them were alone there. His brother could do that, too, she remembered. It was the Lightman charm. That ability to make you feel like you were the most important, no, *the only* person in the world. She smiled at him. "But I'll see you at the reception, won't I?" she asked him. "And your parents, too?"

"No, we're not going to be there," Tanner said. "I'm taking them home. They aren't really up to anything else today. But I know they'd love to see you. Why don't you stop by the house tomorrow?"

"I'd like that." Her eyes searched the crowd and found the Lightmans. They were heading toward the parking lot and something about the way the two of them were walking, with their heads bowed and their shoulders touching, said *We need to be left alone*. Quinn still wrote them a card, every year, at Christmastime. Once or twice, Jake's mom had written her back, but something about her note—the shortness of it, or the close, spidery cursive that trailed unevenly across the stationery—suggested how difficult it had been for her to do so, and, when she'd stopped answering her, Quinn had felt almost relieved.

"How are they doing?" she asked Tanner now.

"It's hard," he said. "My dad's better, I think, but my mom . . ." He lowered his voice. "It's still really difficult for her. Sometimes she goes and sits in Jake's old room by herself . . ." he said, his voice trailing off.

"Oh, Tanner," Quinn said, because there was something awful about that image. Tanner, she could see, thought this, too, and Quinn wanted to comfort him. "Having you, though—" she began.

"Doesn't make it easier," he interrupted, looking away. "But I try. I'm down in Minneapolis. But I get up here at least once a month. And I take my vacations up here too. I'll be here this week." He added, "I stay at Loon Bay Cabins, though." Loon Bay Cabins was a rustic resort with a bar and restaurant, a marina, and a dozen or so cabins on Butternut Lake. "The three of us do better if we give each other some space," he continued. "Especially my mom and I. We don't always . . . get along." The crowd was breaking up now. In the parking lot, good-byes were being said, car doors were slamming, and engines were starting. Quinn watched as a group of high school students who'd been clustered around a couple of nearby picnic tables, talking in low voices and smoking cigarettes, started to move away. Mr. Mulvaney and another man were standing over the dedication stone, admiring it. She didn't want to see the stone close up, though. What she wanted, she realized, was to go somewhere with Tanner, to get in his car, to go to Pearl's or the Mosquito Inn bar, or somewhere else, anywhere, really, where they could have that cup of coffee, or a drink, and just talk. Talk about Jake. Tanner, after all, knew Jake better than anyone. And he'd loved Jake, as she had. But, of course, he had his parents to take care of.

"Hey," Quinn said, remembering the clipping. "Did you by any chance send me the article from the *Butternut Express* about this?" she asked, gesturing around them.

Tanner looked surprised. "No. Why?"

"Someone sent it to me. But there was no return address or note."

"That's odd," he said.

The smell of cigarette smoke drifted over to her, and the queasiness she'd felt earlier returned. She tried to shake it off, but Tanner noticed.

"You okay?" he asked, looking concerned.

She nodded. "I'll be fine once I get something to eat," she said, knowing it wasn't hunger making her queasy.

"There'll be finger sandwiches at the reception," he said, leaning down to give her a good-bye kiss on the cheek. She caught the subtle, spicy smell of his aftershave. "And don't forget, I'm at Loon Bay Cabins. Call if you want to meet up before you leave."

"Thanks, Tanner," she said and started to turn away. "Oh, wait, one more thing. Did you know Gabriel? Gabriel Shipp?"

"Yeah. One of his brothers was in my class."

"Right," she said. "Well, he was a friend of mine. We lost touch, though. Do you know . . . what happened to him? I mean, where he ended up?"

"He ended up right here," he said, looking amused.

"In Butternut?"

"Uh-huh. Not everyone escapes, Quinn," he said with a smile.

"No, I know, but . . . are we talking about the same person?" Because the Gabriel she knew was more likely to be living in Timbuktu than here in Butternut.

"I think so. Gabriel Shipp. He works on people's cars."

Quinn frowned. Gabriel had *known* how to repair cars. His dad had owned an auto shop. But he hadn't particularly *liked* doing it.

"No, it's true," Tanner said. "People drop their cars off at his place. You know that driveway past Birch Tree Bait? The one on the right that says *B. Phipps* on the sign? That's where he lives. Down that drive."

Tanner said good-bye and Quinn watched as he made his way over to his parents. He was stopped, again, before he got to his car by a blond woman—she, too, looked vaguely familiar, but from this distance Quinn couldn't quite place her. She wondered if women were always stopping Tanner. She had a feeling that they were. She smiled to herself, but then her thoughts returned to Gabriel. So, he was here. Living in Butternut. How was that even possible? Like her, of course, he'd been born here. Lived his whole life here. But when they'd become friends in high school at the end of tenth grade, they'd both acted as if they were only passing through, pausing here on their way to somewhere else. Somewhere bigger. *Somewhere better.* She looked, now, out at the lake for the first time since arriving and noticed how dark the water was. A gust of wind ruffled its glassy surface. She wanted to see Gabriel, she realized. But something about him being here, after all these years, made her feel almost afraid. Why hadn't he left? And what if he didn't want to see her? But that was silly. He'd been a good friend once. The closest friend she'd ever had. He'd probably be glad to see her. After all, you didn't have a friendship like that every day. And it occurred to Quinn, as she headed to her car, that she hadn't had a friendship like that since . . . well, since theirs.

CHAPTER 5

Quinn knocked on the cabin's front door. Nothing. She knocked again. Still nothing. She turned and looked at the beat-up red pickup truck she'd parked next to in the cabin's gravel driveway. Was it Gabriel's? She doubted it. Driving a pickup truck was the antithesis of everything he was; he'd be more likely to own a vintage Indian motorcycle or a refurbished 1968 Ford Mustang, like the one Steve McQueen drove in *Bullitt*. Maybe Tanner was mistaken about him living here. Or maybe the truck belonged to Gabriel's roommate or to a friend. But if that was the case, why weren't *they* answering the door? She was about to knock one more time when the door swung open and Gabriel was standing there. In that split second, Quinn felt an electrical current pass through her.

She watched as an expression traveled over his face, like the shadow of a cloud on a windy day. There was surprise, yes, but something else, too, something that she could have sworn was happiness, or maybe even joy. And then it was gone, and his expression was so guarded, his gray-blue eyes so opaque, that she wondered if she'd imagined having seen it.

"Quinn," he said, after what felt like an almost unbearable silence.

"Gabriel," she said, relieved that he had broken some spell between them. She hugged him, hard, a completely different hug from the polite hug she'd given Tanner. She thought he was taken aback, at first, but then he raised a hand and patted her on the back. Patted her cautiously, the way you might pat a wild animal.

She stepped back, wanting to study him. She would have recognized him anywhere. But he was still very . . . *changed*. Some of the changes were easy to see. His hair, which was sandy brown, was cut shorter than he'd worn it in high school, when it was perennially brushing against his neck and falling into his eyes. And where he used to be clean-shaven, he now had stubble on his chin and jaw. His clothes were also different. In high school, Gabriel had favored dark jeans, T-shirts featuring '70s punk rock bands that nobody but him had ever heard of, and Vans sneakers. He'd been cool, there was no other word for it. Today, he was wearing a flannel shirt, faded jeans, and a pair of work boots. Other changes were harder to describe. Where before he'd had a lightness, a quickness, now he had a kind of gravity that she didn't remember him having. Perhaps, though, that was only the difference between him being a teenager and being a man.

"You look different," she said, after a silence.

"You look exactly the same," he said.

"You're the second person today who's told me that."

"You sound disappointed."

"Not disappointed. But do I really look like I'm eighteen?"

"No," he said, after a pause. "The clothes are better."

"They better be," she joked, indicating her long wool coat and high-heeled leather boots. "They cost enough." She'd meant to lighten the mood, but it didn't work. And for a moment she wanted to take it back, the implication that her clothes were expensive. Gabriel raised his shoulders, fractionally, though whether it was a shrug of indifference or worse—a dismissal— she couldn't be quite sure. Either way, she understood now that she wouldn't be getting a warm welcome from him. And the truth was, this hurt, a lot. But she tried to push this aside. Yes, she had lost touch with him. Yes, she hadn't seen him in years, but she hadn't imagined he'd be so disinterested in her when she *did* see him. Despite his lack of warmth, though, she decided to press on.

"Can I come in?" she asked, since he was standing in the cabin's doorway. He tilted his head back, fractionally, and moved aside to let her pass.

When Quinn came into the cabin, she had another surprise. Its interior was as unlike the old Gabriel as the clothes he was wearing. The small living room, dining room, and kitchen, all visible from where she stood, were all neat, but they were otherwise so bland, and so forgettable, that later, back in her motel room, Quinn, who had a mind for details, couldn't re-create them. There was a threadbare couch in the living room, but it wasn't shabby enough to be interesting, and there might have been a rough pine table in the dining room with a few mismatched chairs around it, but it didn't look as if anyone had ever eaten at it before. In the kitchen, there were no real signs of habitation other than a coffee mug on the counter and a folded dish towel hanging on a drawer handle. None of these rooms had any of the things—keys in a bowl, loose change on a countertop, an indented sofa cushion, a stack of books, a sweater tossed on a chair—that Quinn associated with a place where someone lived. *A place where life happened.*

The Gabriel she'd known in high school had been a minimalist. That much was true. But his minimalism had served a purpose. It was to make his few possessions—all of which he loved—stand out. An original poster of the movie *Easy Rider,* which he had scoured the internet for. A vintage working record player he'd bought at a yard sale, and his collection of 78s, also scavenged at yard sales. And there were the other odd, eclectic touches in his bedroom: a dresser he'd made from repurposed lockers, a light fixture fashioned out of chicken wire. Oh, and cameras, of course, including his prized 35-millimeter Nikon. She wondered where that camera was now. And she almost asked him, but something stopped her.

"Can I take your coat?" he asked, and she saw his politeness wasn't so much welcoming as it was habitual. Her father had always liked that about Gabriel. He had nice manners.

"Sure," Quinn said. As soon as she slid it off and handed it to him, though, she realized how chilly the cabin was.

"Do you want a cup of coffee?" he asked, once he'd hung up her coat. "It's already made."

"Sure," Quinn said. More coffee was the *last* thing she wanted, especially since the cup she'd had that morning already felt as if it were burning a hole in her stomach, but she thought it might keep her warm, and, besides, she needed a moment to collect herself. So, when Gabriel went into the kitchen, she sat down on the couch and, suppressing a shiver, tried to rally herself. Yes, the cabin was devoid of personal touches. And no, Gabriel wasn't thrilled to see her, but she wasn't leaving. Not until . . . until what? Until she felt that emotional connection between them that she hoped was still there. It was dormant now, she knew, buried under the years. But it was still there. It had to be. Something that real, and that strong, didn't just disappear, did it? Just evaporate?

"Is this your place?" she called to him while he was in the kitchen.

"No, it's Mr. Phipps's. I rent it by the month," he called back.

"Hey, by the way," she asked, "did you send me the *Butternut Express* clipping for the dedication?"

He reappeared with two mugs of coffee. "Did I send you the clipping? No. I don't even know your address," he said, handing her one of the mugs.

"Someone sent it to me with no note or return address," she said, taking the coffee and setting it down on a worn brown coffee table in front of her.

"Maybe one of your old friends at the *Butternut Express* sent it," he said, of the paper where she'd interned between her junior and senior year in high school. "Are you cold?" he asked. "I could start a fire." He gestured at the fireplace. It was empty now, but logs were stacked on either side of it.

"No, I'll warm up," Quinn said, taking a sip of the coffee. It was black.

"Sorry. No cream," he said, sitting down in a chair across from her and then taking a sip of his coffee. He set it down carefully in front of him and looked at her with an expression on his face she couldn't quite read.

"This is fine," she said, wrapping her hands around her coffee cup for warmth. She couldn't help but notice how classically handsome he'd become. She looked away and searched the small room for something familiar, something from the past. But she couldn't find anything. They were silent for a moment as they sipped their coffee.

"You weren't at the dedication," she said now, turning to him and stating the obvious.

"I'm there all the time, Quinn," he said.

"What does *that* mean?" she asked.

He shook his head. Even he looked surprised that he'd said this. "I don't know. It doesn't mean anything," he said, with a kind of finality that precluded further discussion.

Quinn was baffled; she didn't know what to say. They were quiet again. Communicating with him was difficult, a struggle. That had never been true in high school. The old Gabriel was so easy to talk to. She wanted him back, but she knew that, on some level, she had no right to expect him. Nervously, she took another sip of her coffee.

"Why did you come here?" Gabriel finally asked. "To my place?"

"To see you, obviously," she said.

"But why now, Quinn? Why after all this time?" And the way he asked this, quietly, almost intimately, made her face flush.

"I didn't *want* to wait this long," she said, not quite able to meet his steady gaze.

"But you did," he said, sounding, once again, disinterested, emotionless. She was confused. She couldn't reconcile his questions, which seemed personal, with his general air of detachment.

"I'm sorry," she said. "But you know, you could have looked *me* up, too. I think we're both at fault here," she added, feeling defensive now. "We both let this friendship . . ." *Don't say die.* "I called you," she said, starting over again. "I called you when I got to college. But you never called me back. I mean, you weren't such a great communicator yourself." Quinn had called him *more* than once. Every time she did, though, the call would go straight to voice mail. And when she did leave a message, he wouldn't call her back. She reached him once, early that fall, after her first semester had started, and he'd had little to say. And when she'd called him again, later in the fall, he'd been vague and had found an excuse to hang up. She'd asked him, then, when she could call him back. And he'd said "I'll call you." But he didn't. Then, that winter, when she'd discovered his cell-phone number was out of service, she'd tried to reach him at his parents' house but no one ever answered the phone. After that she didn't call him again. And he'd closed down his old high school Yahoo email account and his MySpace page in the summer after they graduated, so Quinn couldn't contact him that way either. "You didn't make it easy for us to stay in touch, Gabriel."

He shrugged. An admission of culpability, maybe, but then he leaned forward and said, "You're right. I didn't make it easy, Quinn. That was a tough year." He sat back as if he was done, but then he added, quietly, "I could have used a friend."

"Gabriel, I didn't know that. You didn't *tell* me that." The realization that he'd needed her that year, and that she hadn't known that, brought a lump to her throat. "Do you want me to leave?" she asked, trying to control her emotions. "Because if you don't want me here, I will." She started to stand up, but Gabriel, looking apologetic, waved her back down.

"Stay," he said. "Forget about me. I want to hear about you. How's the writing life?" He leaned back in his chair then and stretched his long legs out in front of him.

"It's good," she said, sinking back onto the threadbare couch. Her face still felt warm. She took another sip of her coffee, hoping to gather herself. "It's fine," she added. She didn't want to talk about her writing, though. She set her cup down and looked directly at him. Why was meeting his eyes so hard all of a sudden? She couldn't help but feel that he was looking straight through her, judging her. Or maybe, she thought, she was judging herself.

"Your writing is *fine*?" he asked.

"Actually, I'd rather talk about you. Did you ever go to RISD?" He'd been accepted to the Rhode Island School of Design, in Providence, Rhode Island, in the winter of their senior year, but that summer, after they graduated, he told Quinn he'd deferred his admission for a year. Sitting here in this cabin, however, she realized that he'd never gone.

"You know I didn't, Quinn," he said, as if he'd read her mind.

"But why, Gabriel?" she asked. "You always wanted to go there."

"I couldn't leave here," he said.

"You couldn't leave? You sound like you were being held prisoner here." She was joking, but he looked momentarily taken aback.

"I didn't have the money for school," he said, quickly. "I didn't have the drive, either."

"No money? Gabriel, you had a scholarship. And no drive? You were so driven in high school that you tried to make a case for graduating early. And furthermore, you were—and I'm sure you still are—hugely talented."

"That's debatable." He ran his fingers through his hair and smiled, just a little, as though remembering some internal joke. Then abruptly he was serious again. "Tell me about the memorial," he said.

"The dedication," she corrected him, pulling her sweater a little closer around her. "It was hard. And strange. Apparently, Mr. Mulvaney made the high school junior class attend, so there were all these teenagers there. And Mrs. Fast said hi to me. You know, seventh-grade social studies? But I didn't recognize her right away. It made me feel so old, not recognizing her. Though, I guess, twenty-eight isn't exactly old, is it?" She looked at him when she said this, but he was watching her without any real expression on his face. "And Dominic's dad spoke," she continued. "Which was incredibly sad. And Tanner. Tanner Lightman was there. You know, Jake's brother—"

"I know who he is," Gabriel interrupted. And something in his tone made Quinn stop. It wasn't quite impatience, but she got the distinct impression that he knew all this already. The sun must have come out from behind a cloud just then because the light in the room changed and a patch of it fell across Gabriel, lighting up his gray-blue eyes and the strands of blond in his hair. He leaned forward, closer to her, as though to get out of the sun.

"I didn't think you'd come for it," he said, running his hand along his chiseled jaw.

"Why not?" she asked.

He looked at her, speculatively. "I didn't think you'd want to be reminded of the past."

"Well, you're right, in a way," she said, folding her arms around herself. "I *don't* want to be reminded of the accident. And I didn't want to come back here either. But I made myself."

"You made yourself? Against your own will?" he asked, with mild amusement.

"What I meant is that I thought I *should* come," she said. What she didn't say to Gabriel is what she'd told herself a couple of weeks ago: *You can go back to Butternut and try to figure things out or you can wait for your life to fall apart again.* "I thought it was time to come back here, even though I knew doing it would make me feel . . . sad." And even saying that word, as inadequate as it was, made her feel the sadness encroaching. If she was expecting sympathy from Gabriel, though, she didn't get any.

"Is that all you feel when you think about the accident?" he asked, a quizzical expression on his face. "Sad?"

"What do you mean?" she said. But even as she asked for clarification, she realized she was afraid of what he was going to say.

"I mean—just sad? Do you ever feel guilty? You know, about the night of the accident?"

"Do I feel guilty? Because of . . . what we did?" she asked him. He closed his eyes for a second and then looked away, but not before she saw another emotion flash across his face. Not joy this time, but pain. Seeing that, and knowing that remembering that night was painful for him, stirred something in her that she couldn't quite put her finger on.

"Partly that, yes," he said, finally. "What I mean, though, is do you ever feel responsible for what happened?" He looked directly at her now, and it felt like a challenge.

Quinn felt suddenly anxious. "No. Yes. I don't know," she said. "I don't feel *solely* responsible. I mean, I feel horrible about the night of the accident. I wish I'd done things differently. I wish *we'd* done things differently, but . . ." For the first time since walking into this cabin, she felt a flicker of anger. She had tolerated his standoffishness and his incommunicativeness, but she wouldn't tolerate this. She could hear her voice rising. "The main person, Gabriel, who was responsible for what happened that night was Jake. What he did . . . it was a mistake. It was tragic. But it was his decision to drive his pickup out onto the ice and take his two best friends with him. It was his decision to stop his truck in the middle of the lake. No one told him to do that. No one else is to blame." She looked at Gabriel, but he shook his head, as though she was wrong.

"What? You think *I'm* to blame for it?" she asked. Did Gabriel know what she'd said to Jake that night at the bonfire? No, he couldn't. She hadn't told him. She hadn't told anyone.

"I didn't say that," Gabriel said. "But you left the bonfire so suddenly that night. We never really talked about what happened there. I just wondered if you felt responsible."

"Do you?" she asked him. For a second, he looked stricken at her question. She didn't wait for an answer.

"Never mind," she said, standing up. "I don't want to talk about it anymore." A tumult of feelings crowded in on her—anger, confusion, defensiveness, fear, and hurt—and, as she headed for the front door, she thought, *This was a mistake. Coming here. I don't want to stay for one second longer.*

"Quinn. Stop, okay? Wait a second," Gabriel said behind her, a gentler tone in his voice. She paused, her hand already on the doorknob. "Here, at least take this. You'll freeze without it," he said, coming up to her and holding out her coat. She'd forgotten all about it.

"Thank you," she said, but as she pulled it on she refused to look at him.

"Quinn," he said again, and the affection with which he said her name felt familiar to her. She looked at him. "You don't look back, do you?" he said, with something close to admiration. "You keep moving. If something stands in your way, you go around it."

"That's . . . not true." But even as she said this, she knew that it was *partly* true. Or, at least, *had been true*, years ago. She'd stopped looking back. She'd kept moving. But only because she'd believed that if she didn't keep moving, she'd never move at all. "That's not true anymore," she amended.

"Well, I'll take your word for it."

"I should get going," she said, feeling, for a moment, almost suffocated by the weight of everything—of the town, of the cabin, of him. She opened the front door, and Gabriel, to her surprise, followed her out. He must have been aware of how agitated she was, how upset, because he seemed determined to end her visit on a positive note.

"You look like you're doing well, Quinn," he said, as they walked over to her car. "I'm happy for you. I am." He smiled. The first real smile she'd seen from him since she'd arrived at his cabin. And seeing his smile made her realize how much she'd missed it.

She felt a little better now, outside in the clean, cold air with the sun glinting hard off the little patches of snow in the driveway. She breathed deeply. Maybe she and Gabriel should have gone somewhere else, instead of staying here. Maybe it was the cabin, impersonal to the point of unsettling, that had hobbled them in their conversation. She wanted to try this again, somewhere else.

"Do you want to meet later?" she asked him. "Maybe get a burger at the Corner Bar?"

"I don't think so," he said. But the way he said it was matter-of-fact, not unkind.

"What about tomorrow?"

"I've got some work to do," he said.

"What kind of work?" Quinn asked, realizing that the conversation hadn't even gotten far enough for her to ask this question earlier.

"I'm a caretaker," he said.

Gabriel, a caretaker? Her face must have fallen, a little, because he said, "There aren't a lot of great year-round jobs up here, Quinn, in case you've forgotten."

"No, I remember. Caretaking is a good job," she said. And it was. She only felt sad because it was so far from the kind of work Gabriel had dreamed of doing.

"It's, you know, checking up on cabins in the off-season," he said. "Making sure the pipes haven't burst, or raccoons haven't built nests in the living room, or whatever."

She tried to think of something positive to say. "It sounds—"

"It pays the bills," he interrupted.

Then he said, "All right, well," rubbing his hands together, since he was without a coat. "Good-bye, Quinn." It was he who reached out to hug her this time. Quinn hugged him back. She wanted him to stay that way, with his arms around her, but he stepped back. Still, as he opened her car door for her, she felt a momentary panic. Things weren't right between them, and there wasn't time to fix it. She was getting into her car and Gabriel was waiting, as if he'd been waiting this whole time, since she'd set foot on his doorstep, for her to leave. And then she *was* leaving, driving down the gravel drive, and being careful not to look in the rearview mirror, because she didn't know what would make her feel worse: Gabriel standing there and watching her, or Gabriel going back inside the cabin.

As she turned onto the main road, she realized how unrealistic she'd been. Had she honestly thought that she could come waltzing back into his life, after a decade away, and the two of them would just pick up where they'd left off? As if that night of the accident had never happened, as if they were both back on the blue couch in the communications room at school whiling away the time before they could both leave for college? Yes, on some level, she had. And that was what made the disappointment so bitter.

CHAPTER 6

Quinn stood on frozen Shell Lake, the surface below her crisscrossed with sharp lines cut into the dusting of snow, like those left behind by an ice skater. It was night and the sky was a starless inky black. Quinn was holding a coffee mug that had a chip in the rim and was half filled with red wine. "Quinn!" she heard Jake yell. He was in his blue truck out on the middle of the lake. There was someone else in the truck with him, and although she couldn't see the person, she knew somehow it was Gabriel. But why was he there too? They were far enough away that Jake's voice sounded distant. "Quinn, help us," he called again. "Quinn." He sounded desperate this time. And then she heard it, the splintering crack. The ice beneath her shifted, *and she turned and started running toward the shore, away from the truck. She had to get to land. "Quinn, don't go," Jake yelled. And just as the ice gave way, she fell onto the shore. The mug that had been in her hand was broken, a spill of red wine staining the snow. She looked back over her shoulder, toward the center of the lake, where Jake's truck had been. But it was gone.*

The persistent ringing of her cell phone woke her, scattering the dream. Still, Quinn sat up on the bed and looked around. Her eyes settled on the garish nature photography on the opposite wall. She blew out a breath. She was at the Butternut Motel. She reached for her handbag next to her on the bed and found her cell phone. It was Theo.

"Quinn?"

"Uh-huh?" she answered. She was groggy, but she tried to push the dream out of her head. She needed to stop napping; now the dreams were disturbing her nights *and* her days. And besides, napping always left her feeling irritable.

"Are you okay?"

"Yes. Why?" She stood up, put her cell phone on speakerphone, and set it down on the dresser.

"You sound a little strange," Theo said.

"I fell asleep," she said. After she'd gotten back to the motel from Gabriel's cabin, her feelings of disappointment and hurt gave way to anger. Anger at herself, but also anger at Gabriel. Her visit with him had been so upsetting that she'd opened her suitcase and started packing. Then, overcome by weariness, she'd lain down on the bed and fallen asleep.

She walked over to the closet now and surveyed the clothes still hanging there. As usual, she'd overpacked; she'd brought enough clothes to last a week. "Aren't journalists supposed to know how to pack light?" she asked Theo now.

"Um, well, I guess if you're a war correspondent, that would be a useful skill," he offered.

She tugged a blouse off a hanger, started to fold it, and then gave up and rolled it into a ball and tossed it into the open suitcase on the bed. She yanked a sweater off another hanger and threw it in after the blouse. Now that the grogginess had worn off, the anger she'd felt earlier returned. Ordinarily, Quinn wasn't afraid of anger. Her own or anyone else's. It could be a useful emotion, under the right circumstances. Clarifying. And energizing. But this wasn't that kind of anger. This was as much defensiveness as anger. She replayed Gabriel's accusations over in her mind. Because that's what they were. Accusations. No matter how obliquely he'd made them. First, he'd said she'd been a bad friend. And although he admitted he was partly at fault for them falling out of touch, he'd still laid most of the blame at her feet. Then, he'd asked her if she felt guilty about the night of the accident. And, on top of that, he'd implied that she might have been responsible for it.

Guilt and responsibility. In Quinn's mind, there was a difference between these two things. Guilt could be an interior feeling that didn't correspond to a "crime." Guilt, after all, was entirely proportional to your own moral compass. You could feel guilty about not having been there for someone, not having done something you thought you should have done. But feeling responsibility, for an accident, especially, meant you were partly to blame, meant that in some way you'd caused things to happen. It was true she'd felt both of these things, in varying degrees, over the years. But she'd long tried to push them away. Especially responsibility. After all, the possibility that what she'd done that night, what she'd said that night, caused the whole tragedy was too awful to contemplate. No, she wouldn't think about that.

"Quinn, are you there? Do you want me to call back later?" Theo asked.

"No," she said, startled out of her thinking. "I want to talk now." She walked back over to the dresser, where she'd left her phone.

"How was the dedication?"

"It was difficult," she said, her anger suddenly deflating. "And afterward, I went to see an old friend of mine, Gabriel. Remember? I told you about him," she rushed on. "Theo, he's so changed." She took the remaining clothes out of the dresser and dumped them into the suitcase, then carried her cell phone into the bathroom and, placing it on the counter, started stuffing her toiletries into a cosmetic case.

"Changed how?"

"He's a different person," she said. "Something happened to him." She paused to screw the lid on a tube of toothpaste. "In high school, he was so driven, and talented, and funny. He got a scholarship to RISD. But he never went. He stayed here and now he's taking care of people's cabins . . ." Her voice trailed off. But those weren't the only changes. Gone, too, was his affection and warmth toward Quinn; that was painful as well.

"He lives alone," she added, retrieving her shampoo and conditioner from the shower. "I'm pretty sure he's depressed. The thing is, though, he blames *me* for our losing touch. And he . . . I don't know, I think he implied that by leaving here, I somehow abandoned him. Which isn't fair. I didn't stop him from going to RISD. And if he wanted to hole up in some cabin here, indefinitely, I don't see how that was my fault either." She zipped her cosmetic bag closed and carried it and her phone out of the bathroom.

"I'm sorry, Quinn. That sounds hard. What are you going to do about him, though?" Theo asked from the bed, where she'd set the phone.

"About Gabriel? Nothing. There's nothing I can do."

"You're not going to spend more time with him?" Theo asked.

"*No.* That's just it. He doesn't *want* me to. He practically chased me out of his cabin." She leaned over to zip her suitcase, then changed her mind. "In fact," she said, sitting back down on the bed, "I'm pretty sure he hates me."

"I doubt that," Theo said.

"No, it's true. I don't think I'll see him again. I'm already packed, and I'm leaving," she said. He was quiet for a moment. "Theo," she asked, "are *you* still there?"

"I'm here," he said. "I'm wondering . . . do you think you should try to stay longer, spend more time with your friend? You know, find out what's going on with him? Before you left

Evanston, you told me you were going to . . . I think you said you were going to face things head-on, figure things out, so you don't have another . . ."

"Breakdown," Quinn finished for him. She was a little uncomfortable that she'd told Theo about this episode from her past, a time in college when she'd fallen apart. She traced the bedspread pattern with her finger.

"I'm not sure that's the word I would use," he said.

"Theo," she said, sighing, "I really appreciate your concern, but you're starting to sound more like a therapist than an editor."

He laughed. "You're right," he said. "Sorry about that. Call me when you get back to Evanston, okay?"

"I will, Theo. And thanks," she said, hanging up. He hadn't mentioned again that she write about this experience, she realized. Probably because he didn't want to get her even more agitated than she already was.

She hoped she hadn't been snappish with him. She liked him. She liked him *a lot*. He was supportive and unflappable and smart. And she imagined him as she'd seen him last, in his favorite coffeehouse in Wicker Park, seated at a table in the corner and looking appealingly rumpled as he raked his fingers through curly brown hair, his brown eyes mellow in the soft lighting of that cluttered room. She had a feeling that Theo would be amenable to letting their professional relationship develop into something more. The thought had crossed her mind before too. She was interested in him, but something was holding her back. The truth was, for the last couple of years she hadn't been involved with anyone. No one had really interested her, or interested her enough. She'd gone on a lot of dates, but she hadn't settled into any relationships. Over the years she had gotten romantically involved with a couple of men, but never for more than a year. Her closest girlfriend, Katrina, referred to these relationships as Quinn's "eleventh-month specials." This wasn't intentional on Quinn's part. It wasn't as if she kept an eye on the calendar as the anniversary of their first date approached. It was more like an inner mechanism of hers sensed a shifting of the light, a changing of the seasons. Either way, she was apt to end things before the earth had made a full rotation around the sun.

She looked at her suitcase now. *First sign of trouble and you're ready to take off? What happened to sticking it out, Quinn? You had a plan to stay here for as long as it takes to figure things out. But here you are already plotting your escape.* She stood up and carried her suitcase over to the luggage rack.

What she really needed now was some caffeine, she decided. There was a coffeepot in the motel office. She'd get a cup of it and unpack again. Then, maybe, she'd try writing something.

But when she reached the office door, it was locked. *Back in five*, the note taped to it said. She looked through the glass. Sitting on a low table was the platter of shrink-wrapped breakfast pastries left over from the continental breakfast. Had that only been this morning? Less than six hours ago? How was that possible? She felt as if she'd been here forever. She lingered for a moment, peering into the office, and flashed on an image of Gabriel sitting on his couch in that impersonal cabin.

"Damn it, Gabriel," she muttered, as she turned around and headed back to her room. "What happened to you? Where is the old Gabriel?" she asked aloud as she passed the plastic tables and chairs lining the walkway. *And why are you still here, and why didn't you go to RISD? And why, why, why, did you give up the things you wanted to do?* She needed to know. Tomorrow, she vowed, she would go back to his cabin. She'd see him again even if he didn't want to see her. She remembered now the elation she'd felt when he'd opened his door and she'd seen him standing there. She hadn't realized how much she'd missed him until he was right in front of her. But that wasn't the only reason to see him again, she reminded herself. Theo was right. Actually, *she* was right. All Theo had done was quote her back to herself. She'd told Theo she needed to face, head-on, the spring of her senior year, and Gabriel was a part of that. A *big* part of that. After all, they'd been together the night of the accident. No, she wasn't backing down that easily.

When she got back to the room, she sat down on the chair in front of the window and pulled her laptop out of her computer bag. *Write*, she told herself. *Write about what happened the year leading up to the accident. Write about what Gabriel was like then. Write*—as her creative writing professor had said her freshman year in college—*write like your life depends on it.*

CHAPTER 7

June, Junior Year in High School,
With Gabriel in the Communications Room

G abriel, what are you doing?" Quinn asked, looking up from
her yellow legal pad. She was sitting on the blue couch in
the communications classroom—to the right of the hole that
had stuffing leaking out of it, stuffing that Gabriel cheerfully
referred to as the couch's "intestines"—and Gabriel was standing at the window, opening and closing the blinds against the
late-afternoon sun.

"I'm trying to get the light right in here," he said, looking at
Quinn and making a minute adjustment to the tilt cord.

"And this is important because . . . ?" They were supposed
to be having their Monday after-school brainstorming session

for that week's edition of the school newspaper, which was published every Friday.

Gabriel ignored her. He came back from the window, grabbed his camera off the coffee table, and looked at her through the viewfinder.

"Gabriel," Quinn protested. "No. No photo shoot. Not now. We need to talk about the paper. If I don't start studying for my Spanish final soon . . ." She trailed off. He wasn't listening to her anyway. When he got like this, he didn't listen to anyone, and that included Quinn. She watched as he set up the shot, testing it from several different angles, changing the settings on his camera, leaving to adjust the blinds again, returning to reposition the coffee table that he was sitting on to get the shot, and then repositioning Quinn, too, rearranging her on the couch just as he might have rearranged one of the cushions.

And Quinn sat still, knowing that the sooner he got the shot, the sooner the meeting could start. She looked at the poster that Gabriel had hung on the wall at the end of their sophomore year: a *Shawshank Redemption* poster in which Andy and Red are in the prison yard, with the quote "Get Busy Living or Get Busy Dying" beneath them. After Gabriel had tacked it up there one afternoon, he'd said, "There, now the room is complete."

Quinn looked at Gabriel now. He was still adjusting his camera lens. She smiled. It wasn't that she was enjoying herself. It was more like she was enjoying Gabriel enjoying himself. He was caught up in what he was doing, so oblivious to what was happening around him that the fire alarm could have gone off and he wouldn't have noticed.

A warm breeze blew through the classroom's open windows now, lifting the blinds and bringing with it the sweet smell of freshly mowed grass from the school's athletic fields. Quinn sighed. On the one hand, she loved this time of year. Winters lasted so long in northern Minnesota that spring could make you feel almost dizzy with appreciation and anticipation. On the other hand, it was so hard to concentrate on classes, and exams, and the paper with all that sunshine and warmth beckoning from outside. *One more week*, she told herself. Then school would be over, the last issue of the paper would be printed, and she'd be starting an internship at the *Butternut Express*. And Gabriel? He'd gotten into a summer photography program at the Art Institute of Chicago, where he'd be for several weeks before he spent the rest of the summer with relatives in suburban Chicago. She was a little nervous about his leaving. They weren't boyfriend and girlfriend or anything, but they'd spent almost all their free time together this school year, and now she couldn't quite imagine him being gone for ten whole weeks. What would she do with herself?

"Okay, now, look down," he told Quinn, as he sat on the edge of the coffee table, looking through the viewfinder. "Look down at the legal pad. Pretend to write something on it." She did better than pretend. She wrote *Gabriel is driving me crazy and I want to get this meeting over with* in her neat, slanting script.

"Now, look back up," he said. She did. She didn't smile,

though. She had a feeling that Gabriel was going less for year-book candid, and more for photographic auteur. The camera clicked again.

"Got it," he said, with satisfaction, sliding over from the coffee table onto the couch beside her. "It's going to be cool," he said. "Do you see these stripes?" He indicated the striped shadows from the blinds that were projected onto Quinn.

"I see them," she said, amused.

"I think they should make these photographs interesting. I think I can get these developed tonight," he added, indicating the camera.

"How's the home darkroom coming?"

"It's all right," he said, his enthusiasm ebbing somewhat. Quinn was referring to Gabriel's recent attempt to comman-deer his family's basement laundry room into a space where he could develop his photographs. "My mom doesn't like the fact that I blacked out the windows," he said, brushing hair out of his eyes. "But, I mean, it's not like the space wasn't already dark to begin with. Oh, and another thing. She's worried about the chemicals being cancer causing. And I'm like, no, Mom, that would be your two-pack-a-day Marlboro Lights habit. I'm not giving up on the darkroom, though." Gabriel loved the whole film development process, even at a time when many people were enamored with the immediacy and cheapness of digital cameras.

"She's not going to make you take it down, though, is she?"

"No, I can leave it there." He sighed. "She's not completely evil."

Quinn smiled. Gabriel's mother wasn't evil at all, as far as she could tell. Neither was his dad or his three brothers. But that didn't mean Gabriel's relationship with them wasn't problematic. His family was boisterous and loud, whereas Gabriel was quieter and more circumspect. He liked to talk—he and Quinn had had conversations that lasted all night—but when it came to other people, he only talked when he had something to say. His parents and brothers also loved sports—playing them, watching them, *anything* having to do with them—especially ones that involved speed and danger. Dirt-biking. ATVing. Snowmobiling. And when they weren't *riding* on motorized vehicles, they were *working* on them.

Gabriel, on the other hand, was indifferent to motion and speed, unless it involved photography. He *was* athletic. Quinn, who'd gone to elementary school with him, remembered his renowned dodgeball prowess. But he had no passion for sports or games, except, for some reason, pool. And while he was what Quinn's grandparents' generation liked to call "handy"—he could fix almost anything—he reserved this trait not for working on mud-splashed ATVs, but for tinkering with his cameras. Still, if he'd confided in Quinn once that as a child he'd harbored a secret belief that he'd somehow ended up in the wrong family, he'd now reached a fragile truce with them. His parents had agreed to give him the space he needed, and he, in exchange, had agreed to stay out of trouble. Not that this was that difficult for Gabriel. But his parents appreciated it. What with his brothers' occasional suspensions from school (cutting classes) and minor scrapes with the law (underage drinking), his mom and dad already felt that they had about as much as they could handle.

Although Quinn adored her dad, sometimes she envied Gabriel his large and very extended family. Both her parents had been only children born to older parents and Quinn had hardly known them.

Most of the time, though, Gabriel seemed to think his family was less of a blessing and more of a curse. And Quinn understood. But she could also see things from their perspective, and still imagine how unknowable Gabriel must seem to them. After all, she'd gone to school with him for ten years, and before last spring he'd practically been a stranger to her. She still marveled at the fact that while the two of them were sitting in the same classrooms, eating in the same cafeterias, riding on the same buses, she'd been oblivious to him. If anyone had asked what she'd thought of him then, she would have said he was quiet. And he was. But it wasn't that simple; he was quiet *and* self-assured.

It wasn't until he showed up in the communications room that spring and asked if he could take photographs for the student newspaper that she started noticing other things about him. Like he was smart. Smart, as in, "he didn't study that hard but he still got straight As smart." And he was observant. He noticed things other people didn't notice. Knew things other people didn't know. And he was funny. He could make Quinn laugh like no one else could. And he was talented.

And yet Quinn might never have been aware of any of this if Gabriel's uncle hadn't given him his vintage Nikon FM2 camera the summer before ninth grade. Because once Gabriel had that camera, all he wanted to do was take pictures. He was obsessed. And his obsession led him to Quinn, who was already preparing, at that point, to take over the editing of the school paper and had already changed its name from the *Bobcat Bulletin* to the *Superior News*.

Since that spring, they'd spent almost all their free time together. They'd spent it on this couch in the communications room; in Gabriel's room, where Quinn curled up on his bed, studying, and Gabriel sat at his desk, looking at photos on the desktop computer he shared with his brother; and at the kitchen table at Quinn's house, where they ate microwavable pizza pockets and Gabriel tutored Quinn in precalculus, the one subject that had given her trouble. She liked being with him. But she didn't give their relationship a lot of thought. She didn't need to. It was easy. It was fun. It was *right*. And if her other friends didn't always understand it, Quinn shrugged it off. It was still possible for members of the opposite sex to be friends with each other, she reminded them. She and Gabriel were those friends. Friends *without* benefits.

"All right, let's get started," Quinn said. "Once again, Matty is missing in action." Matty was the paper's associate editor, whose video-game addiction interfered with this role. "But can I run some story ideas by you?" she asked Gabriel.

"Yep," he said, putting a lens cover on his camera.

"All right. Number one: a profile of Northern Superior High

School's bus driver, Bart Walgamott. He's retiring after forty years. I thought you could get a picture of him sitting behind the wheel." Quinn made it a point to include a profile of one of Northern Superior's administrators or employees in every issue. She wanted the paper to represent the whole school, not just the students.

"I can take a picture of Bart," Gabriel said.

"Good," she said, glancing down at her legal pad. "Idea number two: a theater review of the spring play." It was *The Crucible* that year. "I can get Emma Raible to do that. She did a good job on the *Music Man* review, don't you think?"

"Yeah. It was good. Do you want a cast photo? Or something from a performance?"

"Something from a performance. I already got tickets for us for Friday night."

"Cool."

"And, let's see, number three." Quinn studied her remaining suggestions. But she wasn't satisfied with any of them. "God, someday I want to live in a place where more happens," she said, biting her lower lip.

"So make something up."

She raised an eyebrow at him. "That's right. That's the first rule of journalism. 'Make something up.'"

"It works in this country."

"Hmmm. Well, I'm trying to hold this paper to a higher standard," Quinn said. She studied her scribblings on the page in front of her. Maybe she'd go with the article about the current drought? This part of the state was still recovering from it.

She could get Gabriel to get a picture of a local farmer bending down in a field, sifting through a handful of dirt. She had no idea if farmers still did this, but it struck her as uniquely American. Hadn't those photographers who'd chronicled the Dust Bowl taken pictures like that? She started to ask Gabriel but he interrupted her.

"What about an article, no, not an article, more of an intellectual exercise, on why the cafeteria smells the way it does," he suggested.

"What does it smell like?"

"Like some combination of spilled milk and bleach," he said. "Haven't you ever noticed it? Where does that come from? I mean, nobody drinks milk in there, except, maybe, for a couple of football players. And bleach? Nobody cleans that place. Maybe, like, once a week they run a damp mop around it, just for show. But Clorox? I don't think so."

Quinn considered this. "Would you write it?" She'd always wanted Gabriel to write an article. She had a feeling it would be funny.

"I'm not a writer. But I'd take pictures of the cafeteria. In line today, I was looking at the green Jell-O. I like that color. It's kind of . . . violent."

Quinn nodded. "Why green?" she said. "Always green. All the time." She was getting the idea for an article. "And why make it? Still? After all these years? Does anyone *ever* eat it? I can get Woods Fairbanks to do something on that. He's good with humor. He did something about tater tots last year, remember?"

"It was national tater tot day."

"Right," Quinn said, scribbling *green Jell-O* on her legal pad. Okay, so this subject wasn't exactly Woodward and Bernstein material, but she had to work with what she had here.

"Um, Quinn?" she heard someone ask. She looked up from the couch.

It was Emma Raible, a sophomore who wrote for the paper. She was petite, as in *tiny*, with wide brown eyes and a general air of adorability about her. "I finished that article," she said, though she wasn't looking at Quinn. She was looking at Gabriel. "The one on high school dress codes? I emailed it to you."

"Good, I'll read it tonight," Quinn said. "I might have something else for you this week too."

"How do you feel about green Jell-O?" Gabriel asked her. He'd been lying down on the couch but now he sat up.

"Green Jell-O in what way?" Emma asked him, looking more serious than the subject required.

"In every way."

Quinn made some notes on possible articles while the two of them chatted. She wanted to do an article on what colleges seniors were attending in the fall, and a companion article about juniors and their summer plans. But when Emma left, Quinn gave Gabriel a dirty look.

"What?"

"Why do you torture her? You know she likes you." And in that moment, looking over at Gabriel lounging beside her, Quinn understood exactly why Emma had a crush on him.

"No, she doesn't," he said.

"Gabriel, you can't be that clueless . . . Ask her out."

"No. She's, like, fourteen."

"She's sixteen. And she's so cute. She looks like a little doll."

"Not all men find that attractive."

"No?" She raised an eyebrow, but he didn't notice. He was unscrewing the lens cap on his camera. She reached for her overloaded backpack, on the floor beside the couch, and unzipped it, stuffing the yellow legal pad inside. "Do you want a ride?" she asked.

"Yeah, thanks. Aiden won't be done with track for another hour," he said, of his middle brother.

She started to get up, then stopped. Gabriel was preparing to take another picture of her, and whereas before he'd been animated, now he was quiet and meditative. "Did I tell you about this tradition at Northwestern?" she asked him. She'd been online again last night, researching Northwestern University's journalism program. "It happens on the Sunday night before final exams start. At nine P.M., all the students stick their heads out their dorm windows and scream as loud as they can. It's supposed to release tension," she added, imagining what her father might think if she tried this at home.

"Do you think they do it at RISD?" she asked him.

"Maybe," he said. He was looking at her through his viewfinder, adjusting his lens.

"I don't know," Quinn mused. "At RISD students are probably too busy hanging out in cool coffeehouses or something to stop and scream."

"Maybe," Gabriel said. She heard the shutter click. "Hey, Quinn," he said, "turn your head. A little to the left."

CHAPTER 8

After Quinn finished writing this memory, she felt both exhilarated *and* exhausted. How she could feel both, she didn't know. She'd never written anything like this before. It was a memory—or as true to that memory as she could get with the distance of ten years—and it was deeply personal to her, but it wasn't even close to a *personal essay*. No, she'd written it in the third person. She'd heard this described as fictional memoir, but she hadn't consciously planned to do this. It was simply that doing it this way—writing her memories like a story—made it possible to do it at all.

A few minutes later she put on her coat and headed over to the Corner Bar. She wasn't going to make the same mistake she made last night, when she skipped dinner. She was sitting in a booth and was glancing through a red leather-bound menu that she still knew by heart when the waitress approached her.

"Hey. What can I get for you tonight?" she asked Quinn. She was a blond middle-aged woman whom Quinn didn't recognize and whose name tag identified her as *Dawn*.

"I'll have the Corner Burger, medium rare," Quinn said, closing the menu and handing it to her. "And a glass of pinot grigio, please."

Dawn hesitated. "Can I see your ID?" she asked.

"*Really?* I'm twenty-eight," Quinn said. She extracted her wallet from her shoulder bag and, flipping it open, let Dawn examine her license. "You're the third person today who told me I look like I'm still in high school."

"No, you don't," Dawn said, scribbling on her check pad as Quinn put her wallet away. "You look like you're in your twenties. It's just that I don't know you, and Marty, the bartender here, is a real stickler about carding people."

"Of course he is." Quinn smiled. She knew Marty. Or rather *had known* Marty when she'd lived here before. The way you knew most people in a town like Butternut. He was an institution. Either the only bartender the Corner Bar had ever had, or the only bartender anyone could ever remember the Corner Bar having. Either way, he would forever be married in Quinn's mind with the extra maraschino cherries—at least a half dozen of them—he'd put in her Shirley Temple when her dad had brought her here as a child. When she'd come in this evening, she'd seen him behind the bar, polishing glasses, and had almost said hello to him, but she'd decided it was too complicated and had taken refuge in a back booth instead. She wanted to be anonymous, for now.

"Okay, I'll bring you your pinot," Dawn said, with a smile. "And just remember, when you're my age, on the *other* side of forty, you'll miss getting carded."

"Probably," Quinn said. Dawn left her, and she looked around the room, which, at five o'clock in the evening, was still quiet. There were a few men sitting at the bar watching a NASCAR race on a flat-screen TV, a family sitting in another booth, and, across the restaurant, two couples sitting at a table. Quinn recognized the female half of one of the couples, who was seated facing her; it was Butternut's mayor, who had spoken at the dedication today. The man sitting next to her, Quinn assumed, was her husband. The couple across from them had their backs to her so she didn't know whether she would have recognized them or not, but there was something about the way the four of them were sitting—hunched forward—and the quiet intensity of their conversation that gave Quinn pause.

"Here you go," Dawn said, interrupting her gaze as she put the glass of wine on the table. "Your burger will be right up."

"Thank you," Quinn said. She took a sip of the wine and sighed with satisfaction. It was delicious, and, to prevent herself from gulping down the whole thing, she pulled her laptop out of her computer bag. She wasn't sure she wanted to write anything more tonight. But it wouldn't hurt to read over her memory of that spring afternoon in the communications room with Gabriel. She reread her file while she sipped her wine. It was faithful to that time in their lives, she decided. Sometimes she found her memory for details irritating; if someone told her, five years ago, about an appendectomy they once had, she could recite the story verbatim today. She was grateful now, though, for that ability to recall, and when Dawn brought her order, she thought some more about that afternoon in the communications room as she munched on her burger and fries. She had spent so much of her last year of high school in that room. Well, until the accident. Still, she reasoned, Gabriel was only half of that year. Jake was the other half. And writing about one without writing about the other was like . . . like telling half the truth. She nudged her plate, empty but for a parsley garnish, away from her, and was reaching for her laptop again when Dawn reappeared.

"Can I get you anything else?" she asked, taking Quinn's plate. "Another glass of pinot grigio, maybe?" She nodded at her empty glass.

"No, thank you. That was delicious, though. If you don't mind, I think I'm going to work a little," she added, gesturing at her laptop.

"Go right ahead."

Quinn wanted to write about Jake, even if there was a part of her that was afraid to. Still, there were things that *needed* to be remembered, no matter how difficult remembering them would be. She hadn't been aware of Jake until high school. He'd grown up in Winton and although it was only fifteen minutes away, they had a separate elementary and middle school. The image that came to her now was of the first time she'd seen Jake, walking down the hallway at Northern Superior High School at the beginning of ninth grade. He was coming toward her, his backpack slung over his shoulder, and while Quinn was at an age where she worked very hard not to be impressed by anything, she was impressed by him. He was good looking and rumored to be a gifted athlete. But it was more than that. He was confident, and while he didn't have the swagger of, say, Seth Worcester, a senior and the quarterback of the football team, he had something better. An ease. A comfort in his own skin. Quinn tried not to stare at him. He caught her eye, anyway, and smiled at her, a killer smile.

She smiled back, but she'd already classified him. He wasn't her type. He was a jock. Her interests lay elsewhere. She doubted they would spend much time together and she was right. Over the next three years, their paths only occasionally crossed, and although they were friendly enough, they were each caught up in their own separate worlds. Their own high schools *within* a high school. Besides, Jake usually had a girlfriend.

And even now, ten years after leaving Butternut, she was surprised they'd ever gone out with each other, let alone stayed together for nine months. Their relationship wasn't only *not* predestined; it was a fluke. It would never have happened if she hadn't had an internship at the *Butternut Express*.

The newspaper's offices were in a converted two-bedroom apartment above the variety store. There were three window-mounted air conditioners, which were often on the fritz, and a half-dozen potted plants, which managed to limp along, though Quinn never saw anyone water them. And, of course, back issues of the newspaper were stacked on desks, in corners, in closets, on the stairs, and even in the cupboards of what had once been the kitchen and was now a meeting room. Like so many small-town papers, the *Butternut Express* operated on a shoestring with only two full-time employees, Bryan Walsh, the editor in chief, and a sales manager, both of whom did a little bit of everything, and two part-time reporters. There was also a freelance photographer they used when necessary. Although, in Quinn's opinion, he was nowhere near as good as Gabriel.

She'd started the summer there with a burst of ambition, pitching story ideas to Bryan. But while she begged to write a story on someone like Rusty Brooke, a local raconteur who was running for town mayor, or a piece on the controversial dredging of Butternut Lake's shoreline, she ended up with features on the closing of Deb's Bear Den, a local beauty salon, and the volunteer fire department's purchase of a new truck.

Quinn didn't get discouraged, though. She didn't stop pitching, either, until one afternoon when she realized she was getting on Bryan's nerves. She left him alone after that, and, when he found her, three days later, reorganizing the storage closet—more back issues of the paper—and asked her if she wanted to do a profile on the high school cross-country star Jake Lightman, she recognized this for what it was: a peace offering. And she jumped at the chance.

CHAPTER 9

Late June, Summer Before Senior Year, Interviewing Jake

It had been a wet spring, and the summer was so lush that as Quinn walked from Northern Superior High School's parking lot to the bleachers she discovered that the tidy, cultivated grounds she'd left behind a couple of weeks ago had been transformed into something different, something verdant and wild. The grass on the athletic fields had grown long and shaggy, the shrub roses that edged the bleachers were in riotous bloom, and even the willow trees seemed ready to collapse under the weight of their foliage. The sunny day would have been hot but for a breeze that was strong enough to carry the scent of roses on it, strong enough, too, to make the leaves on the aspen trees shiver and quake.

It was, in short, a perfect summer day. But something about

it—its heaviness or its sweetness—had the effect of making Quinn drowsy, and, as she settled onto the bleachers to wait for Jake Lightman, the classmate she was interviewing, she sipped the iced tea she'd ordered at Pearl's. She'd gotten an extra-large and added five packets of sugar to it, hoping that the one-two punch of caffeine and sugar would boost her mental alertness. She checked her watch. She was five minutes early, as usual. Her punctuality was either her most endearing or her most annoying quality, depending on how you looked at it. To Gabriel, it was endearing.

She slipped her cell phone out of her back pocket and checked the screen. Nope. Gabriel hadn't returned her call yet. He was probably in class at his summer program at the Art Institute of Chicago. She took out a pen and the yellow legal pad she'd written the interview questions on. She'd meant to review them, but now she wondered instead about Gabriel. Would he meet a girl there this summer? And if he did, would he tell Quinn about her? It was hard to say. Girls were one of the only things he didn't talk to her about.

She was surprised at how much she missed him. How dependent upon him she'd become. How much she wanted him to be here. It was funny how that had sneaked up on her. She remembered the night before he'd left for Chicago. They'd started at the Mosquito Inn, where they'd ordered rum and Cokes. The Mosquito Inn was a dive bar, but unfortunately, it was a dive bar that carded, so they'd ended up driving around and listening to music. Then, after Quinn's curfew, she got permission from her dad for Gabriel to stay late so they could watch *The Shawshank Redemption*, one of their favorite movies. They'd talked for hours afterward, until Quinn's dad said Gabriel had to get home and get to bed.

A gust of wind ruffled the pages on her legal pad, and, as she smoothed them down, she saw Jake approaching the bleachers. "Hey," he said, lifting a hand in a wave. She waved back. His body was lean and light, a runner's body, or so her internet research last night had told her, and he was obviously coming from the locker room, because his wet hair was combed down, and a gym bag was thrown over one shoulder. He had a tan for so early in the summer, and it made the dark gold color of his eyes stand out. He smiled up at her as he climbed the bleachers and Quinn thought, *He's got it. Whatever* it *is, he's got it.* For some reason, it irritated her.

"You're late," she said, matter-of-factly, as he sat down on the bleacher across from her. He glanced at his watch. She didn't know this yet, but it was a Garmin watch, a gift from his parents after his cross-country team won the state championship last season. It was his favorite, his *only*, accessory.

"Just by a couple of minutes," he pointed out. "I could have been early, but I was so sweaty from my run I thought it would be rude not to take a shower." He smiled again, but Quinn only nodded. She was determined to be professional, even if he was one of her classmates. She studied her legal pad, trying to decide which question to start with.

"Mr. Drossel said you called him last night," Jake said. She looked up. Mr. Drossel taught U.S. history and coached the cross-country team. "Lou and Griffin said you called them, too." They were both friends of Jake's on the cross-country team.

"I did. When I interview someone for a profile, I try to interview at least five other people connected to them first."

"Why?"

"It gives you a different perspective on your subject, and it helps shape the questions you're going to ask them."

Jake nodded, obviously impressed. "When the *Duluth News Tribune* did an article on me, I was the only person they interviewed."

"I probably have more time than their reporters," Quinn said, thinking of her self-imposed exile to the supply closet. "Do you want to get started now?" she asked, studying her notes again.

"Fire away," he said.

"Okay, let's see." She started with a list of necessary, though to her not-terribly-interesting, questions. Cross-country was his main sport, but he also ran indoor track in the winter and track in the spring. She asked him about what events he competed in, what his best times were, what his training regimen was like. "How'd you get started running?" she asked, her pen poised above the pad.

He paused. "My brother," he said.

"He was a runner?"

"No, he *wasn't* a runner. That's the point."

Quinn looked up, waiting for more information.

He shrugged. "You know who Tanner is, don't you?"

She nodded. Everyone knew who Tanner Lightman was. He was in twelfth grade when Quinn was in ninth. It was almost a rite of passage to have a crush on him. He was like a composite character from the classic 1980s high school movies that Quinn loved. The handsome athlete who falls for the insecure, quirky girl. He'd been something of a daredevil, too. That year he'd been famous for driving his truck on Shell Lake on April Fool's Day—it was the latest anyone from their high school had ever driven out on the ice before. But all Quinn said to Jake was, "He was athletic, wasn't he?"

"He played two varsity sports. If he could have cloned himself, he would have played three. I saw early on, when I was, like, *eight*, that I wasn't going to have his hand-eye coordination. I could run, though. I could always run. My mom said I skipped walking. I went straight from crawling to running. So I figured that was the way to go."

"Your brother can't be your whole motivation," Quinn pointed out.

"He's not."

"Why do it then? I mean, why do you love it?"

"I don't love it."

She paused in her writing.

"No, it's true. I hate it."

Quinn must have looked skeptical.

"*What?* Have you ever been to a cross-country meet in mid-October?"

She shook her head. She'd never been to a cross-country meet, ever.

"Okay, then. Let me set the scene," he said, warming to the topic. "First, cross-country means hills. Second, at that time of year, in Minnesota, it means cold, and rain, and mud, and . . . more mud. Basically, miserable conditions. And, if you're me, you're running uphill, fighting cramps and dehydration, covered with mud, your feet freezing cold, and another runner is coming right up behind you, so slowing down is not an option."

"That sounds awful," Quinn said. "But if you hate it, why do it?"

"Because I only hate it seventy-five percent of the time. The other twenty-five percent of the time, I love it. That's common, by the way, among distance runners. That love-hate relationship."

"Do you get runner's high?"

"Absolutely."

"What's it like? I've never run far enough to get it," she admitted. She hated running. Always had.

"It's worth it."

"The cold? The wet? The mud?"

"All of it."

"So the twenty-five percent of it you love is about the runner's high?" she clarified.

"No," he said. "It's not that simple. The high, that's like a bonus. It's not the whole thing. I love running because . . . well, I'm good at it, for one thing. That's common too. There may be bad runners out there who love it, but I've never met any of them. And—this is harder to explain—but I like the mind-set part of it. The mental toughness, I guess you'd call it. If you don't do well, there's no one else to blame. You can't blame the referee or another player or the coach. It's you. You leave it all there on the trail or the track. If you do well, though, you feel like you can do *anything*."

"That's interesting," Quinn murmured, writing this down. But she didn't know if it was the running or Jake that was interesting. He was so different than she'd imagined he would be. He was more introspective. And articulate.

"What about college?" she said, trying to focus. "I assume you've been recruited?"

"Madison," he said, of the University of Wisconsin at Madison. "You can't put that in the paper yet," he added, quickly. "They can't make me an official offer until July first. Right now, it's a handshake agreement."

"Why Madison?" she asked.

"Tanner goes there."

"You're competitive with him. Are you close, too?"

"Close?" He looked confused. "We're brothers," he said, as if this were self-explanatory.

"Not all brothers are close," Quinn said. She was thinking of Gabriel's relationship with his brothers. He couldn't have been more different from them, or less close to them.

"That's true, I guess. But *we* are close. Sort of. Most of the time. When we're not trying to kill each other," he joked. "You know how it is."

"I don't. I don't have any siblings," she said.

"No? Well, it's complicated. We're . . . pretty competitive with each other. But, yeah, I want to go to the same school as him. It would feel weird not to."

Quinn nodded, though sibling dynamics were often a mystery to her.

"What about you?" he asked. "Where do you want to go to college?"

"Me?" She was scanning her questions to see if she'd missed anything. "I want to go to Northwestern," she said. "It's a stretch, though."

"You'll get in," he predicted. She looked at him. His hair had dried and a cowlick had popped up. She smiled. He smiled back. She loved his smile, but she would only admit it to herself. "Okay," she said abruptly. "I think that about wraps it up. Except for the photo. I already gave your contact info to our freelance photographer. His name is Josh Hartley. I don't know what he has in mind, but you two can work that out. If you want to give input, that's fine. He's good at listening to suggestions. Do you have some time available tomorrow?"

"Yeah, have him call me."

She reached for her backpack, though she didn't want to leave.

"So that's it?" Jake asked. He ran his hands through his hair, messing it up a little more.

"Uh-huh. Unless . . . there's something you want to add?"

"No, I'm done talking. But what about you? I don't know any more about you than I did when we started."

"You're not supposed to," Quinn said. Instead of looking at Jake, she closed her legal pad and looked briefly over to where some kids were kicking a soccer ball on the far side of the field.

"I'm still curious, though," he said. Quinn looked back at

him. His eyes caught the afternoon light. There was another smile from him. *Did he have to keep smiling at her like that?* "Come on. Tell me something about you," he said.

"There's nothing to tell. We've been going to high school together for three years. You already know all the basics."

"That's almost nothing."

Quinn laughed. She was the least mysterious person she knew.

"No, it's true," Jake said. "All I know about you is . . . you run the paper. You're always in the communications room. And you hang out with that guy. Gabriel. By the way, what's up with you two? Are you guys friends or . . ."

"We're friends," she said. But she knew in the past that people had wondered if they were a couple. Well, that was high school for you. A girl couldn't be friends with a boy without people wondering. "And now I feel like you're interviewing me," she said to change the subject.

He ignored this. "Did you grow up in Butternut?"

"Born and raised."

"And what about your family? I know you don't have any siblings. What about your parents?" *Here it comes*, Quinn thought.

"It's just me and my dad," she said.

He started to ask her something else and then caught himself.

"My mom died when I was little," she said. It was best to get that out there right away.

"I'm sorry," he said. "How old were you?"

"I was eighteen months old. I don't remember her." And this was true. But Quinn had formed an image of her based on photographs her dad had taken and stories her dad had told her.

"She must have been beautiful," Jake said, surprising Quinn.

"Why, why do you say that?"

"Because she had you," Jake said. This could have—perhaps *should have*—sounded cheesy, but somehow, coming from him, it didn't. She was flustered. She'd fielded questions about her mother for most of her life, and the script, by now, was well known to her. This was the point at which most people asked *how* her mother had died, although they were always careful to couch the question in an apology. *If you don't mind my asking . . . I hope it's not too personal . . . I don't mean to pry.*

"She died from a head injury," Quinn said to the question Jake hadn't asked. "An epidural hematoma." What she didn't tell Jake until months later was that one morning, when her dad was at work, and her mom, Celia, was home alone with a napping Quinn, she'd climbed a ladder to put something on top of a storage shelf in the garage and had fallen and hit her head. Afterward, she'd felt dizzy for a few minutes, and then she'd felt fine. In the late afternoon, though, she'd felt dizzy again, and by the time Quinn's dad came home from work, she'd told him she needed to go to the hospital. He'd left Quinn with a neighbor and called an ambulance. By later that night, her mom was in a coma, and by early the next day, she had died.

Her dad told Quinn that one day he had a wife whom he adored, and the next day she was gone. For the year after she'd died he'd been bereft. And not only that, but Quinn's maternal grandmother—known to Quinn as "Grandmother Shaw"—had insisted that Celia be buried in a family plot in Chicago. So her dad could only visit her grave if he traveled five hundred miles away.

"My dad was a good dad," she said to Jake now, again un-prompted. "Still is, actually."

"I can tell," Jake said. "Is he . . . like both parents to you?" he asked. "I heard that's what happens when you have one parent. They have to be both."

"Is he a dad *and* a mom?" Quinn asked. She laughed. "No. He's just a dad." She had no idea whether or not her mother would have been more domestic than her father, but she could hardly have been *less* domestic than him. That hadn't stopped her dad from finding creative solutions for running a household. Once, when he was teaching a nine-year-old Quinn how to do laundry, he'd instructed her, in all serious-ness, to cram as much clothing into the washing machine as it would hold. Another time, when Quinn wanted him to put her hair in a ponytail and he couldn't find a hair elastic, he was delighted to discover that a plastic cable tie made an accept-able alternative. And then there was his cooking, which not only didn't improve over the years but seemed to get worse. One of his favorite fixes for a bland meal, and they were *all* bland, was to melt cheese over everything on the plate. It was years before Quinn discovered that not everyone ate dinners that came buried beneath a bubbling sheet of Velveeta. "But we do all right," she said to Jake. *More than all right.* And, realizing how much more she'd told him than she'd intended to, she said, "Now that we've covered my childhood, I think *this* interview is over too."

"One more question," he said. "I swear. That's it."

"What?" she asked, a little curious about what it would be.

"Why don't I ever see you outside of school?"

"What do you mean?"

"Why don't you ever go to parties?"

"*Oh*. Well, because they're not my thing. *Big* parties, I mean. I hang out with Gabriel, and some of our other friends, and we watch movies or play pool. Sometimes someone brings something to drink, but it's not . . . a scene. You know, like Leigh Downer's parties." Leigh Downer, who was in their class, was the undisputed party queen. It helped that she lived in a big house and that her parents were never home. "The last time I went to one of those," she said, "everyone was so drunk, they couldn't even stand up. There was no one there I could have talked to."

"You could have talked to me," he said. "I don't drink."

"Never?"

"*Almost* never. I don't want it to interfere with my training. Plus the last time I got drunk, a couple of years ago, I acted like an idiot."

"In what way?"

"I jumped out of Dom's second-story window. It was after a snowstorm. I thought the snow would break my fall."

"Did it?"

"Uh, no. I broke my arm. My dad was so pissed." He shook his head. "He said if I'd broken my leg, my running career might have been over." It was getting windier now, and a succession of white, puffy clouds were crossing over the athletic fields. Quinn could track them in Jake's eyes, his gold irises darkening and lightening as they moved into and out of the shade.

"I should get going," she said, without much conviction.

"Can I walk you to your car?"

"Okay," she said, again surprised by his seriousness. His chivalrousness. This wasn't a side of Jake she'd seen at school. Then again, *that* side of him was never alone; it was always surrounded by friends. It was easygoing, outgoing, extroverted. He was different now. Quieter. More thoughtful.

They climbed down the bleachers and headed for the tunnel that linked the locker rooms to the football field. It was cool and dim inside, and Quinn thought about how it was one of the places on campus couples went to make out. When she and Jake came out the other side, into the green sea of summer, they still said nothing. Jake looked relaxed, but Quinn felt agitated. Too much caffeine. Too much sugar. She was acutely conscious, though, of her body in space, and of his body, too, near to hers, near enough to be touching hers, but not touching hers.

When they got to her car, he said, "Do you want to go to the beach sometime?"

"Let me . . . think about it," she said.

He smiled. His smile was even better now, if that was possible. A smile he'd saved for her. "Don't think too hard about it, Quinn," he teased. And then he took the pen and pad she was still holding and wrote his number across the top. "Call me," he said.

"It was nice interviewing you," she blurted. (That night, replaying the scene, she cringed at those words. Had she really said them?)

"It was nice being interviewed by you," he said. She was standing close enough to him to smell the soap he'd used in the locker-room shower.

"Bye, Jake," she said, getting into her car. By this point, she didn't really want to go. And maybe he didn't either. His truck was parked only a few spaces from hers, but he didn't get into it. He stood there and watched until she'd driven away.

CHAPTER 10

"Hello, Quinn."

Quinn, startled, looked up. While she'd been writing about Jake, the Corner Bar had gotten more crowded. Dominic Dobbs's mother, Theresa, was standing beside Quinn's booth.

"Mrs. Dobbs," Quinn said. She started to stand up to greet her, but Dominic's father, who'd joined his wife, waved her back down again.

"Don't get up, Quinn," he said, apologetically. "Theresa just came over to say hello. We're going to go back to our table." He gestured at the table across the restaurant where the mayor and her husband were still sitting.

Quinn smiled at the Dobbses. "I thought the ceremony today was so moving," she said, still trying to find her bearings. To have been so deep into her memories and writing, and then

catapulted to the present and the Corner Bar was disorienting. But there was something else giving her pause. Something
about Theresa Dobbs's appearance. She looked both as if she
were having difficulty focusing on Quinn, and as if she herself
were out of focus. Her silk blouse was wrinkled and her mascara was smeared.

"Thank you," Mr. Dobbs said now. "We thought the ceremony was moving too." He took his wife by the elbow and tried
to steer her back to their table.

"We didn't see you at the reception," Theresa said, shaking her husband's hand off and lurching to one side with the
effort. "Why weren't you there?" she asked. Her words were
slurred.

She's drunk, Quinn thought. "I was planning on going to
the reception," she said, feeling regretful now that she hadn't
gone but also wondering why it was any of Theresa's business
whether she had or not. "But I went to see a friend of mine,
someone I'd lost touch with," she explained, though she realized this would mean nothing to Theresa.

"So you had better things to do?" Theresa asked. Quinn felt
confused.

"No, that wasn't it—" she started to explain, but Mr. Dobbs
interrupted.

"Theresa, Quinn came to the dedication," he told his wife,
speaking to her the way he might speak to a recalcitrant child.
"Obviously, there were things she needed to do afterward." His
hand closed over her elbow again, but Theresa wouldn't be
budged. Quinn glanced over at the mayor's table, where there

was a flurry of activity as the mayor and her husband settled up the bill and gathered their belongings together. Although neither of them looked over at the booth, Quinn got the impression they both knew why Theresa was there.

"I'm sorry I wasn't at the reception," Quinn said. "I spoke to Tanner after the dedication, and when he said his parents weren't going, I thought . . ." She stopped. She didn't want to use the Lightmans as an excuse.

"You'd do something more fun," Theresa finished for her, her hands resting on the table as if to steady herself. It was impossible to ignore the contempt in her voice. Mr. Dobbs looked embarrassed. "Theresa," he said, pulling on one of her arms. "Come on. Let's go. *Please.* I asked you not to come over here."

Theresa, though, gripped the side of the table now, her expression a grimace of concentration that made her wrinkles— the furrow lines on her forehead, the commas around her mouth—appear even deeper. The table wobbled a little, and Quinn reached out a hand to steady it. What the hell was going on? she wondered, her heart beating faster. Why had Theresa wanted to come over when it was obvious she didn't like Quinn? Or was that *why* she'd wanted to come over? It was hard to imagine why she disliked Quinn so much, though. She barely knew Quinn. Aside from saying hello a handful of times at high school events, they'd never spoken to each other.

"Theresa, I think it's time we went home," Mr. Dobbs said, a different, harder tone in his voice. "It's been a long—" he started to add, directing this at Quinn.

"A long ten years," Theresa interrupted. She swayed forward. "Thanks to you," she said to Quinn.

What? Me? Thanks to me? Quinn almost said, her face flushing. But she wondered if she'd heard her correctly. Mr. Dobbs, with a twist of Theresa's elbow, finally succeeded in steering her away from the booth. "Please excuse us," he said, heading to the exit. Theresa stumbled as she walked, then turned to watch Quinn, her mouth moving as if forming words that wouldn't come. The mayor and her husband hurried after them, trailing winter coats and murmured apologies, though who the apologies were for Quinn didn't know; they never acknowledged her.

Dawn came over when they were gone. "Jeez, what was that about?"

"No idea," Quinn said. She felt overwhelmed.

"Do you know her?" Dawn asked.

"I did, once. But even then, not really."

"Wow. I'm sorry." Dawn said. "Do you want something else? Another pinot grigio? I bet Marty would comp it."

"What? No, thank you," Quinn said. "Just the check."

"Right," Dawn said. "I have it right here, dear." She put it down on the table next to Quinn. When she left her alone, Quinn touched a finger to her cheek, almost as if Theresa had struck her there. *My God, did she actually say that to me?* she thought. *That it had been a long ten years because of me? Does she believe I'm somehow to blame for Dominic's death? Is that what she meant? And not just Dominic's death, but Jake's and*

Griffin's as well? No one had ever blamed her before. At least, not that she knew of. Although, of course, in her darkest moments she'd blamed herself. After all, there was the question of what had happened between her and Jake the night of the accident. But no one knew about that but the two of them. All anyone else knew was that three young men—one of whom, in Theresa's case, was her son—had died needless, useless, and heartrending deaths. And nobody could change that fact.

Well, not now, a voice inside her said. *Not anymore. It's too late. Too late to undo what you said and did that night. Too late to take back what you and Gabriel did.* The question that Gabriel had asked her earlier that day, about guilt and responsibility, came swirling back into her head. And, without caring who saw her in a bar that was now crowded, Quinn put her head in her hands. She had held up so far, but she didn't know if she could anymore.

LATER, BACK IN her motel room, with her coat still on and the lights still off, Quinn sat in a chair by the window and watched as the occasional car glided past on the highway. She pulled a Kleenex out of her coat pocket, and, as an eighteen-wheeler rumbled by, she dried her tears. She hoped she was done crying. The trouble was that in the hour since she'd left the Corner Bar, the shock of Theresa's words had worn off, but the pain they'd caused had not. She wanted to leave Butternut, she realized. And what better time to do it than now, under cover of darkness? But something made her stay in that chair.

And not only stay, but dig in a little. She couldn't leave. She knew this. Even if this was *all* that she knew. There was simply too much at stake.

How much was at stake had become increasingly clear this past winter, when she'd driven by a car accident, or, rather, driven past the *aftermath* of a car accident. It was a January evening, freezing cold, and she was returning to Evanston after an interview she'd done for an article she was writing. The traffic had slowed to a crawl and then, finally, inched past the scene of an accident. It must have happened recently: flares still burned on the road, debris and glass were everywhere, and an ambulance, its lights flashing, was still on the scene. So was one of the vehicles involved: a blue pickup truck.

It was empty, and it had a shattered windshield and a crumpled hood, grill, and front bumper. And maybe it was the uncertain light of dusk, or the weird pink light being thrown by the flares, but the truck looked uncannily like the one Jake had driven. "*That's it,*" Quinn had murmured, seized by the entirely irrational belief that it *was*, in fact, Jake's truck. Without thinking, she'd pulled over, gotten out of her car, and walked up to a police officer who was talking to an EMT. "Excuse me, Officer," she'd said, tapping him on the shoulder, "is the driver of that truck okay?" He turned to her, startled. "Ma'am, you can't be out here," he'd said. "This is an accident scene. You need to get back in your car." "But, Officer, is the driver all right?" she'd asked, again, pleading with him. "He's at the hospital," he'd said, curtly. "Now move along." He'd pointed her in the direction of her car, and she'd gone back to it, meekly. She'd known better than to argue with him. She'd driven home, then, a little unsteadily, but it wasn't until she'd gotten back to her apartment that she'd let herself fall apart. She'd sunk down on the kitchen floor, shaking uncontrollably.

She'd had one of the dreams that night. She'd been having them for years, off and on, but once she'd seen the mangled blue pickup, she started having them more frequently. Afterward, she couldn't fall back asleep and was tired the next day. She'd kept up with her daunting freelance workload, but, increasingly, she'd felt gripped by a strange kind of inertia. It was an uphill battle to get out of bed in the morning, and, once out of bed, to keep her day in motion. So those days became a series of mantras. *Brush teeth. Make coffee. Pour cereal in bowl.* And these mantras continued, from morning to night, when all she really wanted to do was to crawl into bed, pull the covers over her head, and stay there, indefinitely.

She'd felt this way once before, during her junior year in college. She'd had what her therapist had referred to as a kind of breakdown, though to Quinn it had felt more like she was *shutting down* than *breaking down*. Whatever the terminology, the experience had frightened Quinn enough so that when she felt it beginning to happen again in January, she knew she needed to do something. But what? She understood that accident on Route 45 had brought up buried feelings and memories about Jake's death, but knowing this did not mean she knew what to do about it. She'd thought about trying to find a therapist to talk to, but then, a couple of weeks ago, the anonymous newspaper clipping had come in the mail. And it had felt to Quinn like a message, a sign, that she needed to return to Butternut.

So here she was. And here she would stay. For how long exactly, she didn't know. But she was going to need to stay beyond the weekend. That much was clear. She'd found her encounters with Gabriel and Theresa so upsetting that they made her want to leave, but then perhaps that was all the more reason to stay. *No one said this was going to be easy*, she reminded herself.

As for what Theresa had said to her, well, she didn't know what to think. She'd blamed Quinn for the misery of the last ten years, which meant she was blaming Quinn for the accident. Why would she say that? Well, she'd been drunk. Was it possible she'd wake up tomorrow morning with no memory of what she'd said?

Of course, Theresa could have been motivated by pure anger. She'd wanted someone to lash out at, and Quinn, who'd been Jake's girlfriend at the time of the accident, had presented herself as a convenient target. Perhaps Theresa had been offended that Quinn hadn't gone to the reception. Or perhaps her behavior was better explained by grief alone. She was hurting; she was a mother who had lost a son. Quinn could only imagine how debilitating that must be. Maybe, then, her words to Quinn were the result of a toxic mix of all these things—alcohol, grief, and anger.

As Quinn got up, turned on her bedside table lamp, and pulled the curtains closed, she settled on this as an explanation. And, as she got ready for bed, she thought of the other parents she knew who had lost a son, Jake's parents. She did not believe they would treat her the way Theresa had. She would go see them tomorrow, she decided. And after that, she'd go see Gabriel. If she was lucky, she wouldn't run into Theresa again during her stay in Butternut.

CHAPTER 11

The next morning, Quinn sat in one of the back booths at Pearl's, a now-tepid cup of coffee and a half-eaten order of blueberry pancakes in front of her. She picked up her fork and poked at the remaining pancake left on her plate. How did Caroline Keegan, the owner of Pearl's, do it, she wondered, concocting this impossibly fluffy creation, part pancake, part pillow, and, months before berry season, studded throughout with plump, purplish blueberries? Quinn had no idea. She'd never graduated beyond the Bisquick mix herself. She gave the pancake a final prod and set her fork down, too preoccupied to eat any more.

"Quinn? Is that you?" Caroline asked, coming up to the booth.

"Caroline!" Quinn said. She slid out of the booth and gave her a hug.

"What a nice surprise," Caroline said.

"I wanted to say hello when I first came in, but you were so busy," Quinn said, noticing that Caroline—a pretty, strawberry-blond woman in her forties—looked the same as she'd looked ten years ago. Quinn had once written a profile about Caroline for the school paper in which she'd described her as the de facto mayor of Butternut. But she was much more than that. And there were few people in town whose lives she hadn't touched.

"Your dad and Johanna were up here last summer," Caroline said. "He told me that you're writing and living near Chicago. Good for you, Quinn. I couldn't be prouder of you."

"Thanks, Caroline. I love what I'm doing. Hey, how's Daisy?" Quinn asked, of Caroline's daughter, who'd been three years behind her in high school.

"She's married. She got married last summer. She married Will Hughes—he's from Winton. And, just between you and me, she's pregnant. *Newly* pregnant. The baby is due in the fall."

"That's wonderful, Caroline," Quinn said. "I'm so happy for her." But just as she said this, there was a crash from the kitchen.

"Oh, dear," Caroline said. "I'm training a new employee." She gave Quinn a quick kiss and was gone. *Daisy is going to be a mother?* Quinn marveled, sliding back into the booth. Although Quinn had always imagined she herself would have children one day, she couldn't imagine being ready for them now. And even though she was three years older than Daisy, she hadn't yet had a relationship that was serious enough for

her to broach the subject of having a family. She signaled the
waitress for her check and ordered a to-go cup of coffee.

A FEW MINUTES later, Quinn stood outside of Pearl's, sipping
her coffee and listening to the Sunday bells ringing from the
Lutheran church down the street. A few cold droplets of water
from the overhead awning dripped onto her hand. The weather,
again, was clear and cold. But it was fractionally warmer than
the day before, and those few added degrees of warmth were
enough to encourage a thawing of sorts on Main Street. Melting ice and snow dripped from awnings and sent rivulets of
water gurgling through the gutters. It was spring, technically,
but it didn't feel like it yet. Not when the trees were bare and
the flower boxes empty. There wasn't a bud or a shoot in sight.
But the thaw, the thaw was real. And spring would eventually
work its way this far north.

Quinn was loosening her scarf when she saw a woman in
a navy peacoat and her blond-headed son coming out of the
IGA grocery store down the block. The boy shot past Quinn
as he ran up the street, and Quinn studied the mother. She
recognized her. Her name was Annika. Annika Bergstrom.
She was from Winton. She'd been two years ahead of Quinn
in high school, and she'd also been a waitress at Pearl's during
Quinn's last year in high school. Quinn remembered her as an
unusually gloomy presence there. But something else about
her gave Quinn pause. Annika was the blond woman who'd
stopped Tanner at the dedication yesterday before he'd gotten
into his car.

As Annika approached her, she shifted her grocery bag in her arms and looked at the businesses across the street. For a second Quinn wondered if she should simply let her pass. But her curiosity got the better of her.

"Annika?" she said.

Annika turned and looked at her. "Oh, hi," she said. She looked distinctly uncomfortable and it occurred to Quinn, too late, that Annika may have been hoping to avoid her. If it hadn't been for the fact that she'd barely known Annika back in high school, she might have been offended. But they hadn't been friends; they'd barely been acquaintances.

"You're still here," Annika said now, as she juggled the grocery bag she was holding.

"Yes, for a few more days," Quinn replied, sipping her coffee. Annika, she realized, must have seen her at Shell Lake yesterday. "What did you think of the dedication?" Quinn asked her now.

Annika looked briefly up the street to where the little boy had stopped. "I didn't want to go at first, but now I'm glad I went," she said. A gust of wind rattled the awning above them and sent Annika's blond hair flying. She caught it and pulled it back off her face, revealing her pale complexion and light blue eyes. *She's pretty*, Quinn thought, pretty in the way that women of Scandinavian descent—women like her stepmother, Johanna—often were.

"I know what you mean about the dedication," Quinn said. "I felt the same way."

A customer came out of Pearl's then, sending the little bells that hung from the door into a frenzy of jingling. "You used to waitress here," Quinn said, gesturing at the door as it swung closed. "Do you still?"

"Oh, no. I work at Loon Bay Cabins now. I'm the manager," Annika said, pulling the collar of her peacoat closed. Quinn nodded, remembering that Tanner was staying at the cabins this week. That must be how he and Annika knew each other.

"Do you live there too?" Quinn asked, though she had the vague impression that Annika needed to get going.

Annika hesitated. "Jesse and I have one of the cabins there," she said. Quinn looked up the block at the boy. He was bouncing one of those Pinky rubber balls that they still sold in the vending machine outside the hardware store. Quinn had loved these as a child, and she and her dad could rarely pass by the hardware store without Quinn wanting a quarter for one. She shuddered to think of how many near accidents she must have caused when she'd lost control of one. Jesse was bouncing his ball with great skill and total absorption, though. It made her smile. She loved the way kids that age could be so oblivious to the adult world unfolding around them.

"He's cute," Quinn said, of the uncomplicated *boyness* of him, and of that need, she still remembered, to be in a state of unending motion. "How old is he?" she asked, watching as Jesse made a dramatic dive to catch the ball.

"He's nine. He'll be ten in August," Annika said, and then she looked down into the bag she was holding as if she might find more information there.

"He's in fourth grade, then?"

Annika nodded and smiled a barely there smile. "Well, nice seeing you," she said, and she started to move away.

"Wait," Quinn said. "How are the cabins at Loon Bay? I'm staying at the Butternut Motel," she explained, "but I'd love to move somewhere else for the next few days."

"The Butternut Motel?" Annika asked, turning back to Quinn. She wrinkled her nose.

"Yeah, it's pretty depressing," Quinn agreed. "What about Loon Bay?" she persisted. "Do you have any cabins available?"

"We do," Annika said, pulling her hair back.

"How are the rates there?" she asked.

"We have a midweek rate of seventy-nine dollars a night now." Annika looked up the street again, trying to spot her son, who was looking in the window of the variety store.

"That's good," Quinn said, of the price, especially since she didn't know if she could face another night in room 6. At Loon Bay, at least, she'd have a whole cabin, albeit a tiny one, to herself. And if she didn't feel like going out to eat, she wouldn't be limited to chicken-flavored soup from a vending machine either. The restaurant there—if that wasn't overstating what it was—overlooked the lake. She and her dad had gone there when they'd wearied of his indifferent cooking. It was nothing fancy, and the menu had been limited, but she remembered it as being cozy in the winter and busy in the summer. Thinking about this, a little nostalgically, made her want to check in to Loon Bay Cabins right now.

"Could I get a reservation there for tonight?" Quinn asked.

Annika looked surprised. "How long are you planning on staying?"

"I don't know yet. But not more than a couple of days."

"We have cabins available now. Check-in is any time after three o'clock," Annika said. "I've got to go. Nice to see you." Then she headed up the sidewalk toward Jesse.

"Bye, Annika," Quinn called after her. Annika waved back. As Quinn drained the last of her coffee and tossed the cup into a nearby garbage can, she watched as Annika took Jesse's hand and the two of them crossed the street to their car. *That was odd*, Quinn thought. Not odd in any definable way. Annika, of course, was different than she'd been in high school. She was certainly politer than she'd been back then. But she still wasn't exactly friendly. *Maybe she's shy*, Quinn speculated, *or reticent*. Scandinavians might be blessed with natural good looks, but they could also be maddeningly reserved. *Or maybe she's one of those socially awkward people.* Or maybe, after ten years away, Quinn—who'd always prided herself on her social ease—was the one who was awkward. Now there was a thought.

CHAPTER 12

As Quinn walked back to the Butternut Motel, she formulated a plan. She would check out, pay a visit to Jake's parents, and then go see Gabriel again before checking in to Loon Bay Cabins. When she got back to the room, though, she reached for her laptop and flipped it open. There was something she wanted to write about. Bumping into Annika this morning had unearthed another memory from ten years ago, though it was a memory that Annika had played only a tangential role in. This was a memory that was mostly about Gabriel.

September, Senior Year, Gabriel (and Annika) at Pearl's

"One iced tea," Annika said, putting the glass down on the Formica-topped table a little too firmly. She turned abruptly and left the table before Quinn could ask for an order of fries.

She watched as Annika crossed the room and deposited some dishes, roughly, into a dishpan behind the counter. Annika had graduated two years ago. And since then Quinn hadn't seen much of her, until recently, when Annika had started waitressing at Pearl's.

"She does *not* like you," Gabriel said, smiling for the first time since Quinn had slid into the booth at Pearl's five minutes ago.

"You mean, 'she doesn't like us,'" Quinn corrected, reaching for the first of the five packets of sugar she put in her iced tea.

"No, I mean she doesn't like *you*," Gabriel said. "She was perfectly pleasant when she took my order. In fact, she was more than pleasant. Before you got here. Late."

Quinn frowned. Gabriel was still rankled about her being late. She was *never* late. Not to their afternoons together after school. Usually, they met in the communications room—when they were rushing to get the newspaper out—but today they were meeting at Pearl's.

She watched as Gabriel squirted mustard onto his open-faced burger and flipped the top bun back into place. He didn't take a bite of it, though. He looked out the window instead. It was raining, for the third day in a row. And it was not a gentle rain, either, but a hard, unforgiving rain that sent the few people who were out on Main Street scurrying from one business's awning to another in a vain attempt to stay dry. The bells on the front door of Pearl's jingled, and another customer came in, closing their dripping umbrella, the rain still running off their raincoat.

"Another lovely day," Quinn said, under her breath, dumping another packet of sugar into her iced tea. Weather like this—this wet, for this long—made her feel claustrophobic. The simplest act—getting from school to your car in the parking lot, for instance—was fraught with difficulty. And nothing stayed dry. The cuffs of her blue jeans were wet, her Converse sneakers were positively soggy, and the plateglass window in front of them was starting to cloud with moisture from the inside.

But the weather, of course, wasn't why Gabriel was in a bad mood. The reason for that, Quinn suspected, was Quinn. Or, more specifically, Quinn *and* Jake. Quinn had told Gabriel back in July that she'd gone out on a couple of dates with Jake, and he'd been surprised. More than surprised, actually. "Jake Lightman? Seriously," he'd said. "What do you two even have in common?" At the time, though, she'd made light of it. "Not a lot," she'd said. "But he's fun." And she'd left it at that. The truth was she was as surprised as Gabriel at her growing attraction to Jake. Still, she tried not to dwell on this in her conversations with Gabriel. She sensed that he was not interested.

But by the time Gabriel had returned from his summer in Chicago, a couple nights ago, Quinn had heard Jake refer to her as his girlfriend and Quinn had told her dad Jake was her boyfriend. She'd gone to see Gabriel the day he got back and she'd told him this too. "I thought this was a summer thing," he'd reminded her. And when she'd said it was more than that, he'd been silent.

"Have a little iced tea with your sugar," Gabriel said now, watching her pour another packet of sugar into it.

"Hey, you know me. I'm a five-sugar girl," she said, picking up a spoon and stirring her drink vigorously. "It's all about the viscosity. I want it right at the point of changing from a liquid into a solid."

This didn't get a smile from him, though. He picked up his burger. She noticed his hair had gotten a little longer this summer, and his face was a little tanner. There was something else—in the ten weeks that he'd been away he'd changed. It was almost imperceptible. But it was still there. He seemed older. More worldly? Was that even possible? Quinn wondered. After all, he'd only been two states away.

"Hey, you've barely told me anything about the summer program," she said now, sticking a straw into her iced tea and taking a long pull on it. "And I don't mean what you learned, either. Didn't you say something about a girl in your class? The one who kept flirting with you. What happened with her?"

"Nothing, really," he said, taking a bite of his burger.

"Nothing, really? What does that mean, Gabriel?" She said this part teasingly, but she was also curious.

"Forget it, Quinn. Nothing happened. She wasn't my type."

"What is your type, by the way?" she asked him, again teasing. "Because you said Emma Raible wasn't your type either."

He looked at her, a wary expression on his face.

"Never mind," she said, lifting a french fry off his plate and popping it into her mouth. She realized she needed to tread carefully here; Gabriel and girls was one subject they only discussed superficially.

"Quinn, tell me again. How did it happen, you and Jake?" he

said, pushing his plate away. And he looked at her, *really* looked at her, for the first time since she'd slid into the booth.

"I told you," Quinn said. "I wrote a profile of him for the *Butternut Express.*" The truth was, she'd started seeing him less than two days after she'd interviewed him. He'd pursued her then. There was no other word for it. It was a new experience for Quinn. No one had done that to her before, not with that kind of intensity.

"So . . . you did an interview, and then what?" Gabriel asked.

"After that," Quinn said, "he stopped by the *Butternut Express* office and asked if I wanted to go for a swim." It had been a sultry afternoon, and she was alone in the office, the air conditioner on the fritz, as usual, and she'd had nothing to do. Before he'd shown up she couldn't stop yawning. Afterward, she'd felt like she'd drunk three iced teas, each with five packets of sugar in it. The two of them had gone to the town beach, and after they'd come out of the water, they'd lain on a blanket. As the sun was setting, Jake had leaned down and kissed her. She'd never been kissed like that before; it wasn't your usual polite or tentative first kiss. It was *so* sexy. The next week, she'd gone out on two dates with him, and after that they'd started seeing each other several times a week. By mid-August, they'd fallen into a pattern, a pattern both languorous and thrilling. Late-afternoon swims at the beach, after she was done working and he was done training. Evenings driving over to another town for dinner. Nights spent back at the beach, on a blanket, under the stars, or, weather not permitting, at his house, on the couch, watching

DVDs in his family's basement rec room. He'd told her during their time together that she was beautiful and intelligent and utterly unlike anyone else he'd ever known. He'd told her he couldn't stop thinking about her. Couldn't wait to be with her. And when he *was* with her he couldn't be with her enough. If Quinn were to be blunt—he wanted her. And here was the thing: she wanted him right back.

"Are you there, Quinn?" Gabriel asked, breaking into her reverie.

"Sorry," she said.

"So that's it. You went for a swim with him. That must have been one hell of a swim," Gabriel said now.

Quinn rolled her eyes and helped herself to another french fry. She knew that her having a boyfriend was an adjustment for Gabriel, the same way that his having a girlfriend would have been an adjustment for her. After all, she and Gabriel *had* spent all their time together. That might change now. Maybe, she reasoned, it would be easier if the three of them, she and Jake and Gabriel, did something together, something outside of school. They could come here. But then she remembered that Jake didn't like Pearl's. He wouldn't even come in here with her to get an iced tea.

"Look, Quinn. Forget it," Gabriel said. "I don't need to know the details. I just . . . I mean, it doesn't matter if he's your type, or whether I think he's your type. But do you think you can trust him? Is he, you know, trustworthy?"

"Well, yeah. I think so. Why would you even ask that, though?"

"I don't know. It doesn't matter." He polished off the rest of his hamburger.

"It does matter. You wouldn't have said anything about it if it didn't. Why did you ask me if I could trust him?" she persisted.

He pushed his plate away as if he already regretted saying this. "Because I saw something once. Or I *heard* it."

"What? Tell me."

"It was last year. Like, in September, I think. I was studying in that alcove outside the library and I heard Jake and Ashlyn arguing in the hallway." Ashlyn was a girl that Jake had gone out with in tenth grade and had broken up with sometime last year. "She said . . . she said a lot of stuff to him. But the thing she kept saying was that he was lying to her."

"And you just happened to remember this now?" Quinn asked, suddenly tense.

"I remember it because Ashlyn was crying, Quinn. I felt sorry for her."

Quinn shook her head. She didn't want to hear this. She didn't want to hear about Jake's past relationships. "Gabriel, we don't know what happened between them," she said now. "We don't know the whole story."

Gabriel looked at her for a long moment. "You're right," he said, picking up his camera from the seat next to him and putting it on the table. "Maybe Ashlyn was wrong. Besides, I can't imagine a guy lying to you anyway. Not Quinn LaPointe." He gave her a playful kick under the table, and Quinn smiled and kicked him back. She was relieved. The tension between them had dissipated. Gabriel would see, her being with Jake didn't have to interfere with their friendship. She honestly didn't know how much time she could spend with Jake anyway. At least during cross-country season. He trained *all* the time. He was training right now, running eight miles outside in this weather. She glanced out the window where a car was driving down Main Street, sending a cascade of water up onto the sidewalk. She would have to drive back to school in this rain soon. She was picking Jake up after practice. And if this was like yesterday, there would be making out, she knew, in the parking lot when they got into her car, and more, again, before she dropped him off at his family's house, the rain sheeting down the car's windows, the music barely audible on the radio.

"Are you done with this?" Annika asked Gabriel, reappearing at their table. She was joking; the only thing left on his plate was a tired scrap of lettuce.

"Yep. Thanks," he said, smiling at Annika. Was he flirting with her? Quinn wondered. Annika picked up his plate and, ignoring Quinn, whisked her still half-full glass of iced tea away. Quinn almost called after her.

"I wasn't done with that," she said to Gabriel instead.

"I told you she doesn't like you," Gabriel said.

"I think you might be right. I have no idea what I did to her. Or what *you* did to her to get her attention."

"She's pretty." Gabriel shrugged. For some reason this annoyed Quinn. She raised an eyebrow at him.

"What? She is." He picked up his camera and popped off the lens cap. "I think she's a lifer, though. Like my brothers."

"What do you mean?"

"That's what I call someone who never leaves here," Gabriel explained.

"But how do you know?"

"It's just a feeling," he said.

"Well, I love Butternut," Quinn said. "But I don't want to be a lifer."

"Me neither. Another year, and I'm gone," he said. He looked at her through his camera and adjusted the lens.

"Don't forget about me," Quinn said.

"How could I," he said, still fiddling with the lens.

"I missed you this summer. It's been weeks since I've been in one of your photo shoots."

"Look at me," he said. "Look right into the camera."

CHAPTER 13

Quinn finished writing. She slid her computer into its bag and rounded up her things, then took a last look around room 6 of the Butternut Motel. It would be good to get out of here. Just the thought of waking up in a cabin at Loon Bay, the morning light reflecting off Butternut Lake, was enough to cheer her up. *A little.*

"Did you have a nice stay?" Carla asked when Quinn set her room key down on the reception counter. "I mean, as nice as it could be, under the circumstances," she amended. Carla was so pale in the late-morning light streaming in through the office windows that Quinn could see the spidery web of veins at each of her temples, like tiny bluish bruises.

Quinn smiled politely but didn't answer the question. *It had only been nice if by "nice" Carla meant "depressing as hell."*

"So you're heading home to Chicago?" she asked Quinn. "That's, what? A twelve-hour drive?"

"Closer to ten," Quinn said, glancing over her shoulder at her car. Her packed suitcase was already in the trunk. "But I'm not leaving yet. I'm moving over to Loon Bay Cabins," she added, hoping Carla wouldn't be offended. She wasn't.

"Oh, I *love* Loon Bay," she said. "Especially the bar there. They have *great* pizza. I mean, it's frozen and everything, but they put it in this special oven, or maybe it's not special, but, anyway, they put it in this little oven, and it comes out really good."

"I'll have to try it," Quinn said, wondering at her enthusiasm. Then again, if all Carla had at the Butternut Motel was chicken-flavored soup, frozen pizza might be delightful in comparison.

"So have you decided to take a vacation here in Butternut?" Carla asked.

"Not exactly. I have some things to do here," Quinn said. It was at this moment, however, that Quinn felt something nudging at her ankle and looked down to see Hank Williams there, a leash looped around his neck. She let out a little yelp and jumped back.

"Oh, sorry," Carla said, blithely, picking up the other end of his leash and reeling him back over to her. She picked him up and put him under her arm, like a ferret pocketbook, and tickled him under his chin. "He's being very frisky today, aren't you?" she chided him.

This was Quinn's cue to leave.

"Quinn?" Carla asked, as Quinn was pushing open the door. She paused and turned back.

Carla hesitated. "I hope it's all right if I say this. But I remember you and Jake together," she said, almost shyly.

"You do?"

She nodded, snuggling Hank Williams. "Uh-huh. I remember once, when I was in middle school, I was supposed to meet my brother at the high school, and I saw you and Jake in the locker-room tunnel. You guys were like . . . *wow*. You were . . . *so hot*. Just . . . making out, basically, I guess, but acting like there was no one else around. Which there wasn't, I guess, except for me. I had to walk by you to get to my brother's football practice. Anyway, after that, I couldn't wait to get to high school. I thought, when I do, I want to have a boyfriend like Jake." She smiled, some welcome color coming into her face, but Quinn must have been looking at her strangely, because Carla caught herself and said, "Oh, sorry. I don't know why I'm bringing that up."

"No, it's fine," Quinn said, buttoning her coat. "I'd forgotten about that day. I've got to get going, though."

"I hope . . . I hope I didn't upset you," Carla called after her, but Quinn let the door swing shut behind her and hurried to her car. She wasn't upset. Not exactly. She was dazed, instead, by the sudden specificity of that memory, by the almost granular recall of an autumn afternoon she hadn't thought about in years. Sitting in the front seat of her car, a minute later, the engine humming and the heat piping in, Quinn tried to envision the memory before it slipped through her fingers.

October, Senior Year, Meeting Jake in the Athletic Tunnel

Autumn comes early in northern Minnesota, and, by mid-October, as Quinn stood in the late-afternoon chill in the tunnel that led from the high school's locker rooms to its playing fields, she regretted not wearing anything warmer than a jean jacket. Still, she loved this time of year. Loved the way the golds and oranges and reds of fall first touched, as though casually, and then consumed, completely, the leaves on the trees, loved the way the air smelled like some combination of damp earth, gentle rot, and sour apples, even loved the way her Converse sneakers crunched over the early-morning frost in the grass as she walked out to her car on her way to school.

She'd been leaning against the side of the tunnel, but she straightened up now as, several yards away, a locker-room door swung open and a few boys straggled out, gym bags slung over their shoulders. Their hair was still wet and Quinn imagined that they trailed shower steam and the smell of industrial soap behind them as they came into the tunnel.

"Hi, Quinn," one of them said. The other two nodded at her. She was Jake's girlfriend, and his cross-country teammates, out of respect for him, treated her with politeness. She waved back at them, then edged farther down the tunnel.

"Jake will be out soon," one of the boys, Griffin, called to her over his shoulder.

"Thanks," she said, a little self-consciously. She looked ridiculous standing here, she knew, waiting for Jake after practice. He'd already told her that when it was over, he'd come find her in the communications room, where she'd stayed after school to put the finishing touches on that week's edition of the paper. But the truth was, she didn't want to wait that long. Besides, she couldn't stop thinking about him long enough to concentrate on proofing that week's articles. So she did something she'd done once before; she'd come down to the athletic tunnel to wait for him. The last time she'd done this she'd caught him between his practice and his trip to the locker room for a shower. He'd been a little sweaty—okay, *a lot* sweaty—but Quinn hadn't minded. Even his sweat, she'd discovered, was somehow clean. The football team had been at an away game that afternoon, and Quinn and Jake had gone under the bleachers and made out, until he'd had to tear himself away and go shower before they closed the locker rooms for the evening.

Quinn shivered in the damp tunnel and kicked at a way-ward crimson leaf that had blown in. Gabriel was right, she thought. She'd become a cliché. (He'd teased her about this recently.) Making out under the bleachers. Cheering for Jake at his cross-country meets. Sitting with him and his friends, Dominic and Griffin, at their table in the cafeteria. Even go-ing to a bonfire at Shell Lake on a Saturday night and sipping cheap beer—Jake abstained—as music blasted from iPod speakers and everyone piled more wood onto the fire. Later, couples took blankets and made their way down to the beach, into the woods, or back into the cars in the parking lot.

As she was thinking this, the locker-room door popped open one more time and Jake came out. He smiled when he saw her.

"Hey," he said, swinging his gym bag up on his shoulder. "How long have you been here?"

"Not long. I tried to catch you after practice but . . ."

He dropped his gym bag at their feet and reached for her, his hands sliding under the hem of her T-shirt and around to the small of her back.

"I hope you don't think I'm stalking you," she said, as he pulled her toward him and kissed her.

"I don't. But I wish you would. Stalk me, I mean," he said. "Because I would love to be stalked by Quinn LaPointe."

She laughed, and as she pressed herself to him, she felt the wetness of his chest through his cotton T-shirt. "Didn't you dry off?" she asked.

"Not very well. I didn't have time. I wanted to see you."

He backed her up a little and she felt the concrete side of the tunnel, smooth and cool, against her back.

He kissed her again, in that way that he had, that way that told Quinn there was nothing else in his mind, nothing else but her and his kissing her. It reminded her of what he'd told her that day in the bleachers about running, the day she'd interviewed him. There were at least two things, then, that he did like that. Did with total concentration.

She shivered.

"You're cold," he said.

"A little, but I don't care," she said, because she wanted to keep kissing him. His hands slid into her back pockets, and she put her hands into his wet hair. He'd combed it down in the locker room, but already that familiar cowlick was starting to pop up. She rumpled it, then reached around him and pulled him closer, seeking warmth through the dampness of his T-shirt, under which she felt his heart beating, as smooth and fast as it did after he'd stopped running.

"Quinn," he said, "I talked to Griffin."

"Griffin?" she repeated, as though she'd never heard of Jake's friend before.

"Griffin Hoyer, Quinn. I talked to him about the cabin." This was Griffin Hoyer's family cabin on Butternut Lake. The Hoyers had a house in town, but like a few of Butternut's more well-to-do citizens, they kept a cabin for hunting season and for ice fishing and for summertime.

"Oh, right, the cabin," she said. She put her cheek on his chest.

"He said it's fine. He said they almost never use it anyway. We can go there this Saturday night."

Quinn nodded. "Okay," she said.

"We don't have to," he said. He kissed the top of her head. "And if we do, we don't have to . . ."

"No, it's not that," she said, looking up at him. She wanted to be alone with Jake. And there weren't many places they could be alone together. "I don't know what to tell my dad," Quinn said.

"About where you'll be?"

She nodded.

"Couldn't you, like, make something up?" Jake asked. "Like, make up that you're going to a girlfriend's house, or something."

"No, I can't. I don't lie to him."

"Ever?"

She shook her head. "It's different with us. We're honest with each other. But not so honest that . . ." She shrugged. "Not so honest that I can say, 'Oh, by the way, Jake and I are staying at Griffin's family's cabin so I can lose my virginity.'"

Jake laughed. "Well, if you're going to put it that way." But the words she'd said had had their effect on him. He started kissing her again, differently this time. With more urgency. "Isn't there something you can say to him?" he asked, a few minutes later.

"I'll think about it," Quinn said, as he kissed her again. But what she was thinking about was how she was going to get from the tunnel back to where she'd left her backpack in the communications room when she didn't want to stop kissing Jake for even one single second.

CHAPTER 14

"Would you like some more tea, dear?" Mrs. Lightman asked.

"No, thank you," Quinn said. "I'm still drinking this." She picked up her half-full cup for emphasis. Taking a sip, she smiled at Mrs. Lightman. "It's wonderful, by the way. I'll have to get the name of it before I leave."

"It's Lipton's English Breakfast Tea," Mrs. Lightman said.

"*Oh*. Well, it's delicious. Good old Lipton's," she said, with a cheery smile, thinking that everything she'd said since she'd arrived at the Lightmans' house fifteen minutes ago had sounded inane. Which was unusual. Quinn was good at talking, both talking to other people *and* getting other people to talk to her. Neither of these traits was in evidence now, though. And that was a shame, because it was so quiet in the Lightmans' living room that it made her want to fill the silence or, if not fill it, at least break it. She put her cup back in its saucer now, just a little too hard, and its clinking sound startled Mrs. Lightman.

"Sorry," Quinn said, in something close to a whisper. She'd finished writing about Jake an hour earlier in the parking lot of the Butternut Motel but the memory of that fall afternoon had lingered: the vivid patch of blue sky at the tunnel's end, the crunch of leaves beneath her feet, the feel of Jake's warmth against her. Having summoned it forth, she found that she didn't want to let it go. But the present was calling, and it was the present that had prompted her to go visit Jake's grave at Prairie Oaks Cemetery in Winton. She'd visited it several times in the spring of her senior year, and she had little trouble finding his gravestone. It was at the end of a long row, flanked on either side by small black spruce trees. Jake Lightman, "taken from us too early, forever in our hearts," the epitaph read. She'd brushed some fallen twigs off the gravestone. Then she'd made the short drive to the Lightmans' house. It wasn't until Mr. Lightman had answered the door, smiled, and hugged her warmly that the spell of that fall afternoon was broken. She'd felt grateful and relieved that Mr. Lightman was happy to see her.

Quinn broke off a piece of cookie and nibbled on it.

"Those are Pepperidge Farm," Mrs. Lightman told her. "Raspberry Thumbprint. There's more in the kitchen," she added, though Quinn still had three of them left on a little plate beside her teacup and saucer. She smiled her thank-you, though, and Mrs. Lightman disappeared back into the kitchen, presumably to get some more. Quinn exhaled and looked around the living room as if she were seeing it for the first time. And, in a way, she was. She and Jake had seldom come in here. As she studied it, she realized it had an odd, almost . . . *padded* quality to it. The wall-to-wall carpeting was gingerbread thick, the curtains were heavy, and even the furniture seemed entombed in its own upholstery. Was that why it was so quiet in the room, she wondered, because everything in it absorbed sound? But it was more than the room's silence that disturbed her. Because while it was clean—there were fresh vacuum lines on the carpet, and not a speck of dust on the cabinet that held Jake's trophies—the room had an unused, airless feeling to it. Maybe Jake's parents never came in here, either, she speculated, unless they had guests. *Or maybe their whole house feels this way, as if the two people who still live here live here in such a way as to not disturb the past.*

"Here you go, dear," Mrs. Lightman said, reappearing. She set another plate of cookies down on the coffee table, right next to the identical plate of cookies she'd already brought her, and Quinn, unsure of what else to do, popped a whole one into her mouth.

Mrs. Lightman waited, as though she was used to waiting. She was still attractive, Quinn thought. Her auburn hair showed no trace of gray and was swept back, off her face, and then twisted in an elegant knot and held in a clasp at the back of her neck. She was wearing pale pink lipstick, and her outfit, a beige-edged white blouse with a beige wool cardigan and dark gray wool slacks, was no less chic for being so conservative. As Quinn swallowed her cookie, the dry crumbs catching in her throat, she had an image of Mrs. Lightman putting on her lipstick in front of her bedroom mirror every morning. She would do it without a feeling of anticipation or enjoyment. She would do it because, in her mind, it needed to be done. She would keep up appearances, though Quinn couldn't help but wonder at the effort it must cost her to keep them up.

Now Mr. Lightman came into the room and sat down on the edge of the sofa. He smiled at Quinn, and she tried, again, to start a conversation. "I thought the dedication was so moving," she said to them both. But it was Jake's mother who responded.

"It was more of a warning than a dedication, wasn't it?" she asked Quinn, a frown wrinkling her brow.

"In what way?" Quinn asked, taken aback.

"Oh, students, you know. They're still talking about driving out on the ice at Shell Lake. Not in the winter. Not when it would be safer. But in the spring. When it starts to melt. You know, kind of like a dare."

Quinn must have looked astonished because Mr. Lightman chimed in. "No, it's true. None of them remember Jake, of course. Not personally. But they all know the date he died. It's become something of an urban legend, I suppose you'd say. Or, out here, a rural legend," he added. "Anyway, last spring, when we were having an early thaw, some seniors were going to drive out there, to prove what, I don't know, their own stupidity, I guess. But someone called the police and they got down there before they followed through. That's when Mr. Mulvaney started talking about the dedication. He thought it would be a kind of deterrent. He never said as much, to us, but I think he hoped it would be one in the future."

Quinn nodded. So this was why he'd required the junior

class to go to the ceremony. And she remembered the girl with too much eye shadow, standing next to Quinn and scrolling down her iPhone screen.

"Well, obviously, I don't want young people driving on the ice," Mrs. Lightman said, as if someone had just accused her of wanting this. "I don't want an accident like Jake's to happen to anyone else. But the truth is, I'll never go visit that stone. Before yesterday I hadn't been to Shell Lake in ten years. When I want to pay my respects to Jake, I go to his grave."

"That makes sense," Quinn said. And here she took the opportunity to tell the Lightmans about her own visit to his grave before she'd come here. They nodded politely. But when the conversation fell silent again, she said, "I spoke to Tanner at the ceremony. He looked well."

"We don't see him that often," Mrs. Lightman said, and she looked briefly down at her hands.

"No?" Quinn said, surprised. Tanner had told her he came up here at least once a month. She looked at Mr. Lightman, as if he might clarify the situation, but he only nodded in agreement.

"I'll probably see him again," Quinn said, trying to keep the conversation moving. "He told me he's staying at Loon Bay this week, and I'm checking in there tonight."

Jake's parents exchanged looks. Had she said something wrong? She remembered Tanner at the dedication saying he and his mom "didn't get along," though she had no idea what he'd meant by this. But she got the distinct feeling sitting here in the Lightmans' living room that there was indeed some kind of conflict between them.

Mr. Lightman started to say something, but Mrs. Lightman intervened.

"I had no idea you were planning on visiting for this long, Quinn. Surely you're very busy back home. There can't be much for you to do in Butternut."

"Oh . . . well," Quinn said, surprised, and a little confused, that Mrs. Lightman seemed to be discouraging her from staying longer. "I thought I'd spend a little more time in town. I've been away for so long," she said, feeling this explanation was lame. But how could she explain to Mrs. Lightman her need to be in Butternut right now and how much of that need had to do with her son and the accident?

"Well, of course, you should do what you want," Mrs. Lightman said. "But why would you want to stay at Loon Bay?"

"The price is right?" Quinn suggested, with a smile.

"That may be so, dear," Mrs. Lightman said, leaning forward. "But you can stay here with us, if you'd like. We'd love to have you. And you wouldn't have to pay for a room."

"Oh," Quinn said, feeling anxious at the thought. Mrs. Lightman wasn't suggesting she stay in Jake's old room, was she? "No, no, thank you," she said. "That is so kind of you to offer, though. But I'm doing some writing while I'm here and I might be keeping odd hours. I don't want to disturb you. And, um, I'm only going to be here for another couple of days." She hurried on. "I wanted to spend some time with a friend of mine, Gabriel Shipp. He lives on Butternut Lake. I saw him yesterday." *And he is so changed*, she almost said. But it felt wrong to be sharing her worry over Gabriel with someone whose own unhappiness was already boundless. And she remembered with a sting having explained to Theresa that the reason she hadn't gone to the reception was so she could see him. There was a long pause while Mrs. Lightman considered Quinn's excuse. Or maybe she was considering the imaginary crumb she was now brushing off her cardigan.

"I see, dear. If you change your mind, though, there's always a room for you here," she said. She looked sad when she said this and then looked down at her hands folded in her lap. *The days must be so long for Mrs. Lightman*, Quinn thought. And she wanted to hug this frail but beautiful woman or take her away somewhere, anywhere but here. But of course it would make no difference. She'd take her grief with her wherever she went.

"Maggie," Mr. Lightman said, putting a hand on her shoulder, "are you getting tired?"

"I am, Paul." She turned to Quinn. "Sorry, dear. I need to rest every afternoon." And Quinn saw her eyes drift, as though foreshadowing her retreat.

"Of course," Quinn said, standing up. She was ashamed at how relieved she felt by the prospect of leaving this house. "Thank you for the tea," she said. "And the cookies."

Mr. and Mrs. Lightman rose, too, and then Mrs. Lightman surprised Quinn by taking her hands and holding them in her own cool, dry hands that felt, somehow, as unused as this room. "You look so lovely, Quinn," she said. And for the first time since Quinn had arrived Mrs. Lightman looked directly into her eyes. "You know Jake made some mistakes. But he loved you very much," she said. "He was planning on the two of you still seeing each other on weekends in college. He told me once he wanted to marry you. He was so happy with you, dear." Her blue eyes were shining.

Quinn was stunned. When she looked at Mr. Lightman, though, he nodded his agreement, as if he, too, had been privy to this information. Obviously, Jake's parents had never found out that she'd broken up with him the night he'd died. Well, she wouldn't be telling them this now. And, for a moment, she felt almost light-headed with tiredness. She had to get a good night's sleep sometime soon. Mrs. Lightman had her scheduled nap to look forward to every day. And for her, even an hour of unconsciousness must have felt like a sweet gift.

"Paul will walk you out, dear," she said to Quinn now, giving her hands another squeeze. "And don't forget, you're always welcome here."

CHAPTER 15

After Quinn left the Lightmans' house, she drove around aimlessly, until she found herself at Butternut Lake's town beach. The lake was beautiful. The water was glassy, a perfect mirror for the great northern pines that fringed the shore. She was relieved to have a place to pull over, and she parked where she could see the large flat gray rock that jutted out into the water, the same rock she and her friends used to sunbathe on in high school. The Lightmans weren't angry at her, she reflected, looking out at the lake. In fact, they still loved her. She could tell. Unlike Gabriel and Theresa, they weren't blaming her for anything. And she felt a small reprieve, though this was complicated by what Maggie had said about Jake wanting to marry her one day. She and Jake had never discussed marriage.

There had been the matter of the ring, though. The promise

ring. Jake had given it to her in December of that year. They'd been dating for almost six months, and the make-out sessions in Jake's pickup truck and in the Lightmans' rec room had turned into stolen afternoons and evenings at the Hoyers' cabin on Butternut Lake. The Hoyers, Griffin Hoyer's parents, had bought it when they'd moved to Butternut a few years earlier. It was meant to complement the house they owned in town, to be a weekend escape. But they must not have felt the need to escape, because the cabin—which they'd planned to tear down and rebuild one day—remained in much the same condition it had been in when they'd bought it, lock, stock, and barrel, from the previous owner. It was unused and unloved, or it would have been, if Quinn and Jake hadn't both used it and loved it.

It was a funny little place, with a living room, a kitchen, and two bedrooms. The floor in the living room sloped from one end of the room to the other, the books in the bookshelves gave off an ancient, musty scent, and the kitchen cupboards were full of mismatched crockery.

But Quinn found everything about it delightful. The way the fireplace smoked a little, so that when she went home at night, her hair, her clothes, and even her backpack smelled faintly of woodsmoke.

She'd never told Jake that after the first time they'd gone there together, on a rainy evening in late October, she'd gone home that night and slept in the T-shirt she'd worn that day. She didn't want to take it off. It reminded her of the cabin, of Jake, and, of course, of what had happened between them.

She loved, too, the ancient patchwork quilt they'd found in

one of the cabin's closets. It was so worn its pattern was almost invisible, but it was so soft that when they'd spread it before the fireplace she wasn't even conscious of the scratchy living room rug beneath them. All of it—every rickety piece of furniture, every chink in the china, every crookedly hung painting—was wonderful to Quinn. But the real world did not stop at the cabin's front door. It was there in that funny little place whether Quinn had wanted it to be there or not.

December, Senior Year, Jake and the Promise Ring

It was bitterly cold outside that night—they were calling for snow—and the fireplace was smokier than usual after Jake lit the fire, making Quinn's eyes burn and water. She didn't complain. Tomorrow was a school day, and they only had a few hours before they both needed to be home. They were on the leather couch, which was no doubt older than the two of them put together, and Jake had just helped her out of her sweater, when he remembered something.

"What is it?" Quinn asked, watching him unzip his backpack.

He pulled out a bottle of red wine.

Quinn raised an eyebrow. "Are we drinking?" Jake didn't drink when he was training, and Jake was *always* training.

"Why not?" he said. "I don't have a meet this weekend"—he meant an indoor track meet—"and tonight is special."

"In what way?" Quinn asked.

"You'll see," he said, handing her the bottle. She smiled. It did feel special. Jake was often in a good mood, but tonight he was especially so. He'd been touching and kissing and teasing her before they'd even gotten through the cabin's front door. "Any chance they'll have wineglasses here?" he asked, over his shoulder, heading for the kitchen.

"Not a one," Quinn called after him. She read the wine bottle's label. It meant nothing to her. Her dad, when he drank, favored beer.

Jake returned with a corkscrew and two mugs. "You were right about the wineglasses," he said. "No luck. But at least they have a corkscrew." He sat down next to Quinn, put the mugs on the coffee table, and took the wine bottle from her.

"Where did you get wine?" Quinn asked, watching him uncork it, mangling the cork a little in the process.

"At the back of my parents' liquor cabinet," he said. "The *way* back. I don't think my dad will miss it."

At the mention of Jake's dad, Quinn frowned. She was thinking about a conversation she'd had with his dad that day after school. She'd been trying to put it out of her mind, but now she couldn't. "Jake?" she said, as he filled each of their mugs with wine.

"Uh-huh."

"I saw your dad today," she said. She took the mug he offered her.

"Did you?"

She nodded. "I was coming out of the drugstore."

"What'd he say?"

She took a sip of her wine. It was rich and heavy tasting. "He said . . . No, it wasn't what he said, it was what *I* said.

Remember, you told me you were going to have to run errands with him after school? I asked him where you were, and he said he had no idea. He said you hadn't run errands with him since you were a kid, and even then, the only way to get you to come with him was to bribe you." This whole encounter had reminded Quinn of a time in early November when Jake said he couldn't meet her after school because he had to help Griffin with something. But then she'd seen Griffin with his girlfriend at Pearl's. She'd never asked Jake about this discrepancy, though. In fact, she'd forgotten about it until today.

"That sounds about right." Jake smiled. He took a drink of his wine. His mug, she saw, had a little chip in the rim.

"No, I mean, why did you say you couldn't see me until tonight because you had to run errands with him?" Quinn said, the uneasiness she felt asking this offset by wanting—needing—a simple explanation.

Jake's face fell. Or maybe she imagined it, because in the next moment he recovered. "Does it matter?" he asked, with a shrug.

"It does to me."

He put his mug down on the coffee table and pulled her into his arms. "Okay, I didn't run errands with my dad." He kissed her on the neck, but she was preoccupied.

"Why would you lie about that?" she asked, remembering what Gabriel had told her months ago about the conversation he'd overheard between Jake and Ashlyn, his old girlfriend.

"Because it was a little lie," Jake said, pulling back from her. "A white lie. I couldn't tell you because it's a secret."

"I don't like secrets," she said.

"All right, all right," Jake said, smiling. But then his expression turned serious. "Look, I couldn't tell you where I was going after school without giving this away." He reached behind the couch cushions and pulled something out from behind them. He held it out to Quinn. It was a ring box.

She looked at it, and then back up at him. "Jake," she said. It was silent, then, in the cabin, except for a loud popping sound from the fire.

"Take it," he said, his gold eyes warm and liquid in the light from the fireplace. "And don't worry. It's not an engagement ring."

"It's not that," she said. It was that no one had ever given her a piece of jewelry before. Not even her father. She took the box from him and opened it. Nestled in the box's satiny lining was a gold ring with a pale greenish-blue stone that sparkled in the firelight.

"It's an aquamarine," he said. "I know it's not your birthstone, but—"

"I love it," she said, enchanted. "It's beautiful."

"Here," he said, and, taking the box from her, he lifted the ring out. "It's a promise ring." He slipped it onto her right ring finger. "That's why I couldn't tell you where I was going. The salesman said that you could wear it on your right finger or, if you want, you can wear it on a chain around your neck."

"No." Quinn shook her head. "I want to wear it here," she said, twisting it around on her finger. It was a little loose.

"I didn't know your ring size," Jake said.

"I don't know it either," Quinn said. She couldn't stop look-ing at the stone. It was so bright. So beautiful.

"We can go back to the store together," Jake said. "They can make it smaller."

"Where did you get it?" Quinn asked, looking up at him.

"In Duluth. I went last week. The day practice was canceled."

"I thought . . . you said you got it today?"

"I *ordered* it last week. I picked it up today," he clarified. "No more questions, though, okay?" He took her right hand, turned it over, and kissed her palm.

And then he smiled at her, as only Jake could. And, suddenly, it was almost too much. The fire, the wine, the ring, and the warmth of the room. She felt a little dizzy. Was she drunk? No, she'd taken one sip of her wine. But she still felt as if she could float away. Jake held her against him now, and his mouth found hers. It was quiet in the room, except for the crackling sounds of the fire.

CHAPTER 16

When Quinn finished writing, she sat for several minutes in her car. It was overheated now and smelled like stale coffee. She turned off the heat and opened the window a few inches before backing out of the parking space. She was less aware of the sun glinting off the lake and the melting snow in the parking lot than she was of the memory of Jake giving her the ring. She'd loved that ring, she thought, as she pulled onto Butternut Lake Drive. *What had become of it?* Was it even now somewhere in the shallows of Shell Lake, a narrow band of gold resting among the silt and fallen leaves and waterlogged birch tree branches? She'd never know.

And here was, perhaps, another unanswerable question: *Had Jake been lying to her that day? About where he'd gone after school?* She'd never know this, either. Thinking this, though, reminded her of the day of the accident. *Why had Jake's truck been parked outside that house on Scuttle Hole Road?* When she'd asked him why, his answer had been improbable. She was pretty sure he'd lied. But even this, she couldn't know for certain. And Quinn was still thinking about this as she turned down Gabriel's driveway. She saw him, at the end of it, getting into his pickup truck, and she pulled up beside him and rolled down her window.

"Hey," she said. "It looks like I caught you just in time."

"I didn't know you'd be coming by again," he said, coming over to her car. Quinn sensed his wariness.

"Well, neither did I," she said, aiming for breezy. "You didn't think you'd be getting rid of me that easily, though, did you?" She rolled up her window, turned off her engine, and got out of the car. She wanted to give him a hug but he seemed so unapproachable that it wasn't possible.

"How long are you staying?" he asked, and she realized he'd left his pickup truck door open, as if he thought he might still make a quick getaway.

"A couple of days, at least. I'm checking in to Loon Bay."

His eyebrows quirked up. "Really?"

"Uh-huh. I'm going for the midweek rate, but I'll stay for the frozen pizza. Word on the street is, it's good. As in, not to be missed."

He looked at her for a moment, his expression unreadable. She couldn't help but feel that he was holding back something. And she missed, more than ever, the easy rapport they'd once had with each other.

"Are you sure that's a good idea?" he asked. "Staying at Loon Bay?"

"Why? What's wrong with it?"

"Nothing. I never go there, though," he said then, as if washing his hands of the subject. "I've got to get going."

"Where are you going?" she asked.

"I need to open a cabin," he said, zipping up his jacket. "The owners are coming up for the season this weekend."

"It's a little early in the season, isn't it?" she asked.

"They're from Arizona," he said, as if this explained everything.

"Do you always work on Sundays?" she asked.

"Whenever I need to."

"All right, well, mind if I come with you?"

"To open the cabin? It's not going to be fun, Quinn."

"Who says I'm looking for fun?" She smiled at him. He didn't smile back, but something in him relented, because he gestured at the truck. "Get in. You can leave your car here. But this is work, all right? I'm not promising any witty conversation."

"Got it," she said, and she hurried to get into his truck before he changed his mind. As they bumped along the gravel driveway, Quinn yanked her seat belt on and Gabriel fiddled with the radio. *He said no witty conversation. He didn't say no conversation.* But she wondered what to talk about. She wanted to ask him, again, why he hadn't gone to RISD, but she had a feeling he'd give her the same answer as yesterday. And they couldn't talk about the accident, either. Discussing that yesterday, even obliquely, had been much more upsetting than she'd imagined it would be. She'd never told anyone what happened between her and Jake that night, and she didn't think she was ready to do so now. She decided to stick to a safer subject.

"How's your family?" she asked.

"All right."

"Parents still live in Butternut?"

"Yep," he said, settling on an oldies station. It was something he would never have listened to in high school, when he was always scouring the internet for new music.

"What about your brother?"

"Uh, which one?" he asked, pulling onto the main road.

"I don't know. I don't have a favorite, Gabriel. How about all three of them? What are they doing?"

He sighed. "Aiden is married, has three kids under five, and works at the lumber mill in Ely. When I see him at my parents', during the holidays, he's asleep on the couch and there are a couple of kids crawling all over him. Colin got a job, lost a job, got married, got divorced, had a few more things not work out for him. Now he lives with my parents and works with my dad at the shop. And Brody is married, has three-year-old twins, lives in Bemidji, and works on a loading crew at a warehouse there. How's that?" he asked when he'd finished this recitation. Quinn wanted more details, and ten years ago, she would have gotten them. But this would have to do for now, she thought.

"It's a start," she said. "God, I can't believe your parents have *five* grandchildren."

He nodded. "Oh, yeah. A few years ago, there were babies all around."

"I take it you're not a hands-on uncle?" she asked, in a gentle chide.

"No," he said, after a pause. "I don't see my brothers that often. We don't have that much in common."

"But more than you used to, right?"

"Meaning what?"

"Well, your jobs . . ." She trailed off, feeling self-conscious.

"Oh, I see. You mean because we all work with our hands?" he asked, putting a mocking emphasis on the words *with our hands*.

"No, I didn't mean that," she said, more irritated with herself than with him. "I meant, now that you've all grown up, maybe you've found more . . . common ground with one another."

"No," he said. "It didn't happen that way." He didn't sound angry, though, and Quinn, relieved, didn't ask him any more questions. She told him, instead, about her dad and Johanna, and about the Airstream trailer and the quilting shows, and about their Thanksgivings together in southern Minnesota, during which her father always insisted on grilling a whole turkey, with mixed results.

"My father always liked you, Gabriel. You know that, don't you?" she asked, watching his profile. He said nothing, but he nodded, in acknowledgment, which was probably the best Quinn was going to get from him right now. That didn't stop her, though, from wanting to break through his aloofness, and she made a silent pledge that she wasn't leaving him today until she did.

"By the way, I visited the Lightmans this morning," she said. "You know, Jake's parents."

"I know who the Lightmans are, Quinn," Gabriel said, casting her a wary glance.

She looked over at him but he was watching the road. "Mr. Lightman seemed okay," she said. "But Mrs. Lightman . . . It broke my heart to sit there with her. I don't think she's ever recovered. It's as though her life is at a standstill."

"*Of course* her life is at a standstill," he said, with an intensity that surprised Quinn. "She lost a child. Could anything be worse? Nothing will ever fix that." She stared at him, trying to read his expression, but once again his eyes were fixed on the road.

"Have you ever talked to her? I mean, do you ever run into her?" she asked, thinking that his comment implied some kind of connection to Mrs. Lightman.

"God no," he said. "Of all the people in Butternut, she's the one I'd most like to avoid."

"Why?" Quinn said.

"Quinn, I need to focus on the road. Okay?" he said, impatiently, as he took a sharp turn. He reached over and turned up the radio. And Quinn, who'd brought them up, was not sorry to stop talking about the Lightmans. She and Gabriel were quiet for the remainder of the drive.

"Here we are," he said, as he turned down a driveway and the cabin came into view. Quinn frowned at it, disapproving. It was big, new, and, to her mind, ugly, its pine siding still not yet darkened by the elements, its sprawling design making it look more like a resort than a home.

"Do the people who own this call it a *cabin*?" she asked

Gabriel. "Because the last time I checked, the word *cabin* con-noted something small, and, preferably, quaint."

"I try not to argue semantics with my clients," Gabriel said, as he pulled up in front of it. He cut the engine and grabbed some work gloves out of the glove compartment. He got out of the truck and lifted a ladder out of the back, and Quinn scrambled after him as he headed around the side of the cabin. "What are we doing?" she called out, stepping over a tree root, and stopping to untangle a low-hanging branch that had snagged on her hair.

"Checking the power lines and the phone lines," he called back, not slowing down. "Checking to see if any trees came down, checking to see if there's any damage to the roof or the gutters, making sure the back deck's in good condition."

"Okay," Quinn said, determined not to bother him as he worked, and she watched, at a respectful distance, as he po-sitioned the ladder under the cabin's eaves, and climbed up on the roof, only to reappear a moment later and drop down the ladder in one fluid motion. *God, he is fast*, she thought. Whatever he was doing with his free time, he wasn't sitting on the couch watching TV. She followed him up the steps to the cabin's back deck, which was huge. *Why so big?* she wondered.

"How many trees do you think they had to cut down to get this view?" she asked Gabriel, at one point, but he ignored her. And Quinn forgot to be critical, for a moment, and simply admired Butternut Lake's unsurpassed blueness. Gabriel was oblivious to its beauty, though, and soon they were off again, down the steps and around the other side of the cabin until Gabriel had completed his inspection.

"Now what?" Quinn asked, as he put his ladder back in the truck. "Are we done?"

"No. Now we go inside," he said, pulling a key ring out of his pocket as he headed for the front door.

"Oh, good," Quinn said, anxious to get a look at the cabin's decor, which, from the outside, was hidden behind shutters and blinds and curtains. She looked over Gabriel's shoulder as he unlocked the door, but when he pushed it open, he gestured for her to enter first. "It's cold," she said. And it was dark, too, and gloomy, with no sunlight coming in through the windows. She squinted and, several feet to her left, almost at eye level, she saw a bear's face.

"*Jesus*," she said, giving a little start backward, right into Gabriel.

"It's okay, Quinn," he said, amused, and, as he flipped on a set of light switches, the bear's head revealed itself to be attached to a bearskin rug hanging on a nearby wall. "Have you forgotten about North Woods decorating?" he asked her, with the closest thing to a smile she'd gotten from him since she'd turned down his driveway that day.

"I haven't forgotten," she said. "I just don't see the aesthetic value of it. I mean, who wants to bump into that thing in the dark?" She gestured at the rug. But Gabriel had walked over to a wall-mounted thermostat, the complicated kind where you could program different temperatures for different zones, and he'd started punching numbers into it.

Quinn felt the heat begin to kick in as she trailed him through the cabin's many rooms. She watched as he turned on lights and checked for leaks and mice. Everything in the cabin was oversized—enormous fireplaces, gargantuan couches, a banquet-sized dining table—except for all the tchotchkes scattered about. There were signs that listed CABIN'S RULES ("Eat s'mores" and "Count the stars" were two of them), and log cabin tissue box covers, pinecone bookends, birchbark cocktail coasters, and hand-painted duck decoys.

As Gabriel checked the damper in a fireplace almost large enough for him to stand in, Quinn wandered over to the couch and retrieved a needlepoint pillow from it. "Look," she said, holding it up to Gabriel. "It says *If you're lucky enough to live by the water, you're lucky enough.*" She smiled at him.

Gabriel barely glanced at it. He came out of the fireplace, wiping his hands on his jeans. "I've got to go down to the basement," he said. "You can wait up here if you want."

"What, and be alone with him?" she said, of the bearskin rug mounted on the wall. "No, thanks. I want to come with you."

He headed down a set of stairs into the basement, a utility and storage room with concrete floors, cedar storage cabinets, and enough oversized pool toys to fill up the entire bay the cabin was on. Quinn hoisted herself up onto a washing machine and watched as Gabriel checked the pilot light in the hot water heater.

"So," Quinn said, bumping her heels against the side of the machine, "other than being a caretaker—which, by the way, I can see you're good at—what have you been doing over the last ten years?"

Gabriel kept working, but he spared her a single, inscrutable look.

"*What?*" she said. "You can't have spent all your time with pilot lights. Come on, tell me one thing you've done since I've been away. One thing"—she held up a finger—"that didn't involve work. Really, I want to know."

"Hmmm," he said, turning a valve on the hot water heater. "Okay, how about . . . I got married. The marriage only lasted for about a year, though."

She thought, for a moment, that he was joking, but when he saw the skeptical expression on her face, he shrugged and kept working.

"Gabriel, you were *married?*" she said. *You were in love?* she thought.

"Yep," he said, not looking at her.

"And you're just going to drop that fact, casually, into our conversation?"

"You wanted to know something I'd done."

"I did. But is that all you're going to tell me about it?"

"You were always so curious," he commented, replacing the cover on the water heater's access panel.

"That's right, I was. *I am.* But now I get paid to be. So what happened? Tell me the story."

"It's a pretty short one," he said, adjusting the thermostat.

But she was too impatient for him to tell it to her in his own time. "Who was she? How did you meet her?"

He came over to the big sink beside the washing machine and dryer and turned on the hot water tap. Nothing happened at first, and then there was a gurgling sound and a spit of brown water from the faucet.

"Her name was Callie," he said. "Short for Callista. I met her at a diner. In Hibbing. She was waitressing there."

"And?" she prompted. "You started dating . . . ?"

"Uh, no," he said, looking down at the sink. The water was running clearer now. "Not exactly. She came home with me that night. The night of the day I met her. And then . . . she stayed. Six months later, we got married."

"Wait. Back up. She moved in with you before you'd ever been out on a date with her?"

"Technically, yes. But it didn't feel like that, though. It felt kind of natural."

"In what way?" Quinn frowned.

"In every way, I guess. I mean, you don't need to make it more complicated than it was, Quinn."

"I think moving in with someone is pretty complicated, though. Don't you? Or, if not complicated, then at least serious." And she thought about a couple of boyfriends she'd had over the years who had casually suggested eventually moving in together. But the thought of taking that next step had filled her with anxiety. Then again, neither relationship had lasted long enough for them to have a more serious discussion anyway. "Didn't you think that living with her was a big step?" she asked Gabriel now.

"In retrospect, maybe," he said. "But not the day I met her. I came into this place for a cup of coffee, and I ended up staying all afternoon. She was . . . she was pretty and funny and easy to be with. She still is, I'm sure. And she was new to the area. She didn't know many people. She'd moved out here from Colorado with her boyfriend and then they'd broken up. She was renting a room in someone's house and hating it, so I said, 'Get your stuff, I've got more than enough room for both of us.'"

Quinn considered this, wanting, and, at the same time, *not* wanting, to ask him more questions. Had they been romantically involved, right from the start? Had they just fallen into bed with each other that first night? But of course they had. And was that so surprising? Gabriel had said she was attractive, and God knows he was too. She wondered if he had brought her back to the same cabin she'd been to. And if he had, had it been different with her there? And Quinn tried to imagine the cabin looking if not cozy, then at least *lived in*. Another towel hanging on a hook in the bathroom, a bra trailing out of a top dresser drawer, or a magazine open on the kitchen table, a half-drunk cup of coffee beside it. It was almost impossible, though, to imagine Gabriel living intimately with anyone in that cabin, that cold, impersonal cabin, but it made her feel better to think that, for a little while anyway, he might have.

"What?" he said, watching her. He turned off both water faucets.

"Nothing," she said. "I was thinking."

"You looked sad for a second there," he said, and then, as if he'd decided he'd said too much, he looked away.

"No, not sad," she corrected. "Surprised. I mean, when did you do this? When did you get married?"

"Three years after high school. I was twenty-one."

"Wow, that's so young. How old was she?"

"Nineteen," he said.

"An old nineteen?" she asked, remembering herself at nineteen. There was no way she'd been ready for marriage.

"No, she was a young nineteen. I think that's why she wanted us to get married. She was young enough to think it would change things between us, I guess."

"And did it?" Quinn asked.

"No," he said. She wanted to ask, though, what those things were that Callie had wanted to change between them. But instead she asked what might be a harder, more personal, question to answer.

"Did you love her, when you married her?"

He leaned back against the sink, his eyes searching for something, and not finding it in a far corner of the basement. "I'm not sure it was about love," he said, looking back at Quinn. "She was lonely and I was . . . tired of being alone."

Quinn nodded. She understood, but she couldn't imagine doing this herself, getting married to relieve loneliness. Then again, she couldn't imagine getting married at all. She couldn't stay in a relationship for more than a year. And it occurred to her that Gabriel's marriage had only lasted a year too.

"How did it end?" she asked.

"She went back to Colorado," he said, leaving the sink for the hot water heater. More valves needed to be adjusted.

"Why, though?" she pressed.

"She said she was lonelier with me than she was without

me. Oh, God," he said, "that sounds like the title of a country music song."

"Maybe," Quinn acknowledged. "But why was she lonelier?"

"Have you shifted into your journalist mode now?" Gabriel asked.

"Does that mean you're not going to answer my question?" Quinn said, hopping down from the washing machine.

"She said I was inaccessible," he said, starting for the stairs. "Can you believe it?"

There was a trace of humor in his voice, but as Quinn followed him up the stairs she was circumspect. He *was* inaccessible, inaccessible in a way he'd never been when she'd known him before. Then again, he might not have been alone in this. Because as Gabriel locked up the cabin, she wondered if *she* might have become inaccessible in some ways too.

"So," Quinn said as they got into his truck, "she left and that was the end of married life?"

"Yes, Quinn. I didn't have a second impulsive marriage," he said, looking at her with a wry smile. "Anyway, I'm not proud of it. Though I've done other things I'm much less proud of," he added.

"Like what?" Quinn frowned.

Gabriel waved his hand as though dismissing the subject. *What, in the relationship department, could be worse than having an impulsive marriage that didn't work out?* Quinn wondered. *Did he get some girl pregnant?* No. She couldn't imagine that.

On the drive back to Gabriel's cabin, the two of them settled into silence, and Quinn wondered if he felt he'd revealed too much to her. She stole a look at his profile; he didn't look upset, but he seemed moody again.

"Can I see you tomorrow?" Quinn asked, when Gabriel turned into his driveway.

"I've got to be somewhere until late afternoon."

"Where?"

"You don't need to know, Quinn," he said, with more weariness than unkindness.

"What about when you get back? Around four o'clock?" she asked as he parked his truck in front of the garage.

"You sure you want to stay in Butternut that long?" he asked as he got out of the truck. She grabbed her bag and got out of the truck, too, hurrying around to the other side.

"I'm sure."

"You're exhausting," Gabriel said, shutting his truck door. But he smiled, just enough, for Quinn to feel encouraged.

"Thank you," she said. She gave him a hug, and he gave her a quick hug back. After she got in the car and pulled onto the main road, she felt happy. More than happy. She hummed to the radio all the way back into town.

CHAPTER 17

Later that afternoon, Quinn checked in to her cabin at Loon Bay and was relieved to find it free of both clutter and kitsch. Whoever had furnished it—and she suspected it was Annika—had understood that guests didn't need to be reminded that they were, in fact, where they already understood themselves to be: in a cabin in the North Woods. The single room was rustic but clean, with a queen-sized bed with a Hudson's Bay point blanket on it, and an older-model TV mounted on the opposite wall.

In the sitting area was a small but serviceable fireplace, a red Aztec-inspired rug, and two well-broken-in red leather wingback chairs that Quinn wanted to take back to Evanston; there also was a kitchenette with all the necessities. But the cabin's main feature, of course, was the windows, which looked out over Butternut Lake. She would be comfortable here, she thought, swinging her suitcase onto the luggage rack and hanging her coat up in the closet. She'd bought a few grocery staples at the IGA in town, and she put them away now in the kitchenette and went to light the already laid fire in the fireplace.

Once that got going, making the already cheerful room even more cheerful, Quinn went over to the windows and admired the view of the lake through the trees. It was late afternoon now—after she'd left Gabriel she'd gone back into town for lunch and for groceries—and the lake was a different color than it had been earlier; it was colder, darker, and, somehow, bluer. But still, of course, beautiful. Always beautiful. She had grown up on this lake but she never, ever, got tired of looking at it. She'd planned to go running on one of the trails that edged it this afternoon, but given the warmth of the cabin and the comparative coldness of the day, she decided to stay right where she was instead.

She turned back to face the room. It was, she knew, a perfect place to write. She tried to organize her thoughts about Gabriel, tried to shape them into something resembling a meaningful narrative, but she kept coming back to just one thing: *Gabriel had been married.*

Obviously, he had changed since high school. But she *still* couldn't square *this* person, the person who had married both young *and* impetuously, with the person she had known then. She thought about what an eighteen-year-old Gabriel would have said about someone who had ordered a cup of coffee at a diner and ended up bringing the waitress home with him. For six months. Until he married her. It would have been beyond his understanding. The Gabriel she'd known in high school had never *mentioned* marriage to her. And yet, three years later, he'd gotten married, at twenty-one. *Twenty-one.* An age at which Quinn had still been in college, living on ramen noodles, hanging out with friends in coffeehouses, and pulling all-nighters at the library.

He's got you beat there, Quinn, she thought. She was no closer, she knew, to being ready for marriage now than she had ever been. Which wasn't to say that Gabriel had been ready for it either. The marriage, after all, hadn't lasted long. What had he said, though, when she'd asked him why he'd done it in the first place? He'd said he was tired of being alone. Which was strange. The old Gabriel had always been comfortable being alone, and, what was more, he'd had plenty of friends to call upon when he hadn't wanted to be alone anymore. So there was that mystery. Why couldn't he be alone? And then there was the mystery of why he'd never left Butternut. That, too, was unsolved.

She got up and walked over to the windows again and looked out on the trees, etched ever more darkly against the sky's changing light. It would be a clear, cold night. A good night for the fire that was already burning. So why not just enjoy it? She wasn't, after all, going to understand Gabriel's last ten years in twenty-four hours. She could, though, take heart from the progress she'd made with him today. His mood had thawed, he'd let her tag along, and, more than that, she felt as if she'd gotten somewhere with him. She'd seen flashes of the old Gabriel. His wry tone, his sly smile, what she used to think of as his sardonic sweetness. And she remembered then his smile when she'd jumped at the bear rug on the wall. That had been pure Gabriel. What was more, he'd said she could see him again, tomorrow afternoon.

It occurred to her, not for the first time, that spending time with Gabriel might be helping her come to terms with her senior year. And, maybe, she could help him, too. Help him jumpstart a life that appeared to be stalled. She rested her forehead against the window. Yes, she felt better. She felt hopeful for the first time since arriving on Friday.

She saw someone out the window, a man, walk into the resort's little bar and restaurant, visible from her cabin. She looked around at the half-dozen or so other cabins she could see from the window. Was one of them Tanner's? And would she see him later if she had dinner at the bar? He'd said he'd be up here for a week. If she didn't see him tonight, maybe she'd call him tomorrow. And they'd have that cup of coffee. She'd go by herself to the bar tonight, she decided. And later, when she got into bed, she'd find something dumb to watch on TV, something that would put her to sleep.

She left the window and went to make a cup of decaf. Doing this brought Theo to mind. So much of their relationship so far had consisted of meeting for coffee that she almost couldn't picture him without a cup of it attached to him. She thought about calling him now, telling him of her decision to stay in Butternut for a while, but decided against it. She'd call him tomorrow and bring him up to date on things. He would be pleased, she knew, that she'd gone to see Gabriel again, though she knew he wouldn't say so. He was careful not to have any clear or articulated expectations of Quinn. *Personal expectations*, that is. Instead, he gave the impression that whatever she did was fine with him. Which was a good thing. *An attractive thing*, to Quinn's mind. Professional expectations, on the other hand, were a different story. He kept her steadily employed writing articles for his online magazine. He did, however, have an annoying tendency to push her to write more about herself. And, as if in response to his silent prodding, she brought her coffee cup with her over to the bedside table, set it down, and turned on the reading light. Then she took her laptop from her computer bag and, getting comfortable on the bed, thought about Gabriel. *Why didn't you go to RISD? It was the one thing you wanted to do. More than almost anything.* She tapped her fingers on the keypad, remembering the December that Gabriel had gotten in, early decision, to RISD. *I was there when he got accepted*, she thought. *Not there at the very moment, but right after.*

CHAPTER 18

*December, Senior Year, Gabriel Gets Acceptance
Letter from Rhode Island School of Design*

At four o'clock on a gray, slushy afternoon, when the day-light was already leaching out of the sky, Quinn parked her car in the Shipps' driveway, and, bypassing their front door, headed for the kitchen door instead. She only had an hour before she had to meet Jake, but she wanted to see Gabriel. She felt like she didn't see him enough these days, and some-times it made her feel funny, off-balance. The kitchen door was unlocked, as she knew it would be, and once she'd pulled it shut behind her, she was enveloped in the chaos that was the Shipp household. She passed the laundry room, where mounds of clean laundry waited to be folded—they would never be folded—and the kitchen, where a stack of empty pizza boxes sat on the counter—did any family, *ever*, consume as much pizza as this family? Once in the living room, she encountered the Shipps' three dogs, lab mixes who hadn't heard her come in over the noise of the unwatched hockey game on TV, and the rap music thumping from Aiden and Colin's open bedroom doorway, but who now flung themselves at her with abandon. She petted them, then stepped over a jumble of hockey gear, video-game consoles, and displaced sofa cushions scattered across the living room rug and made her way to the hallway, where two of Gabriel's brothers were playing soccer.

"Head's up, Quinn!" Colin shouted, and she threw herself against the wall to avoid a flying soccer ball.

"Is Gabriel home?" she asked. But they didn't answer. They were savagely athletic, and they were never happier than when they were inflicting the maximum amount of damage on their home or on each other. She unflattened herself from the wall, and, pausing to straighten a childhood picture of the four boys that was hanging askew, she knocked on Gabriel's door.

"Go away," he called out. This wasn't directed at her, though. This was directed at his brothers.

"It's Quinn," she called back.

"Come in."

She opened the door, not to the familiar scene of Gabriel sitting at his desk, scrolling through his photos on his desktop computer, but to Gabriel lying on the floor, staring up at the ceiling. She came inside, amazed, as always, at the contrast between the rest of the house and Gabriel's bedroom. In here, it was eclectic, minimalist, uncluttered. And quiet. *Blessedly quiet.*

"Ahh, I can hear myself think," Quinn said, letting her backpack slide to the floor and coming over to lie down beside Gabriel on the rug. "What are we looking at?" she asked, following his gaze up to the ceiling.

"That," Gabriel said, pointing up at a rectangle-like crack. "I've never noticed it before. But it's the exact same shape as Utah."

"Really?" Quinn studied it. "Hmm. I don't know. All those big, squarish western states look the same to me." She slipped her hand into her blue jeans pocket and touched the ring she'd put there before getting out of her car. Jake had given it to her the day before, but she was nervous about showing it to Gabriel. She thought he would think things had gotten too serious between her and Jake. She hated this, not telling him. But Gabriel's opinion of Jake hadn't changed since September. She would have to tell him eventually, though. Maybe she'd do it tomorrow.

"That's definitely Utah," Gabriel said.

Quinn looked sideways at him. "We haven't hung out in days," she said. "Why didn't you wait for me after school?"

"I thought Jake would hijack you," he said. There was a crash from outside the room as one of his brothers collided with a wall.

"Well, he didn't," Quinn said. "And he's not the only reason I've been busy. I've been working on my college applications. We didn't all apply early decision." She turned on her side, propped herself up on one elbow, and studied his profile. "And speaking of early decision, shouldn't you be hearing from RISD soon?"

He was silent, looking at Utah, but one corner of his mouth twitched.

"Wait. You haven't . . . heard already?"

He smiled.

"You got in," she breathed.

"I got in."

"Gabriel!" Quinn yelped. She grabbed him and hugged him with such force that he laughed.

"When did you find out?" she asked, when she let go of him.

"Today. My mom was home when the mail came."

"You idiot," she said with a smile. "Why didn't you text me?"

"I wanted to tell you in person."

"Okay, fine. But did we have to have a geography lesson first?" she asked, pointing at the ceiling. She sat up. "Come on. I want to read the letter." She held out her hand for it, and Gabriel got up, opened his top desk drawer, and handed her the envelope. She sat on the floor, leaning her back against his bed, and slid the sheaf of papers out of the envelope. She read the acceptance letter with a glowing satisfaction. Truth be told, when she got her own acceptance letter to Northwestern, almost four months later, she was no more excited than she was right now. After she'd read the letter again, she shuffled through the rest of the documents, including his financial aid offer. It was a generous scholarship, but not a full ride. "Can your parents help you with the rest?" she asked.

"I've got three brothers, Quinn. But there are student loans."

Quinn nodded, putting the papers back into the envelope. "So you'll figure out the finances, but what about you?" She looked at him carefully. His gray-blue eyes gave nothing away. "Why aren't you more excited?" she asked. "This is your dream. I thought you'd be bouncing off the walls when you got this."

"No, it's good," he said, coming to sit next to her on the rug. "It's just . . ."

"What?"

"Have you ever gotten that thing you wanted and worked for and prayed for and then felt . . . I don't know, nervous? Like, what if it all gets taken away from you? Or, worse, what if you can't, you know, live up to your own dream?"

"Gabriel, that's ridiculous. You'll probably surpass your own dream," Quinn said.

"Yeah. You're right. It's ridiculous," he said. He smiled at her. "I'm talking nonsense."

"I'll miss you. I'll come visit you," Quinn said.

"But you'll be in the Midwest. It won't be that easy," he pointed out, referring to her first choice of Northwestern University.

"That's true. But there are these things called airplanes. I hear they've revolutionized travel."

"Why don't you apply to Brown?" he asked.

"Because I'm not Ivy League material. As it is, I probably have a better chance of getting hit by a meteorite than I do of getting into Northwestern."

"You'll get in," he said.

"I'm glad you're so confident." She bumped her knee against his. "I want to see your portfolio," she said. He'd promised to show it to her before he submitted it with his application, but somehow he'd kept putting it off.

"It's standard art school stuff," he said with a shrug.

"Gabriel, nothing you do is standard. Come on. Please? I want to see what the admissions committee saw," she said.

He got up and started to go toward his desktop computer and then changed his mind and reached instead for a portfolio case on the shelf above his desk. He stood there for a moment, as if debating whether or not to let her see it, then handed it to her. He sat back down on the floor across from her. She unzipped the portfolio, extracted the stack of photographs from it, and started to shuffle through them carefully, so as not to leave any fingerprints.

"Gabriel," she said, looking up at him. He was watching her.

"These are . . ." she murmured. "These are of me." There were twenty of them, all eleven by fourteen inches, all black and white, and all of them, every single one of them, of Quinn. What amazed her, though, was how different they nonetheless managed to be. They were taken during different seasons, at different times of day, in different settings, and in different lighting. And the different moods they captured ranged from serious to playful, melancholy to joyful.

"You remember my taking them, don't you?" he asked.

"Most of them," she said, feeling distracted. Because Gabriel was always taking photographs. Of everything. There was never a time, it seemed, when he *wasn't* taking them. Yes, she'd known some of them were of her. But she'd gotten the impression, somehow, that he took these when he was experimenting with different lenses, or different filters, or different lighting. She had no idea that he'd developed so many of them, or that they looked so polished, or, in one or two cases, so deliberately *un*polished. And yet all of them were astonishingly professional. This wasn't yearbook stuff. This was in a different category altogether.

She held up one he'd taken in the winter of their junior year. Quinn, in the lower left-hand corner of the photograph, was running in the snow, her hair a blur, speckles of hoarfrost on the branches of the pine tree behind her glinting in the sun, a fence in the background dividing the photograph on a diagonal, leading, almost like an arrow, to the upper right-hand side of the frame where a crow, all blackness against the sky, was sitting on a branch. She put the photo back into the stack and selected another one, this from the spring of that same year. In it, she was sitting on the blue couch in the communications room, bars of light and shadow from the window blinds alternating across her. Her hazel eyes, though, were in a slice of sunlight, and they stared dreamily out into the room beyond. She remembered that day; she'd wanted Gabriel to put away his camera so their meeting could begin. She was glad he hadn't. Another photograph, from early last summer, was taken before Gabriel left for Chicago. The two of them had spent a lazy Sunday afternoon driving around in her car, listening to the radio, and stopping, at one point, to explore an abandoned barn. Gabriel had taken pictures of her then, and here was one of them. Quinn was standing next to an empty horse stall, her hand resting on the open gate, a broken chair overturned in front of her, drifts of hay scattered around on the floor, and pinpricks of sunshine coming through the holes in the barn wall behind her, casting a spectral light. The last one was a photograph of Quinn sitting in a rowboat on Butter-nut Lake. It was taken the previous June, at dawn, a few days before Gabriel left for Chicago. The mist was still rising from the lake, and the sun was lighting up Quinn's hair and part of her face. She had one hand resting on the oarlock, and she was looking away from the camera. She wanted a copy of this one.

She looked up at him. "Gabriel, I look beautiful in this."

"That's because you are beautiful."

She shook her head and shuffled the pictures around a little more. "Why are they all of me?" she asked. And when she looked back at Gabriel, she was struck by how different he looked now. Maybe it was the light in the room, but it was as if he'd changed, in some way she couldn't put her finger on. He had an opaqueness, a mysteriousness, that was new, or per-haps she'd never noticed it before. She wondered what it would be like to reach over and touch his face, but she pushed the thought away.

"I wanted to do a photo essay," Gabriel said. "One person. Over time. And you're the person I saw the most. You know, took the most pictures of. The photo essay is called *Quinn*, by the way. That was a tough one."

She smiled and looked back down at the photographs. "You've immortalized me. When you're famous, I'll say, 'His RISD application was of me.'" She put the photographs back in the portfolio and handed it to him. They both stood up, and she gave him a hug. "God, I'm going to miss you," she said into his shoulder. "I love you," she added, without thinking. And she did.

If her words threw him off-balance, it was only for a moment. "I love you, too," he said, still serious.

"I gotta go," Quinn said. They pulled away a little awkwardly. She was meeting Jake at his family's house for dinner. At the moment, though, she wanted to stay here, in Gabriel's room, with him. But instead she grabbed her backpack and waved good-bye and ran the gauntlet past his brothers, who were wrestling now, or maybe just throwing each other up against the walls with as much force as possible. By the time she got back into her car, it was almost dark outside.

CHAPTER 19

Quinn, startled by a knock on the cabin door, flipped her laptop shut. "Who is it?" she called out.

"It's Annika."

Quinn rubbed a kink in her neck. If she was going to write this much, she'd have to start doing it at a desk, she thought, getting up and going over to the door.

"Wow, Annika," she said, when she'd opened it. "I've seen you more in one day than I saw you all during high school." Annika looked embarrassed and Quinn realized that she might have sounded sarcastic. "I mean, come in," Quinn said, with a smile.

"I brought you these," Annika said, holding out a stack of towels. "The housekeeper told me that you needed a couple more."

"Thanks," Quinn said, taking them from her. "These are great."

"I didn't wake you up, did I?" Annika asked, with a slight

frown, looking over Quinn's shoulder into the cabin. Quinn turned to look too. It did look as if she might have been napping. When she'd started writing, it had been light outside, and the only light she'd turned on was the bedside table lamp. Since then, though, dusk had fallen outside, and, except for the pool of lamplight around the rumpled bed, the cabin was full of shadows, and its corners had receded into darkness.

"Oh, no. I wasn't sleeping," she said. "I lost track of time while I was writing. I'm a journalist," she explained. Annika nodded. Quinn moved around the room, setting the towels down on a chair, turning on lights, and straightening the blanket.

"Would you like to come in for a minute?" she asked Annika, who was still standing in the doorway.

Annika came in, a little tentatively, closing the door behind her. "Do you write every day?" she asked.

"Usually," Quinn said, sitting down on the bed. "I'm not compulsive. It doesn't have to be something weighty or long. But I want to, I need to, write *almost* every day. Even if it's a short description of a person or a place or a conversation. I feel kind of off-kilter if I don't write, kind of out of balance. I feel the same way when I don't run. Which, unfortunately, I haven't gotten to do since I've been in Butternut."

Annika cocked her head, as if she was considering this. She was one of those rare people, Quinn realized, who was a good listener. As a journalist, listening—listening actively and thoughtfully—without interrupting was something that Quinn had had to learn how to do. But some people did it naturally.

"Annika, please sit down," Quinn said. She was making Quinn

nervous standing there, like a fugitive about to take flight. Quinn pointed toward one of the chairs in the sitting area and Annika moved away from the door and sat down on the edge of it.

"Could I ask, though, what you're working on now?" Annika said. "I've read some of your articles in the past."

"Really?" Quinn was flattered. "Where did you come across them?"

"Online. I read one about a woman's professional softball team."

"Oh, the Chicago Bandits," Quinn said, smiling. She'd really wanted to write about them and had had to convince a reluctant Theo to let her. "I had a blast writing that article. Mainly because I got to go out drinking with some of the team at a bar in Rosemont. Suffice it to say, they can hold their own," she said of them. Quinn, on the other hand, had had to be poured into a cab at the end of the night and had woken up the next morning with a deadly hangover.

"It was fun to read, too," Annika said, her animation overcoming her reserve. "And so was the one about the Cape Cod Room closing. I mean, that one wasn't fun. It was sad. But it made me feel like I was there, in those final days."

Quinn nodded. "Say Good-Bye to the Cape Cod Room" was an article she'd written for *Windy City Today*, about the last days of the iconic seafood restaurant in Chicago's Drake Hotel. Her dad had actually taken her there once when she was a kid, when they were visiting Chicago. It was dark and cozy—the tables covered with red-and-white-checked tablecloths and copper pots hanging from the ceiling—and despite the fact it had been known for its seafood, an eight-year-old Quinn had wanted a hamburger.

"You're a good writer," Annika said. "I felt like I was right there in the Cape Cod Room."

"Thank you," Quinn said. "I'm glad you liked my articles. I wonder sometimes if anyone reads them. I'm not writing one at the moment." She went on, "Right now I'm writing about my senior year of high school. I'm trying to re-create it. Not everything, just the most important parts. I've been especially prolific today; I've already written four memories of that year."

Annika looked surprised. "Why do you want to write about your senior year?" she asked.

"I guess I'm trying to understand it better. Writing is the best way I know how to do that. Maybe the only way," Quinn said. "But I'm doing it for me. It's not for publication."

Annika was sitting very still in her chair, almost too still, Quinn thought. The lamplight shone on her blond hair.

"That must be really hard, writing about that year," she said to Quinn. She stood up then and started moving in the direction of the door.

And Quinn, who'd been sitting on the bed, got up too. "It *is* hard. Sometimes I want to write about it. And sometimes I don't. But I'm pushing myself to anyway. So far, I've only written about the good parts of that year. I haven't gotten to the accident yet . . . That will be the hardest part . . . It was a terrible time."

Annika, standing with her hand on the doorknob, nodded in agreement.

"Was it hard for you?" Quinn asked, realizing that all three boys had been from Annika's hometown, and she must have known them, at least tangentially.

Annika put her head down, as though considering this question. "It was a hard year for everyone who lived in Winton," she said. "But I was pregnant with Jesse. So I had to think about that." Checking her watch, she opened the cabin door as she said, "I'd better be going. I told Jesse he could watch a program, but it's almost over now. It was nice talking to you."

Quinn smiled. "Thanks for the towels," she said.

After Annika closed the door, Quinn went to the window and watched her walk away into the darkness. *She's an enigma*, Quinn thought. A bundle of contradictions. She was friendly but guarded, polite but abrupt, interested but not forthcoming. In fact, even as she had settled into the armchair she'd had one foot out the door.

Quinn turned from the window and thought about picking up her writing where she'd left off. She'd lost the thread of it, though, and besides, she'd gotten most of it down, hadn't she? Instead, she wandered around the cabin a little and ended up standing in front of the dresser, staring at her face in the mirror that hung above it. This wasn't Quinn's favorite thing to do, but she looked at her reflection now as if she were searching for something. Had Gabriel kept those photographs he'd taken of her? Were they stored somewhere in that solitary cabin of his? Or were they gone now, another casualty of life? And she wondered what he had seen in them, in her, when he'd taken them. What had he seen in them that she hadn't been able to see in herself?

CHAPTER 20

When Quinn drove over to Gabriel's cabin the next afternoon, his pickup truck was gone and he didn't answer
the front door. She looked through one of the windows. Nope.
Nobody home. The living room looked as impersonal as it had
the last time she'd been here. She checked her watch. It was four
o'clock. She was right on time. He, on the other hand, seemed to
have disappeared into thin air. *And you thought that was your
trick, Quinn, didn't you?* she chided herself, knocking again.

Still, something was bothering her. Something other than
Gabriel not being here. Why hadn't they exchanged phone
numbers yesterday? That would have been the normal thing
for two old friends to do. She gave up on knocking and stuffed
her ungloved hands into her jacket pockets. The problem was,
their friendship *wasn't* normal. Hence, the normal rules did not
apply. What was more, she now understood, Gabriel wouldn't

have given her his number anyway. He didn't trust her. Not yet. And he didn't know if he wanted her back in his life.

Rather than let this knowledge deflate her, though, she paced a little. She had always been lousy at waiting. After a few minutes she walked around to the back of the cabin. She wasn't sure what she was looking for, but she wanted to take a closer look. Was she looking for some clue about Gabriel and his life here? Maybe. That was a journalist for you. Part detective. And part voyeur, she admitted, climbing onto the cabin's back steps and looking in at the kitchen window. But once again, there was nothing to see. Not even a coffee mug on the counter. It was strange. Even her room at Loon Bay, which she'd occupied for less than twenty-four hours, showed more signs of human habitation than this cabin.

She left the back door, planning on returning to her car—she was getting cold—but she caught sight of a shed in his backyard and went to investigate. It was a woodshed, and it was full to overflowing, with more wood stacked at its side and covered under canvas tarps. Was he selling the wood? she wondered, noticing the woodcutting stump he used to split logs on. He certainly wasn't using it himself. He'd had stacks of wood on either side of his fireplace, when she'd first visited him a couple of days ago. But his cabin had been chilly and there'd been no sign of him having had a fire there recently.

She left the woodshed now and headed back around the side of the cabin, passing what she assumed was his bedroom window. It was too high up for her to see into easily. She stopped, kept walking, and stopped again. *Damn it*, she

was so curious. And if he came back while she was trying
to look into his window? Well, she'd hear him. She glanced
around for something to stand on, and, when she didn't see
anything nearby, she hurried back to the woodpile and chose
a wide-bottomed oak log from it. She balanced this under
the window, stepped up onto it, and steadied herself on the
windowsill. There were curtains—an ugly brown-and-orange
check that she knew must have come with the rental—but
they were open wide enough for her to see into the room.
She pressed her nose up against the windowpane, her breath
fogging the glass.

His bedroom, she saw, was like the rest of the cabin. She
sighed, relieved. If there'd been anything personal in it, she
would have felt . . . *icky*. Like she was stalking him or something. But, no, it was bare. Minimalist. Almost monastic. A
bed. A dresser. A closet, the partly open door revealing a few
things hanging up inside of it. She started to get down from
the log, but before her foot touched the ground, she frowned,
and stepped back onto it again. What was on the wall to the left
of the window, the wall that she had to crane her neck to see?
Yes, it was photographs. A whole series of them—maybe twenty
or more—posted on the wall. And she couldn't make them all
out, either, but she could see that they weren't of people. They
were of landscapes, and houses, and buildings. And although
she couldn't get any closer to the photographs, she had a feeling they were beautiful. *So you're still taking photographs,
Gabriel?* And knowing this, she felt oddly elated.

She climbed down from the log and carried it back over to

the woodpile. And then, even though she knew, somehow, that Gabriel wouldn't be meeting her here today, and that he hadn't forgotten and wasn't simply running late, but that he was intentionally avoiding her, she went back and sat in her car for another forty-five minutes, feeling her mood grow heavier. She found a scrap of paper in her shoulder bag and scribbled a message on it. *Gabriel, I missed you. Quinn.* She left it under his door knocker and drove back to Loon Bay.

As she took the turns of twisty Butternut Lake Drive, she felt a sadness she couldn't shake. The note, she realized, hadn't been entirely accurate. She'd written that she'd *missed* him. Past tense. The truth was, she was *missing* him, and everything they had had, right now. Present tense.

CHAPTER 21

Even after she returned to Loon Bay, this feeling of melancholy clung to Quinn. She tried to stay busy. She went for a long run and took an even longer shower. Then she built a fire in the fireplace, thinking to herself that her ability to build a perfect fire—*thanks, Dad*—should have, but didn't, please her.

After that, she settled into the reading chair to answer her emails, and, later, remembering the novel she'd tossed into her suitcase at the last minute, she lay down on the bed and tried to read it. But she was restless. She wasn't used to this much downtime. Or, rather, this much *in-between time*. She knew how to work. She knew how to relax, sort of. It was this *other* thing she didn't know how to do. This indistinct thing in the middle that left her feeling dependent on other people.

Outside, the sky had darkened from a pewter to a gunmetal gray. The clouds were low and heavy. Perfect. Rain clouds.

Soon the weather would match her mood. This wouldn't be one of those pleasant spring rains, either, the kind that brought with it a freshness and a sweetness that put one in mind of summer. This would be one of those dull spring rains that, in this part of the country, were a part of the season's long, slow slog out of winter.

She saw the lights on in the little bar and grill. Should she have dinner now? It was only six thirty, but it wasn't like there was anything else to do at Loon Bay out of season. Then, almost as if it were a reproof to this thought, Quinn heard the familiar, rhythmic sound of a basketball bouncing and followed it with her eyes over to the small court to the right of the bar. It was Jesse, Annika's son, shooting baskets by himself. She hadn't seen him since she'd bumped into him and his mom in town. He'd had a ball with him then, too, one of those Pinky rubber balls. She watched him do a layup now. *Whoa.* He was good. On the sidewalk outside Pearl's he'd looked like a kid. Now he looked like an athlete. A raindrop hit the window. Then another. Out on the basketball court, Jesse paused, squinted up at the sky, and then started dribbling again. *That's right,* Quinn thought, smiling. *Don't let a little rain chase you inside.* She watched as a man in a sweatshirt and blue jeans jogged up to the court, and Jesse turned and threw him the ball. The man caught it, bounced it a couple of times, and passed it back to him. It was Tanner. He'd mentioned that he came up here once a month, so of course he'd have to know Jesse. They were well matched, Quinn thought.

She left the window and sat down on one of the reading

chairs. She wanted to see Gabriel, she realized, wanted to see him so much that she was almost willing to drive over to that cabin of his again. He might be home by now. Or, if he wasn't, she could park on one of those logging roads nearby and stake out the place. A smile trembled at the corner of her lips. Or, if that didn't work, she could break into the cabin and be waiting on his couch, drinking a cup of black coffee, when he got home. The thought of this amused her, and she was still smiling when her cell phone rang a moment later and she picked it up from the bedside table. It was Theo.

"Hey," she said, grateful for the distraction. "What's up?"

"Not much. I was wondering how you're doing. Are you back in Evanston yet?"

"No," she said, tucking her legs under her. "I'm still in Butternut."

"That's good, though, right?" he said. "Maybe you'll get some . . . for lack of a better word, closure?"

"Ugh. I *hate* that word," Quinn said. "And you're sounding like a therapist again. Although, honestly, Theo, I could probably use one right about now."

"What's happening?"

She wasn't going to tell him about her encounter with Theresa. It was too disturbing. And she couldn't tell him about the dreams she'd been having either. Those were too personal. So she told him instead about going to open the cabin with Gabriel and learning about his marriage and divorce. It hadn't quite been like high school, she told Theo. But just being with him again had made her happy. Then, today, he'd blown her off.

"So things aren't perfect. But do you feel like you're getting somewhere?"

"I think so. It's hard being here. But I'm not ready to leave yet."

"Then you'll stay for as long as you need to. Are you writing, though? About that year?"

"I am. And it's helping me to remember."

"That's cool. Do you think it could turn into something publishable?"

"Not the way you mean. I'm not writing it like a personal essay. I'm writing it more like . . . a novel, I guess. I'm trying to re-create everything as faithfully as I can. It's exhausting, sometimes," she confessed, with a little laugh. "You know, having one foot in the past."

There was a pause. "Well, we miss you at *Great Lakes Living*. How much longer do you think you'll be there?"

"I don't know," she said, thinking of Gabriel. "A couple of days? Maybe more."

"Well, I'd love to take you out to dinner when you get back."

Quinn hesitated. They'd never done anything "datelike" before.

"Or not," he said, jokingly. "We could just stick to coffee."

"Coffee might be better," Quinn said. "Things are a little complicated for me right now."

"No problem," he said. "Give me a call when you get back and we'll go over some story ideas."

After she hung up, she felt relieved. It was possible that she'd been nurturing a romantic interest in Theo. But something about being back in Butternut had diminished that interest. Her feelings had shifted. And that was a good thing. Theo was her editor. She wouldn't want to change that. She liked working for him. Besides, she was unreliable in the relationship department these days.

CHAPTER 22

As soon as she'd said good-bye to Theo, Quinn headed over to the bar for dinner. There was no sign of Jesse or Tanner on the basketball court now. It was raining harder, a cold, pelting rain, and, pulling her hood up and keeping her head down, she decided to make a run for it. Her destination, housed in a nondescript, clapboard building, wasn't much to look at by day, but by night, by *rainy* night, the Leinenkugel's Beer signs that twinkled in the windows made the bar look cozy.

She tugged open the door and came inside, lowering her hood. She was right, it was cozy. The single room consisted of a knotty pine bar with windows behind it that faced onto a deck with views of Butternut Lake, and a scattering of high tables with high stools filled out the rest of the room. Old fishing maps papered the walls (leaving space for the obligatory dartboard), a jukebox with 45 records still in it stood in one corner, and the same tabletop shuffleboard game Quinn and her dad had played here when she was a kid stood in another. The few updates to the place, as far as she could tell, consisted of a wall-mounted flat-screen TV and an arcade game called *Big Buck Hunter.*

As she shrugged off her dripping jacket, she tried to imagine this bar in Chicago. She couldn't. It wasn't hip enough to be a hipster bar; it wasn't divey enough to be a dive bar. It just *was.* Unironically. Unselfconsciously. And, God, let's face it, it was refreshing. She was so tired, sometimes, in the media-saturated world she lived in, of everything having to *mean* something, *stand* for something, *be* something, something more complicated than it already was. She wanted to tell this to somebody now. To Gabriel, she realized.

She raised her hand in greeting to the bartender, Gunner, whom she'd met the night before. He was making a half-hearted attempt to wipe down the bar as he watched a hockey game on TV. Watching it with him, his back to Quinn, was the bar's only other customer, and following Gunner's wave, he turned to her now and broke into a smile. "Quinn, Annika told me you'd checked in."

"Tanner," she said, happy to see him. She hadn't realized how much she was dreading spending another evening alone.

He got off his stool and pulled out the one beside him for her. "Come join us," he said. "We're watching the Blackhawks game."

"That's my team," she said, though her interest in hockey was minimal at best. Still, it was good to see Tanner again.

"Have you met my friend Gunner?" Tanner asked, as she slid onto the stool next to his.

"I have. Last night," she said, with a nod at Gunner, who didn't look old enough to drink alcohol, let alone serve it. He hadn't been much of a talker when she'd come in here, though in Gunner's case, that wasn't necessarily a bad thing. Unlike Marty, from the Corner Bar, who'd been around the block a few times, Gunner seemed unaware of where that block might even *be*. His main accomplishment behind the bar, as far as Quinn could tell, was to combine boredom and disinterest in equal parts, and she couldn't help thinking he was counting down the hours to when he could go home to a place where his mother still made his eggs the way he liked them and his dad still scolded him for not taking out the garbage.

"Hey," Gunner said to Quinn, exerting himself. "What can I get you?"

"I'm going to have a glass of pinot grigio and the small veggie pizza."

He nodded, and as if already exhausted by the effort this order would require, he wandered off down the bar.

"The pizza's great here," she said to Tanner, who was already drinking a bottle of Leinenkugel's.

"Oh, I know. It's the special oven. Or so they say," he added, flashing her another smile.

"That's the official line," Quinn agreed, remembering what Carla, at the Butternut Motel, had said about the oven. Gunner brought her a glass and a mini–airplane bottle of pinot grigio and left them on the bar in front of her.

"Jeez," Tanner said, once Gunner was out of earshot. "He could at least pour it for you." Instead, Tanner did it for her himself, twisting the lid off the little bottle and emptying it into her glass.

"Thanks," Quinn said. "Hey, I saw you playing basketball with Annika's son."

"Jesse. Yeah, he's a great kid," Tanner said, peeling the label on his beer bottle.

"Looks like he's almost as good a player as you are," Quinn commented.

"I know. A couple years from now he'll need to find someone better to play with." He took a drink of his beer. "I'm glad you're sticking around, Quinn, and that you ended up at Loon Bay."

"Well, I ran into Annika and Jesse in town yesterday. Plus I've always loved this place."

Tanner nodded. "Did you ever find your friend Gabriel?"

"I did. You were right, by the way. He's renting Mr. Phipps's cabin."

"How's he doing?"

"I'm not really sure," she admitted. "He's changed, but maybe I've changed too. But I'm hoping we'll get to hang out more while I'm here." Quinn took a sip of her wine. She refrained from wincing; it was pretty cheap stuff.

"I hope you're not too picky," Tanner said. "Most people come for the Leinies," he added, using the nickname for Leinenkugel's.

"It will do for now," Quinn said, with a smile. Despite the bad wine, she felt good, and she realized that one of the reasons she did was because she was here with Tanner. Somehow, sitting on that stool beside hers, he managed to radiate an air of well-being that included her within its aura, and that kept at bay, at least for now, the tumult of the last few days. She noticed the spicy tang of his aftershave—*good* aftershave. It was just strong enough to register with her. He was dressed in a T-shirt, a zip-up hoodie, jeans, and the work boots that were de rigueur up here during mud season—but these clothes looked as right on him as the more formal attire he'd worn to the dedication. And then there were those eyes. *Jake's eyes.* No, she reminded herself, they were Tanner's, too. That same gold as the wrapped butterscotch candies Quinn's grandmother Shaw had kept in a glass dish on the coffee table in her living room in Chicago.

Gunner brought her pizza, still bubbling from the oven. "Oh, and I'll have another pinot," Quinn said, wondering if Gunner knew that an empty glass on the bar was the universal signal that a patron might want another drink.

"Right," he said, with a sigh. He brought her another airplane bottle and set it on the bar next to the empty one.

Tanner rolled his eyes.

"Maybe he wants me to keep track of how much I'm drinking?" Quinn suggested.

Tanner laughed. "That's one way to do it, I guess."

"Do you want to split this?" she asked him, of the pizza.

"No, thanks. I already ate," he said as Quinn lifted a slice.

"Do you like '80s music?" Tanner asked, reaching into his pocket and placing some change on the bar.

"Sure," she said, as he picked out the quarters.

"Good. Because this jukebox is like an '80s time capsule," he said, sliding off his bar stool. "I think it's the last time they put new music in it." He went and fed it some quarters, and by the time he came back U2's "With or Without You" was playing.

"I stopped by to see your parents yesterday," she said to him.

"Did you?" he asked. "How'd you find them?"

She hesitated. "They look well. Your mother, especially. But . . ."

Tanner raised his eyebrows, waiting for her to finish.

"But I was only there for half an hour, and, after that, she was tired. She said she needed to take a nap." Quinn couldn't help but remember how pleased they'd been to see her. They'd chased away the feelings that her encounter with Theresa in the Corner Bar had stirred up.

"She naps a lot," he said, taking another drink of his beer.

Quinn nodded. She thought, now, about what Mrs. Lightman had said about Tanner. "We don't see him that often." Which was odd, considering he came up here once a month. "When you're here, do you spend much time with your parents?" she asked, fiddling with the stem on her wineglass.

He considered this, though it was a straightforward enough question. "I usually stop by to see them then." *Usually? If you're not coming up here to see them, then why are you coming up here?* Quinn wanted to ask. But it was none of her business, she knew. Families could be complicated. Still, the journalist in her won out.

"So what else do you do when you come up here?" she asked, coming at the question from a different direction.

"I'm here, mostly, at Loon Bay."

"Just hanging out?" she said, though she was confused as to why he would spend so much time doing it *here*. "I mean, don't get me wrong," she added. "Loon Bay's a nice place. My cabin's been very comfortable." But she couldn't help but feel that Minneapolis or St. Paul had much more to offer, especially for someone their age.

"It *is* a nice place," he said. "But that's not why I come up here. There are a couple reasons. I can't really go into them now," he added, apologetically, and looked away. "But one reason—you might understand this," he said, looking back at Quinn, "is because I miss Jake. And coming up here"—he paused to take another sip of his beer—"makes me feel closer to him. I guess that sounds strange." He brushed his hair out of his eyes. Quinn wanted to comfort him, but there didn't seem to be a graceful way to do this.

Instead, she said, "It doesn't sound strange, Tanner." Though, truth be told, it sounded *a little* strange. After all, Jake and Tanner had grown up not on Butternut Lake, like Quinn, but in the neighboring town of Winton. Why would this place, of all places, make Tanner feel closer to Jake? Then again, there was no logic to grief. And because Tanner was watching her and wanting her, she felt sure, to say more, she told him something she'd never told anyone before.

"I do something, too, that makes me feel close to Jake," she said, taking a sip of her wine. "I run. I started in the spring of my junior year in college. I didn't do it, at first, because of Jake. Believe it or not, at the time, I didn't even make the connection between the two. I did it because I thought it would be a good stress reliever. It wasn't until about six months after I started, when I was coming back from a five-mile run, that I had this moment where I felt, just for a second, like he was . . . *there.* Do you know what I mean? I couldn't see him, or hear him, or anything like that, but I felt his nearness, I guess. His presence. I still feel it, sometimes." What she didn't say was that she felt his presence less and less often. "Now *I* sound strange," she added, feeling self-conscious.

He shook his head. "Not at all," he said. "I know what you mean."

"You know, Jake talked about you a lot, Tanner. He really looked up to you."

Tanner looked pained. "I wish he hadn't," he said. "Looked up to me, I mean."

"Why?" Quinn asked.

"He might still be alive if he hadn't," he said.

"What do you mean?" Quinn asked, confused.

"It's a long story," he said, glancing away. "It's true, though; Jake did look up to me." He took a sip of his beer and put it down on the counter. "When we were kids he followed me around like a puppy dog. I loved it. He was my own built-in fan club. We were close enough in age to hang out and play together, but I was always one step ahead of him—rode a bike first, dated girls first, drank first, learned to drive first. And I think it would have *really* driven him crazy, my being one step ahead of him all the time, except my mom doted on him to no end, and that seemed to balance things out." He paused to drain his bottle of beer. "Sometimes, though, I think he got tired of always being a step behind me."

"Isn't that natural, though?" But all Quinn knew about siblings was what she'd observed in her friends' families.

"Maybe. But I was his older brother. I was supposed to watch out for him. Instead, I encouraged him to try to keep up with me. To follow my lead. Even if what I was doing was stupid. And reckless." He held his beer bottle up, as though inspecting it.

"I don't know about that, Tanner. But I do know you inspired him. You were the reason he pushed himself so hard. He wanted to follow you to the University of Wisconsin."

"Really? I think *you* were the one who inspired him. He had his whole life with you mapped out."

Quinn couldn't help but think about what Mrs. Lightman had said yesterday, about Jake wanting to marry her. Had he told that to Tanner, too?

"I miss him," Tanner said, suddenly.

"So do I," Quinn said.

He signaled Gunner for another beer. "To Jake," he said, when the beer came. He tipped the bottle toward her. "To missing Jake. And to the ways we keep him close."

"To Jake," she agreed, touching her glass to his bottle.

They were quiet, then, Quinn nibbling on a pizza crust, and Tanner watching the end of the hockey game.

"I just realized something," she said, when he looked back at her.

"What?"

"Other than the fact that you live in Minneapolis and you come up here, I know almost nothing about your life now."

"I work. A lot. I own my own business. And what else? I'm single. Those are the basics."

"Have you ever been married?" she asked, thinking of Gabriel's revelation.

He looked surprised. "Nope."

"Ever wanted to get married?" Quinn asked, though she wondered at her tendency to ask people personal questions.

"Not really," he said. "I don't think I'd trust myself to take on that level of responsibility. You know, till death do us part. That, and I realized, at some point, that it's better for me to keep things simple."

"Simple?" Quinn asked.

Tanner nodded. "It's why I rent, instead of buying. And why I have the minimum number of possessions. It lets me preserve the illusion, I guess, that I could move out at a moment's notice. Just . . . go anywhere."

"Or come here," Quinn pointed out.

He smiled.

"You said you owned a business? What kind?"

He took out his wallet, extracted a business card from it, and handed it to her.

LIGHTMAN SAND AND GRAVEL CO.
TANNER LIGHTMAN, PRESIDENT

Underneath this was the company's address and phone number in Minneapolis. She nodded and started to give the card back to him, but he shook his head. "No, hold on to it," he said.

She smiled and slipped it into her back pocket. "I don't know a lot about the sand and gravel business," she confessed.

"No. I didn't think you did," he said, amused. He tipped his beer bottle back and took a drink.

"How does it work, though?" Quinn asked, warming to the topic. "I mean, let's say I wanted to buy some gravel. How do you sell it? By weight?"

He nodded. "It starts at one-eighth of a ton and goes up from there."

"One-eighth *of a ton*? Okay, let's say I wanted that much gravel. I call you up, from Chicago, and I say, 'Tanner, I want one-eighth of a ton of gravel.' Now what? You deliver it, in what, a dump truck?"

"To Chicago?" He shook his head. "No, I'd probably tell you to go with a local guy."

She laughed. *Is it successful?* she almost asked. *Your business?* But she didn't need to ask him. She knew, intuitively, that it was. People wore success, the same way they wore clothes, and if you were observant, you could almost always see it on them. Tanner was successful. Which made it all the more surprising, to her, that he wasn't married. Yet. That he didn't have a family. Or a house in the suburbs. Didn't have, in short, all the trappings of the comfortable, middle-class existence his success entitled him to. And why didn't he trust himself with the level of responsibility those things would have required? She might have asked him—there wasn't a lot she wouldn't ask people—but somehow this seemed too personal.

"Why don't we talk about *your* work?" he said. "I think it's more interesting than mine." He finished his beer and signaled for another one. "I googled you. I ended up reading your article about the creative writing workshop for veterans. I liked it. A lot."

"Thank you. I loved writing that. I'm going to do a follow-up on it, I think. One of the guys I profiled, Angel, is going to have a play produced."

"Really?"

"Or workshopped, anyway. Still, it's a big deal."

"To Angel," Tanner toasted.

"To Angel," she agreed, clinking glass to bottle. She was tipsy now, but it was a good kind of tipsy. A fun kind of tipsy. Especially with the rain lashing the windows outside and Jon Bon Jovi's "Livin' on a Prayer" playing on the jukebox.

"I think I've got some more quarters," Tanner said, when the song ended.

An hour later, after he'd challenged her to a couple of games of tabletop shuffleboard—which she suspected he let her win—they were back sitting at the bar, though Tanner still left occasionally to feed quarters into the jukebox. "Okay, listen," he said, "just listen to the lyrics of this song. They are so perfect." He spoke with the conviction born of the several bottles of beer he'd already drunk that night.

"Is this 'Summer of '69' again?" Quinn asked, listening to the opening chords of the Bryan Adams song.

"Yeah, but listen. Just listen."

She laughed. "Tanner, I've *listened* to it. This is, like, the *fifth* time you've played it."

But he couldn't be reached. He sang along.

I got my first real six-string
Bought it at the five-and-dime
Played it 'til my fingers bled
Was the summer of sixty-nine

Quinn finished her latest glass of wine. She'd lost track by now of how many she'd had; there was a scattering of empty bottles on the bar had she cared to investigate, but she didn't care to. She bent her head toward Tanner's now and sang the chorus of the song with him.

Oh, when I look back now
That summer seemed to last forever
And if I had the choice
Yeah, I'd always want to be there
Those were the best days of my life

"Great song," Tanner said, when it was over. He signaled to Gunner, who was standing down at the other end of the bar playing a game on his cell phone. "You know how much I loved that song when I was thirteen?"

"How much?" she asked.

"I asked for a six-string guitar for Christmas."

"Did you play it "'til your fingers bled'?"

He shook his head. "No. I only ever learned one song on it."

Quinn raised her eyebrows. "'Summer of '69'?"

"Yep."

"*Tanner*," Quinn said. But this struck her, suddenly, as hilariously funny, and Tanner started laughing too. By the time Gunner came over with the beer, they were both doubled over, and Quinn was trying not to fall off her bar stool.

"Here," Gunner said, setting the bottle down on the counter. He looked like he wished they'd call it a night.

"Thank you," Tanner said, recovering himself. He checked Quinn's wineglass and saw that it was empty. "Oh, and another wine, Gunner. Your finest bottle," he called, to his retreating back. Quinn cracked up again.

"WHOA, QUINN. CAREFUL," Tanner said, sometime later. He came over and took the two remaining darts out of her hand. "That last one went a little wide. Maybe the shuffleboard would be safer."

"I *rock* at shuffleboard."

"You said you rocked at darts, too," Tanner teased, before going to retrieve the missing third dart, which Quinn saw now had gone far wide of the board. Good thing it hadn't hit someone. Like the bartender. She looked around. He was nowhere to be seen.

"What happened to Shooter?" she asked Tanner, after he'd put the darts away.

"Shooter? You mean, *Gunner*?"

"Yeah. Where'd he go?"

"Home, Quinn," he said, facing her and putting his hands on her shoulders. His touch was like him, she thought. Light. Easy. "I released him from his responsibility."

"Can you do that?"

"Why not? I paid our tab, and I gave him a big tip. I told him we'd lock up on our way out."

"Do I owe you anything?" Quinn asked, looking around for her raincoat. Her wallet was in the pocket.

"Not a thing," he said, his hands still on her shoulders. She liked them there.

"This was fun," she said.

"It was."

Why were they talking in the past tense? Quinn wondered. The night wasn't over yet.

CHAPTER 23

Early the next morning, as a thin light filled the cabin, Quinn untangled herself from Tanner's sheets and, being careful not to wake him, eased out of his bed. She looked around for her clothes. They were not folded on the nearest chair. It hadn't been that kind of a night. She found them, instead, in a little heap on the floor on the other side of the bed. She picked them up and went into the bathroom to dress. When she was done, she allowed herself one quick look in the medicine cabinet mirror. Her hair was a little wild, her mascara a little smudged, but otherwise she looked almost human. If only she *felt* almost human. As it was, she had the makings of a world-class hangover: ferocious thirst, pounding headache, sped-up heartbeat. She looked around for a cup, and when she couldn't find one, she turned on the cold-water tap, bent over the sink, and drank from the faucet. *Very classy, Quinn.* She splashed some water on her face, and then patted it dry with the corner of a hand towel, avoiding her eyes so as not to leave any mascara on it.

When she tiptoed out of the bathroom, Tanner was still asleep, lying on his stomach, the covers around his waist, one arm dangling over the side of the bed. Even from across the room, she imagined she could feel the warmth emanating off his body. He stirred and mumbled something in his sleep, and there was a part of her that wanted to get back into bed with him. But a bigger part of her wanted to leave, preferably before he woke up. She found her coat in the closet, surprised that one of them, probably Tanner, had had the presence of mind to hang it there, and pulled her boots on beside the front door. And then she opened the door just wide enough to angle herself through it and clicked it shut behind her.

She stood on the steps of his cabin and looked out at the lake, or what should have been the lake, but was now a thick, cottony layer of fog. Everything was silent but for the rain, which fell softly, dripping off the eaves and pocking those few clumps of snow left beneath the pine trees. Even that snow, she knew, would be gone by the end of the day, taking with it one of the last signs of winter. She took the concrete footpath back to her cabin, relieved that there was no one, at this hour, to see her do this. Already she was feeling defensive about last night, though, in truth, the one person, other than Gunner, who might guess where she had spent it, and whom she had spent it with, was Annika.

But as she let herself into her cabin and tossed her coat on the bed, she reminded herself that she didn't owe Annika an explanation for last night. She didn't owe *anyone* an explanation for it. After all, no one was going to get hurt, were they? Not Tanner, and not her. And, as for Jake . . . Jake was beyond anyone's ability to hurt—and had been now for over a decade. She yanked off her boots and went to curl up in the wingback armchair, its leather cool against her pounding temples. She'd had fun, and she'd needed some fun. *Let it go*, she told herself. *Chalk it up to the stress of being back here, or the temporary loneliness of your existence, or to the need to blow off steam, or to the rain, or to the airplane bottles, or . . .*

No, she couldn't do it. She couldn't shake the feeling that what had felt right to her several hours ago through the fog of alcohol felt wrong to her now. And she knew why. She hadn't let herself see this last night, but this morning, in the light of day, she saw it plainly enough. Her attraction to Tanner was grounded in his resemblance to Jake. And not only in his physical resemblance to Jake, in his gold eyes and cowlicky hair, but in his mannerisms, too, his tics, and even his figures of speech. Some of these similarities were hard to quantify; there was a "Jakeness" to Tanner that she couldn't translate into words. (Or maybe, she considered, there had been a "Tannerness" to Jake. He wouldn't be the first younger brother who had imitated his older brother, whether consciously or unconsciously.) But some of these similarities were obvious. The way Tanner, like Jake, closed his eyes when he was listening to a piece of music he loved. The way he tipped his head back when he laughed. Even the way he used the word *ridiculous* to mean that something—a

restaurant, a movie, even a person—was great. Jake had done
these things too. *Oh, God*, she thought.

It was at times like this—times when Quinn was forced
to question her own judgment—that she asked herself if she
might have been different if she'd been raised by a father *and*
a mother. If she'd had more of a "feminine" influence over her
life, would she have made different decisions? Would she have
had different character traits, or life goals, or love interests?
Would she have gone home *alone* last night? She didn't know.
But that didn't stop her from speculating about it.

"You're like a guy," a boyfriend she'd had in college had once
said to her. "What do you mean?" Quinn had asked, surprised.
(By then, she'd long since put her tomboyish ways behind her.)
"Well, you just go after what you want," he said. "You don't apologize, or explain, or worry about doing what you want to do.
You just . . . do it." At the time, Quinn hadn't known whether to
be flattered or offended. She knew what he'd said wasn't entirely
true. Maybe this was what she projected to the rest of the world.
That didn't mean that she didn't wrestle with her decisions and
worry about the consequences of her actions in her head. In the
simplest sense, though, she understood what this boyfriend had
meant. After all, in many ways, her father *had* raised her like a
boy. When she was a child, he didn't buy her dolls; he bought
her Lincoln Logs, an Erector set, and a miniature workbench.
When she fell and got hurt, he didn't coddle her but picked her
up, dusted her off, and said, "Try again, Quinny." He played
catch with her in their yard after school and spent hours explaining the rules of football to her during televised weekend games.

He taught her how to hunt (something she'd never taken to), how to fish (she liked this better, more for the tranquility than the sport), and how to drive his truck on backcountry roads. He brought her to the timber company he worked at, which specialized in reclaimed wood, and took her, step by step, through the business, as though she, too, might be interested in working there one day. She wasn't.

But here was the thing about her dad: he accepted that. Some of his interests became hers; others did not. Still, he told her she could do whatever she wanted to do, have anything she wanted to have, provided she was willing to work hard for it. He encouraged her in her writing. But as for the actual *writing* itself? For that she would have to credit the mother she'd never known.

"Your mom was a writer," her friend Lilly Hess had said to her at school one day, when they were seven years old. They were sitting at a table in the cafeteria, trying to stick their straws into slippery pouches of chocolate milk. "No, she wasn't," Quinn said. "Yes, she was," Lilly said. "She was going to write a novel. My mom told me."

As soon as her dad picked her up from school that afternoon, Quinn asked him, "Was my mom a writer?" "Well, yes. She was," he'd said, taken aback. "Why didn't you tell me?" Quinn asked, affronted that Lilly Hess should have known this before her. "It's complicated," he said. But Quinn wouldn't bend. "Why don't you ever talk about her?" she asked. When he couldn't answer this, Quinn settled into a stony silence. "Quinny," he said, when he'd pulled over. "The year your mom died . . ." He stopped, almost overcome with emotion. He took a deep breath and went on. He explained to her that the year her mom had died he'd missed her so much that he wasn't paying enough attention to the other important thing in his life, which was Quinn. A friend of his had pointed this out to him, and that day he'd decided he needed to try to put the past behind him, and to move forward, and to stop looking back. To do that, he'd needed to stop thinking about Quinn's mother, Celia, all the time. And that meant, of course, that he needed to stop *talking* about her all the time too. "Perhaps," he'd said to Quinn then, "perhaps I overdid it."

Quinn understood, sort of. She was impatient, though. Once her friend Lilly had introduced the subject, Quinn wanted to know more about her mother. She wanted to know *every-thing* about her mother. And not just her name, and where she was born. She knew that already. She'd met her grandmother Shaw—a woman she hadn't particularly liked—a couple of times when she was small. She wanted to hear about *the good stuff*.

Was she really a writer? she asked her dad. Yes, she was. When Gene had first met her, she was working for a free Chicago weekly whose offices were over a pet shop. Did she ever write a novel? Well, no. She didn't. She *wanted* to, but she didn't have time to. How did they meet? At a Chicago Cubs game. She and a friend were sitting in front of Gene, and it was obvious from their conversation that neither of them knew the first thing about baseball. Gene took pity on them and spent the rest of the evening explaining the finer points of the game to them. Her friend liked Gene, too, but at the end of the night, it was

Celia whose phone number he asked for. That was the start, he explained. What was their wedding like? Quinn asked, jumping ahead. It was small. Celia's mom, Grandmother Shaw, wasn't happy about the two of them getting married. Grandmother Shaw had "come from money," her dad said. It was a phrase that fascinated Quinn. And her grandmother had thought that Gene was too "rough around the edges." This, too, was mysterious. Quinn had never known her dad to be rough before, not with anyone else and certainly not with her.

The questions continued, but the answers never satisfied Quinn. Her dad wasn't a storyteller. Which meant that the things he told her about her mother often felt piecemeal or random. She hadn't liked pears, for instance, he'd mentioned once. Or, Fig Newtons had been her favorite cookie. She wasn't afraid of bugs in general, he'd explained, but for some reason she was afraid of beetles. She'd planted a garden when they'd moved up to Butternut, he'd told Quinn, but hadn't known when to pick the vegetables. The zucchinis had grown to be the size of baseball bats before the raccoons had gotten to them. She had the best sense of humor, he said, and always knew how to make him laugh. But when Quinn had asked him to describe her sense of humor, he'd shrugged and said, "Well, you know, she was just funny. I can't explain it."

Later, when Quinn was older, she'd spend hours going through the box of photographs her dad had saved of her mom. She was pretty, Quinn thought. She looked happy. In many of the pictures, she was gazing, fondly, at Gene, and later, at the baby snuggled in her arms, or the toddler sitting on her lap.

Photographs, though, don't unlock the secrets to someone's personality; for these Quinn turned to the yellowing copies of the free weekly paper she'd worked at that Gene had saved. Again, she was disappointed. It wasn't that her mother didn't write well, she did. It was that the subject matter of her articles—a new neighborhood recycling center, a long-running bingo game at a local church—didn't tell Quinn anything about her innermost thoughts. In the end, Quinn concluded, her mother was a fine writer; she was more than fine. (She wrote with what Quinn's high school English teacher, Mrs. McKinley, had called "verve.") But what did Quinn *do* with this? She became a writer herself.

And she felt it now, sitting in the armchair by the window, that ache that was no less of an ache for having been with her for so long. It was different from missing Jake, or Gabriel, different from missing a person she'd known who was complicated, and real, and whole. Missing her mother was more like missing the idea of *having* a mother. Missing something, or someone, you don't quite know *how* to miss. Like missing a language you've never spoken, or an instrument you've never played, or a place you've never been.

Quinn got up and looked out the window. There was Annika's son, Jesse, wearing his backpack and trudging up the driveway to the road. It was a Tuesday; he must be headed to his school bus stop. She should get moving too. She'd take a shower, and then she'd go see Gabriel. Despite the fact that he'd blown her off yesterday, she wanted to see him again. No, she *needed* to see him again.

CHAPTER 24

By the time Quinn left Loon Bay later that morning, the rain had stopped. But as she drove to Gabriel's cabin, the view through her windshield was of a landscape saturated with water. Still, even in her hungover state, she found it beautiful. The mist that had gathered in the hollows along the roadside lent everything a mysterious, primordial quality. She drove slowly through puddles as wide as the road, and turned her windshield wipers on whenever the wind shook another shower loose from the pine boughs hanging overhead.

When she reached the B. PHIPPS sign and turned into the gravel driveway, she rolled down her window. It was warmer now, and the air bathed her face in dampness. There, that was better. She wished, though, that she'd had the presence of mind to bring a bottled water and extra-strength Advil with her. Something to eat before she'd left the cabin would have been a good idea too. In her experience, it was better to confront a hangover on a full stomach. There was a simple breakfast served at Loon Bay—coffee, juice, fruit, baked goods, and cereal—but it was served in the bar and grill and she hadn't been able to face the scene of last night's transgression this soon. She wondered, now, who'd found the scattering of empty airplane bottles she'd left on the bar. Not Annika, she hoped.

She slowed her car as the cabin came into sight. Gabriel's pickup was parked in the driveway, and there, in the garage beside the cabin, was Gabriel. He'd propped open the hood of a car and was working on its engine, but he looked up as she parked. And, as she walked over to the garage, he turned and went back to working on the car, a green Toyota Camry. Even before she reached the garage, she knew that whatever ground she'd gained with him the day before yesterday had been lost.

"Hey," she said, coming over to him.

He didn't look up. "You're still here," he said.

"I wish people would stop saying that," she said, rubbing her temples, which were throbbing from the effort of getting out of her car. All she wanted was a simple *Hi, Quinn, nice to see you.* But she was hoping for more than she was going to get. Gabriel was clearly irritated that she was here. She stood a little distance from him now and surreptitiously studied his profile. It was beautiful. He glanced at her, and she saw that he was paler than usual, and his eyes—more blue than gray in this light— had faint, purplish circles under them.

"Are you okay?" she asked.

"Am *I* okay?" he clarified, and the way he looked at her,

briefly, skeptically, made her wonder if she looked like she was under the weather too. Her hand traveled, almost involuntarily, to her hair, still damp from the shower, twisted into a messy knot on the top of her head. The cardigan she was wearing now—the one full of holes she liked to wear when she was writing—was misbuttoned, and one of her Converse sneakers, she saw, was muddy from a misstep into a puddle on the way to her car.

"Okay, so we both look like hell," she said, trying to shove some loose hair back into her bun.

"I didn't say you looked like hell," Gabriel pointed out, before he turned his attention back to the engine. He put a cap back on what she thought might be the coolant system—her dad had taught her some basics about car maintenance. And it occurred to her that Gabriel wasn't irritated at her. He didn't care enough about her to be irritated at her. He didn't even care if she was here or not. *So, why am I here?*

He looked up, briefly, and shook his head, almost imperceptibly, as if he'd heard her silent question. *Please go*, he seemed to be thinking. *Not a chance*, she thought, looking around for a place to sit and finding it on top of a grimy cooler a few feet away from him. She perched there and watched as Gabriel continued to work. He had a rag in his hand and appeared to be cleaning a part of the engine. She shivered, in the damp, chilly garage, and, as she nursed her hangover, she thought that she wouldn't say no to a cup of his black coffee if he offered one to her. And although she'd first felt miffed by his indifference, now she felt hurt. *No time for feeling hurt, Quinn. Keep going. Don't give up*, she told herself in a little internal pep talk. Searching for something to talk about, she settled on his photography.

"Are you still taking pictures?" she asked. He looked up from the engine and met her eyes before looking down again.

"Yeah. Sometimes. When I'm inspired."

"What inspires you?" she asked, thinking of the photographs on his bedroom wall.

"Things," he said, mysteriously.

"What kind of things?" Quinn asked.

"Inspiring things, Quinn," he said. But she could tell he was joking.

Talk to me, Gabriel, she wanted to say. But he'd resumed working. Everything felt different than it had when she'd seen him two days ago. He'd been almost friendly then. Or, at the least, he'd opened up a little. Today, though, she couldn't find a way in.

"Did you forget we were supposed to meet yesterday or were you avoiding me?" she asked, suddenly. She didn't want to sound injured or peevish, though, in truth, she was feeling both of those things right now.

He didn't answer this. He had a question for her. "Seriously, Quinn, why do you keep showing up here?" he asked, with more curiosity than hostility.

"Because I want to see you, Gabriel," she said. Silence. She was rankled now. She rubbed her temples, again, and decided to change the subject.

"I'm staying at Loon Bay," she said, into the silence. "I like it there. It's been very welcoming. Butternut, on the other hand, not so much." Although she hadn't told him the last time she'd seen him, she started telling him now about her run-in with Theresa Dobbs at the Corner Bar.

"She's a troubled soul," he interrupted her, looking up from his work. "Who drinks. A lot. I would take whatever she said with a grain of salt," he said, going back to work.

She thought about continuing, and telling him exactly what Theresa had said to her, but she decided against it. Only later did she realize why. She was afraid Gabriel would confirm what Theresa had seemed to imply: that Quinn was somehow to blame for the accident.

"I ran into Tanner, Tanner Lightman," she tossed out, changing the subject. "I saw him last night at the bar at Loon Bay." Why had she brought that up?

Gabriel nodded. Something about her tone, though, made him look up at her again.

"I guess he likes staying there," she went on. "He comes up every month or so and checks in to the same cabin." Cabin 9, to be exact. He'd told her it was larger than the others and had a better view of the lake. "At first, I thought it was kind of weird. I mean, it's four and a half hours from Minneapolis, and I don't think he sees that much of his parents while he's here, but he said . . ." She stopped. She didn't want to betray Tanner's confidences about coming to Loon Bay to be "closer" to Jake.

Gabriel was staring at her now. She had his full attention. "And? How's he doing?" he asked.

"Um, he's good," she said. "But, honestly, I got a little tipsy. We ended up closing the place down. If you can call it that—

which, I'm not sure you can—if you're the only two customers there." She felt a flush traveling up from her chest to her neck and then to her face.

"Quinn." He shook his head.

"What?" she said, defensively.

"You didn't . . . the two of you?"

She didn't answer. She didn't need to. Her guilty expression must have said it all.

"Hmmm," he said. He didn't look disgusted, she saw with relief. More mystified. "Wait . . . let me get this straight," he said. "You slept with your dead boyfriend's brother?"

"I did," she said, looking at him, but wanting to look away.

He stared at her for another long moment, but said nothing.

"I know. *I know*," she said. "I don't know what came over me. Over *us*. We were drinking, as I said. And we were having fun. I don't have much fun these days, Gabriel. And it just happened. We didn't plan it."

Gabriel still didn't say anything. But Quinn chafed at her own defensiveness. "Look, it was a mistake. *Obviously*," she said. "It's not going to happen again. But I'm an adult. And it's not like I was cheating on anyone."

Gabriel raised his eyebrows. "Interesting statement, Quinn."

"I mean, I'm not in a relationship," Quinn said now. "And you seem to be forgetting that I'm human. I make mistakes. I never claimed to be perfect. I would think you, of all people, would know that."

He went back to the car engine. "So you think it was a mistake. Do you think Tanner thinks so too?"

"I don't know," Quinn admitted, surprised by the question. "I don't know what he's thinking." She hadn't wanted to wake him this morning, but she hoped that he felt the same way she did, that it would not be repeated.

They were silent while Gabriel worked on the car engine. "You're right, Quinn," he said, finally. "You're an adult. You can do whatever you want."

Yes, she thought, *even if what I've done is the wrong thing.* She shifted on the ice chest, trying to get comfortable. Something dripped, loudly, in the garage, working on her frayed nerves. Every time she blinked, her eyes felt like sandpaper. Dehydration. There was water everywhere, but none for her to drink. It was hard, in fact, to overstate her misery right then. The hangover was bad enough, but what was happening now between her and Gabriel was worse. She felt even further away from him than she had on that first day.

"It's not easy being back here," she said, almost to herself.

"No? Well, you should try never leaving," Gabriel said.

"Then why *didn't* you leave?" she asked him.

"What? And give up all this?" he asked, gesturing around the garage. There was a glint of humor in his eyes, but Quinn was not amused. She wanted to know more and he was making light of it. But before she could press him on this, Gabriel went to get a gas can off a nearby shelf. He unscrewed the lid on the car's gas tank and fitted the can's nozzle into it. *Glug, glug, glug.* Listening to the gas going into the tank, she smiled.

"Remember homecoming, our senior year? Gingy Harris brought the Wolverines quarterback to the dance, and the football team got you to siphon the gas out of his tank so they'd be stranded afterward?" She laughed. It had been such an *un*-Gabriel-like thing to do. "I guess I shouldn't be surprised you're working on cars," she said. "You might not have wanted to learn all the stuff your dad taught you, but you learned it anyway."

The glugging sound stopped. Still, Gabriel didn't move. At all. It was as if he were frozen in place. And his face, or at least the little she could see of it, was startlingly pale.

"Gabriel," she said, feeling a surge of protectiveness. "Are you okay?" But he didn't answer her. It was as if he hadn't even heard her. She got up and went over to him. He was still standing there with the gas container in his hand. "My God, you look like you've seen a ghost," she said. *It's your family, isn't it,* she wanted to say. *I shouldn't have brought them up. Shouldn't have called attention to the fact that you're doing the one thing you said you never wanted to do; you're working on cars.*

Gabriel, though, turned abruptly and put the gas can back on the shelf. Then he removed the hood prop, slammed the hood of the car, and grabbed a rag and started wiping down tools.

"Gabriel, what is it?" Quinn persisted. "I'm worried about you," she said, edging closer to him. "What's going on?"

"I could ask you the same question, Quinn," he said. He moved farther away from her, putting the tools back on the shelves. "What's going on with *you*? I mean, I could see you coming for the dedication. But why are you still here three days later?" He stopped to look at her, running his hand through his hair.

"I'm here because I thought I should spend some time in Butternut," she said.

"Yes, you told me that the first day. That you felt you should be here. But why *should*? Like being here is some kind of an obligation."

"It's not an obligation. But I feel like I need to be here. I need to deal with things I haven't dealt with yet. I know that sounds vague. But that's the best I can do," Quinn said. What she didn't tell Gabriel about was her belief that if she didn't come to terms with her past, particularly the accident, it would forever trip her up. Or worse, it would leave her paralyzed, incapable of moving forward.

"But that's not the only reason I stayed in Butternut, Gabriel. I want to spend time with you, too."

"Are you sure that *want* is not a *should*, Quinn?"

"What? No." Her hangover should have been wearing off, but it wasn't. She felt worse now than ever. And even Gabriel appeared to notice.

"Let me walk you to your car," he said, in a gentler tone.

"Can I come back tomorrow?"

He shook his head. "I don't think that's a good idea."

"Why not?"

"Look, I should have said this to you the first time you came here, after the dedication. I'm glad you're doing well. Not right this minute, maybe"—this was said with a wry smile—"but in general. Your life and your career. I feel like you got what you wanted. And I'm happy for you. I mean that—"

"Do you?" Quinn interrupted him. "Because you don't look happy to me. About anything."

"Maybe I'm not happy for myself. Not everyone deserves to be happy, Quinn. But I'm happy for you."

"What do you mean, 'not everyone deserves to be happy'? Because good people deserve to be happy. And you're a good person," Quinn said.

"You don't know that," he said, looking away.

"Yes, I do," Quinn said.

"Look, let me finish what I started to say," he said, with exasperation. "I wish you well, Quinn, but I don't want to spend time with you. I don't want to spend time with *anyone* right now."

"You 'wish me well'?" Quinn repeated. "Is that what we've come down to? Gabriel, you were my closest friend, and now you 'wish me well'? What does that even mean?" Frustrated by his formality, his remoteness, she added, "And why are you even talking to me this way? It's not . . . it's not you."

"This *is* me, Quinn. And you need to respect it."

"I . . . I can't," she said.

"You've got to, though. And another thing. You don't need to worry about me, okay? I'm fine." Quinn tried to dispute this, but he kept going. "No. Seriously. And if you're feeling guilty about losing touch with me, don't. It's not something you have to make up for by spending time with me now. Forget what I said that first day, okay? Our losing touch wasn't your fault. It was mine, too. I shouldn't have placed all the blame on you like that. You haven't done anything wrong, Quinn, and you don't need to make amends. You can stop coming here. You can go back to Evanston."

Quinn shook her head. He was dismissing her. She didn't want to be dismissed. She wanted to stay here with him, though given his current attitude toward her, she didn't exactly know why.

"You can't do this," she said. "You can't just send me away. Like we were never even friends."

"You have to go now," he said. He sounded weary. And for some reason it touched her. He wasn't being unkind, she saw. Not intentionally. Her anger receded. And when he started walking over to her car, she followed him.

"Could I possibly have your cell-phone number?" she asked when he opened her car door for her.

"No," he said. "That's not a good idea." And then, as if to soften those words, he smiled at her, his eyes full of something she couldn't fathom. "Now go," he said, leaning in to kiss her on the cheek. "Back to your life."

Somehow Quinn made her limbs, heavy with resistance, move. She got into the car.

"Good-bye," she said. Her voice broke.

"Drive safely," he said.

When she looked in her rearview mirror, just before the driveway ended, she saw that he'd already disappeared, whether into the cabin or back into the garage, she didn't know.

ON THE DRIVE back to Loon Bay, Quinn felt her sadness giving way to something else. Depression? No. It was worse than that. It was defeat. She *hated* that feeling. Her father had discouraged it when she was a child, and she had tried to avoid it as an adult, but it was defeat she felt now, staring her in the face. She'd failed to reach Gabriel, failed to reconnect with him. And there was nothing she could do. She was stymied. He'd told her to leave. He'd told her not to come back. He'd told her, point-blank, that he didn't want her in his life anymore. She couldn't very well keep forcing herself on him, turning up unannounced on his doorstep.

And yet he wasn't just one of the reasons, she realized, that she was still here. He was the *main* reason. She'd returned in order to come to terms with the accident, and in doing so she'd unexpectedly found Gabriel again. And seeing him had become, somehow, fundamental to understanding everything. She wasn't sure exactly how, but she knew this, intuitively, to be true. If she acceded to his demand, she'd lose one of the few people in Butternut who mattered to her. And perhaps then she'd lose her purpose for being here. Lose her purpose, it felt for a moment, for being *anywhere*.

As she turned into the driveway at Loon Bay, though, she pushed that thought out of her mind. She was no more comfortable with fatalism than she was with defeat. She parked, and as she approached her cabin she saw a note taped to her door. *Wonderful. More bad news*, she decided, as she peeled off the piece of notepaper and unfolded it. *Quinn*, she read, *I was hoping to see you this morning. I have to go back to the city today, but I'll be back tomorrow afternoon. I need to talk to you. Don't leave yet. Tanner.* He'd left his cell-phone number underneath this.

She folded the note and put it in her pocket. Well, that was one person who didn't want her to leave Butternut. She let herself into her cabin and, needing something to do, went to make herself a cup of coffee in the kitchenette. This was good, she decided. Tanner being away. There was no possibility of a replay of what had happened last night. Tomorrow, when she saw him, clear minds would prevail, or, at least, sober minds.

She wasn't ready to eat yet, but when her coffee was done, she put extra cream in it and carried it over to the reading chair. Something was bothering her. Something beyond the obvious. Yes, Gabriel had said good-bye to her, but it was the *way* he'd said good-bye to her that was nagging at her. She saw now what he'd tried to do. He'd tried to absolve her from any guilt she might have felt over losing touch with him. And he'd hoped, in doing so, to relieve her from any burden she might have felt to keep visiting him. Did he really think that was why she kept turning up at his cabin? Well, he was wrong. But she could hardly go back and tell him that now. He'd explicitly asked her to stop coming to see him. And what had he said? That she could go back to Evanston?

There was just one problem. She wasn't going back. She knew she had unfinished business here. It felt like the *only* thing she knew right now, but it would have to be enough. There was no clear way forward. No obvious next step for her to take. For once in her life, she would have to wait for it to be revealed. That kind of passivity had never suited her. But perhaps, just this once, she would try to be patient. Of course, patience wasn't to be confused with surrender. She was still stubborn, or, as her dad had once pointed out, with more than a little pride, "stubborn as all hell."

CHAPTER 25

Quinn woke, suddenly. She'd had a dream. Not *the* dream. Not the dream about Jake, in his pickup truck, on the frozen lake at night. She'd had *that* dream too many times to count. This dream was different.

She and Gabriel were ice fishing on Shell Lake. But it wasn't Gabriel from high school. It was Gabriel now, with his shorter hair and work clothes on. Quinn, on the other hand, was not the contemporary Quinn, but Quinn in high school. She was wearing the army-green parka that she'd worn nearly every day of her senior year winter. The two of them were sitting on overturned plastic buckets in the shallow area, about twenty feet from shore. Right near where she and her father had gone ice fishing the day of

*the accident. The sky was gray, and it was getting
later; it was almost dusk. Gabriel was concentrating,
reeling something in. "You've got a fish," Quinn said,
excited. He pulled his line out of the water, but there
wasn't a fish on the hook. There was a ring. It was
the aquamarine ring Jake had given her. The fishing line swayed in the wind and the ring glinted as
it caught the light from the setting sun. "You've been
looking for this, haven't you?" Gabriel asked. "I knew
you'd find it," Quinn said. "No, Quinn. You found it."
But before she could reach for it, she woke up.*

Now she sat up on the bed, trying to orient herself. She
didn't know what the dream had meant, but it was the second
time in a week that she'd dreamed about Gabriel, and the first
time, ever, she'd dreamed about the ring. What did it mean?
Was Gabriel going to help her find her long lost ring? If so, that
was odd. Because Quinn had never told him she'd lost it in the
first place. She shivered. The dream had seemed so real. In it,
she could practically see her breath in the air, practically feel
the wind stinging her cheeks. She reached over to the bedpost
for her cardigan, pulled it on, and walked over to the window.
The clouds had burned off and now the setting sun had slipped
beneath the tops of the pine trees. She saw the Leinenkugel's
light blink on in the window of the bar and grill and realized
she was starving. She hadn't eaten all day. She headed over
there.

Once inside, she paused in surprise. The room seemed

to have transformed itself. Last night it had been dimly lit, the jukebox turned up loud, the place empty but for her and Tanner. Now the overhead lights were on, an innocuous pop station played in the background, and three of the tables were already taken. The biggest surprise, though, was the bartender. Where the hapless Gunner had stood, pretending to wipe the bar in between text messaging with his friends, was Annika, who, in her neat ponytail and crisp button-down shirt, looked the picture of professionalism.

"Hi," Annika said to Quinn, smiling her familiar reserved smile. She was polishing glasses with a dish towel, and a few stools down from where she stood was Jesse, sitting at the bar. He had a half-drunk glass of milk, a half-eaten plate of chicken strips, and a workbook in front of him.

"Hey," Quinn said, sliding onto a stool in front of Annika. "Hi, Jesse," she added, with a wave, and he looked up and nodded politely before returning to work, a frown of concentration on his face and the eraser end of a pencil shoved into the corner of his mouth. This was the closest Quinn had ever been to him before, and, she had to admit, he was a beautiful child. He was blond and blue-eyed and pale like his mother, but his eyebrows and eyelashes were noticeably darker, and the contrast between them and the rest of his coloring was striking.

"Math," Annika said, by way of explanation. She put a cocktail napkin and a little bowl of peanuts down in front of Quinn. "He hates it."

"Ugh, so did I," Quinn said, with a shudder. "And here's the thing about math: it only gets worse. Precalculus? Junior year?

My friend Gabriel *carried* me for the entire class." She smiled, remembering how they'd spent many afternoons at her kitchen table while he tutored her. She selected a peanut from the little dish and popped it into her mouth. Why, she wondered, had she brought up Gabriel so soon after he'd said good-bye to her, when the pain was still so new? Maybe, she thought, just for the pleasure of saying his name, and of reminding herself of a time when their friendship had seemed not only durable, but indestructible.

"What can I get you?" Annika asked Quinn, before glancing in Jesse's direction.

"How about a cranberry juice," Quinn said, thinking that she wasn't ready for anything stronger than that yet. As Annika went to pour her drink, Quinn dug into her little bowl of peanuts. She wondered if Annika knew about her and Tanner closing the place down last night. Which made her wonder just how friendly Annika and Tanner actually were with each other. Did Annika, for instance, know that Tanner came up to Loon Bay to be "close" to Jake? This still struck her as a little strange. She'd love to hear Annika's opinion on this. Although, truth be told, Annika didn't seem to offer her opinions very freely. She was too reserved. Quinn decided she would make it her mission to get Annika to open up a little tonight. She would draw her out.

Annika returned with Quinn's cranberry juice. "I should really take your order. What would you like?" she asked.

"Hmmm," Quinn considered, putting a peanut in her mouth. "What did Jesse have?"

"Chicken fingers. They're from the children's menu. But I can waive the twelve-and-under rule," Annika said, with a smile. Quinn smiled back. Maybe she was already making a dent in Annika's reserve.

"I'll have the chicken fingers then," Quinn said. After Annika brought Quinn her dinner, she was busy for the next half an hour, waiting on tables, and negotiating with Jesse, who'd finished his dinner and his homework, and who wanted quarters to play the deer hunter video game. It wasn't until Quinn was done eating that Annika reappeared before her.

"Can I get you anything else?" she asked.

"No, thank you. That was delicious," Quinn said. "It reminded me of the time this guy took me out to this expensive restaurant in Chicago, and all I could think, staring at the menu, was that what I really wanted was the mac and cheese the kid at the table over was having."

"Must be nice," Annika said. "Eating out in nice restaurants, I mean."

"I do that sometimes," Quinn said. "I also eat ramen noodles in front of my computer sometimes. Especially when I'm writing."

Annika nodded. "How is your memory writing going?"

Memory writing. Quinn liked the sound of that. "It's been a couple of days, actually, since I've done any," Quinn said. "I did *a lot* of writing on Sunday, though. In fact, twice when I was in my car, I stopped to write. And it's been amazing. It's actually helping me understand that time. But yesterday and today, I've been more focused on the present." She realized as she said this that her interactions with Gabriel and Tanner were both weighing on her.

"What about you?" Quinn asked. "*Your* present, I mean. Do you like working here, and living here?"

"I do," she said.

"How long has it been?"

"It's been almost eight years since I started working here, and about five years since Jesse and I moved into one of the cabins. That's when I started managing the place year-round. It's not perfect," she said with a shrug, "but it works."

"Jesse must love it," Quinn remarked, looking over at him. He was absorbed in the video game.

"Winters can be long," Annika admitted, tucking a loose strand of hair back into her ponytail. "But summers are fun. A lot of the families who come return every year. And Jesse's friends with the kids. He's on the run all day. I have to force him to sit down and eat."

It sounded nice, Quinn thought. But she couldn't help but wonder if Annika had to do it all alone. It was obvious that Jesse's father wasn't at Loon Bay. But did she still have family here? Quinn wondered.

"What about Jesse's dad? Or your family, are they still around?"

"My family?" Annika asked. "Some of them are around. It's not much of a family, though."

"No? What do you mean?" Quinn asked.

"You've never heard of my father? The 'Crazy Swede'?"

Quinn shook her head.

"Well, the name rings true, at least in Winton."

"How is he crazy?" Quinn asked.

"I don't know about crazy. But he does crazy things. Plus, he's a drunk with a mean temper." She was quiet for a moment, polishing glasses that already looked perfectly polished. "You know how, in a small town, there are all these legends? About haunted houses or a graveyard or whatnot?"

Quinn nodded.

"Well, my dad was like that. Most of the kids who grew up in Winton were afraid of him, but they'd still dare each other to go on our property."

"Kids can be cruel," Quinn said.

"Cruel? Maybe. But they can also be stupid. Because one of my father's favorite things to do was to stand on our porch with a shotgun and threaten—in Swedish—to shoot anyone who came up our driveway."

Quinn was surprised. It was difficult to imagine Annika with a father like that. She was so calm. So reserved. And, obviously, so responsible, managing this place as well as she did. "Did he ever shoot anyone?" Quinn asked.

"No. He was a good shot when he was sober, but he was almost never sober. It didn't make it easy for my sisters and me to have a social life, though."

"No, it wouldn't," Quinn said. "How many sisters do you have?"

"Two. Both older. One of them—her name is Britta—moved away. She lives in Tennessee with her family. She turned out all right. Jesse and I don't get to see her as much as we'd like to."

"And the other sister?"

"Hedda," Annika said. "She stuck around. She's not doing so great. She got married at eighteen to a local guy. A jerk. That was her way of getting out of the house, I guess. Going from one bad place to another. Then her husband left her"—Annika shrugged—"so she lost the guy but she kept the house. She's an angry person, though. We almost never see her. I don't want her around Jesse."

"What about your mom?" Quinn asked, hoping that she wasn't prying.

"She still lives with my dad in the same house I grew up in. She never had the nerve to leave him. He's pretty sick now. So he still sits on the porch, but he doesn't really cause any more trouble. Jesse and I, we don't see him or my mom."

"That must be hard," Quinn said. "But you're like your sister in Tennessee, aren't you? You got away. You may be only one town over from Winton, but to me it looks like you're in a whole different world."

Annika considered this. "You're right, I didn't get very far, but it was far enough, I guess. Loon Bay is our home now. I have Caroline to thank for that."

"Caroline Keegan?" Quinn asked, of the woman who owned Pearl's.

"Uh-huh. She gave me a job at Pearl's when I was twenty. She took me to open a bank account. She taught me how to make a budget. She helped me find a place to live before Jesse was born; I'd been staying at Hedda's house, which was crazy. People were coming there, day and night, to party. And she told me about this job at Loon Bay." Quinn smiled. Caroline had helped more than her fair share of people get a footing in life. And in Annika's case, more than a footing. But Annika needed to give herself credit, too, Quinn thought. She told her this now.

"I don't know about that," she said, laughing a little nervously. "And I don't know why I'm talking so much either." Annika glanced around the room. "Let me get this table their check," she said. "And it looks like Jesse's going to need some more quarters, too." She hurried away and Quinn sipped her cranberry juice. Annika's life was more complicated than she'd realized, but she'd been resourceful enough to put distance between herself and her parents. Quinn thought about what it must have been like growing up in a family like that. She couldn't imagine it. Her dad was the antithesis of the "Crazy Swede."

"We need to get going," Annika said, coming back around the bar and untying her apron. "It's Jesse's bedtime. Gunner will take care of you, though," she said, nodding at Gunner, who was hanging up his jacket. "By the way, do you know how long you're going to be staying here, at Loon Bay?" she asked.

"Oh," Quinn said, surprised by the question. "No. I don't. Not yet." She had no idea how long she was staying. *Why* she was staying was a whole other question. "Do you need my cabin?" she asked her.

"No. We're not completely booked until Memorial Day weekend." After Annika left, Quinn tried to settle her bill with Gunner. But he shook his head. "Annika said it's on the house."

After Quinn walked back to her cabin and let herself in, she brushed her teeth, peeled down to her underwear and a

T-shirt, and crawled into bed. Thanks to her marathon nap, she wasn't tired. She turned over on her back and stared up at the ceiling. She thought about Annika, for a little while, and what she'd told Quinn about her life tonight. How difficult it must have been to bring a child into the world with no family to help. But she'd had a friend, Quinn reflected. She'd had Caroline. That's what had saved her. A friend who was there for her. And this made Quinn think about her friendship—or lack of friendship—with Gabriel. He'd been her closest friend. Until the night of the accident. After that, she couldn't go back to the way their friendship had been. And she couldn't go forward into what their friendship had become. Instead, she'd avoided him, she'd avoided everybody. She been too overwhelmed with guilt. The problem was that in avoiding Gabriel, she'd failed him.

What was clear now, ten years later, was that she still cared so much about him. The painful part was that he no longer cared about her in the way he once had. You couldn't *make* someone care about you. But she wasn't ready to give up on Gabriel yet. She'd think of something tomorrow. She'd stay for a couple more days, maybe get some more writing done. She'd come up with something. She had to.

CHAPTER 26

The next morning, Quinn stood in the bread aisle of the IGA and considered the selection. There seemed to be as many different kinds of bread as there were people in Butternut to eat them. She'd come into the store to pick up a *Minneapolis Star Tribune* and a cup of cheap coffee before heading over to the Butternut Library to write, but she'd ended up roaming the aisles, curious to see what had changed. There was a tiny gluten-free section now, and some half-hearted organic selections in the produce department. Quinn was about to leave the bread aisle when she saw Theresa Dobbs come around the corner. Her first impulse was to hide. Her second was to run. She went with the second. She turned and headed in the other direction down the aisle, brushing past an older man who'd stopped to pick up some rolls. She made it as far as the crackers—walking as fast as she could without attracting attention—before she heard her name being called.

"Quinn. *Quinn!*"

Oh, God. Not this again, she thought.

"Quinn, wait!" Theresa called from directly behind her. Quinn stopped. *Best to just get this over with*, she decided. She turned around. Theresa, who was holding an empty grocery basket, looked better than she had several nights ago. She was wearing a Minnesota Wild T-shirt, a pair of skinny jeans, and a quilted down coat, and her hair was pulled back in a pony-tail. When she came up to Quinn, though, and stood much too close to her—what was it about this woman ignoring personal space?—Quinn saw that her nose and cheeks were covered with tiny, spidery red veins. *Gin blossoms*, they were called, though in Theresa's case, *vodka* blossoms might have been more accurate. Quinn could smell it on her breath. Gabriel had said Theresa drank a lot, but he hadn't mentioned she started before noon.

For some reason, Quinn saw an image of Jake's mother, Maggie, sitting on her living room couch three days ago, her hair in an elegant twist, her clothes neat and chic as she sipped her Lipton's English Breakfast Tea and made polite conversa-tion. Who would Quinn be, who would *any* woman be, she wondered, when faced with the kind of loss these two women had suffered? Would they start their day applying lipstick in the mirror, or downing a fifth of vodka? Or would they mud-dle along somewhere in between the two? Probably the latter.

Though, on the worst days, she thought, it might be tempting to take the vodka-for-breakfast route.

"Quinn, you're still here," Theresa said now, taking her arm. She didn't seem angry anymore. She seemed, instead, possessed of a fierce sense of urgency. "I've been meaning to talk to you again."

"I have some errands to run," Quinn said, taking a step back. She tried to shake her arm free of Theresa's hand, but Theresa didn't appear to notice. It was almost as if, having placed her hand there, she was no longer responsible for it.

"What happened that night, Quinn?" she asked, leaning closer. "The night of the accident? I never got a chance to ask you before. You left. And then you didn't come back. Until now. And I want to know what happened."

"You *know* what happened," Quinn said.

"I wasn't there," Theresa said.

"Neither was I. When it happened. I left before . . ." *Before Jake drove out on the ice.*

Theresa shook her head with vigor. There was a strange gleam in her eye, almost as if she'd caught Quinn in a lie and she relished the opportunity to confront her with it.

"No, before that, Quinn. What happened *before* you left that night? I know some of it. Dominic called me on his cell phone. From the lake. Did you know that?" she asked, as if she was goading her. "Did you know I talked to him that night?"

Quinn shook her head. She *hadn't* known that. And she realized she didn't *want* to know that now.

"Oh, he did," Theresa said, breathing in Quinn's face. A

woman with a little boy passed them and the little boy looked back at Theresa. "He called me," Theresa continued. "He *always* called me if he was going to be late. That's the kind of kid he was. He'd call and he'd say, 'Mom. Mom' . . ." Theresa appeared to lose her train of thought here, and Quinn wondered if she was done. A woman walked by the two of them, pushing a grocery cart, and Quinn longed to follow her, wherever she was going. Anywhere was better than here.

Now Theresa shook her head, as if clearing it, and continued. "Dom called and he said, he said, 'Mom, Jake and Quinn got in a fight. And Jake's drunk.' And I was like, 'What? Jake doesn't drink.' And he said . . . something about he's drunk because he was fighting with Quinn, and he's acting crazy, and then he said something about a ring being lost. He said, 'Jake won't leave the lake until we find that ring. I'm gonna help him find it.' Then he had to go. And I said . . . I can't remember what I said. I probably said something like, 'Dom. Come home. It's late. And you sound like maybe you've had a little too much to drink too.' He hung up, though. That was it." She looked at Quinn as if she still couldn't believe it. "That was the kind of kid he was. Always helping people. You know what I mean? Those kids?" Her animosity was gone now. She was waiting, it seemed, for Quinn to agree with her about the kind of kid Dom had been.

Quinn couldn't speak, though. The mention of the lost ring had made her feel ill. It was that hot, cold, prickly sensation that had come over her at the dedication. This was worse; this feeling had come with a new knowledge she hadn't had before.

She hadn't known that Jake was planning to look for the ring that night after she left.

"Was it your ring he was looking for? Is that what you and Jake were fighting about?" Theresa asked her now. But she seemed to discount this last question as soon as she asked it because she then said, "It doesn't matter. You fought with him and he got drunk. If he hadn't been drunk, my Dom would be alive right now." And she seemed to be looking not at Quinn, but just past her.

"Theresa, I have to go," Quinn said, brushing her hand off her arm. "I need to leave. I shouldn't have stayed."

Incredibly, this seemed to cheer Theresa up. "Oh, you can't leave, Quinn," she said, a strange smile on her face. "You can't just go away. You're stuck here. With the rest of us."

That's crazy, Quinn thought. She turned and walked as quickly as she could down the aisle, past the checkout counter, and into the parking lot, where the blacktop felt soft and putty-like beneath her shoes. She didn't check to see if Theresa was following her. She got in her car and pulled out of her parking space, her hands clumsy on the steering wheel. One quick look in her rearview mirror showed Theresa standing now in the front of the IGA. Quinn stepped on the gas and tore out of the parking lot before she realized what she was doing and slowed down.

Theresa had accosted her twice now, Quinn thought. Once in a restaurant. And once in the IGA. And both times she'd overstepped boundaries; both times she'd said things that were inappropriate. "It's been a long ten years. Thanks to you," she'd said at the Corner Bar. And what had she said a few minutes ago? "You're stuck here. With the rest of us." What had she meant by that? *Who knows.* Maybe she didn't even know herself what she was saying.

Except . . . except that she'd mentioned the ring. The lost ring. And that Dominic was going to help Jake look for it. Was that true? She'd never heard this before. That didn't mean that Quinn hadn't been haunted, over the years, by the possibility that Jake had driven out on the ice that night to find the ring.

"Oh my God," she murmured. She drove without thinking and pulled over on a residential street. She couldn't keep going. She couldn't make her hands do what she wanted them to do. She looked at them. They were shaking. She felt ill. And she felt dizzy, too. Only her dizziness was more like vertigo. It was like the feeling she had in dreams, the ones where she was standing on the edge of something. A building ledge. A cliff. A yawning abyss. One wrong move, and she would fall.

And in that moment, Quinn thought she understood Theresa's smile. It was a smile of triumph. Theresa had finally found someone to blame for the accident. *It was you, Quinn,* that smile had said. *It was your fault. All of it. You set it in motion.* Was Theresa right? Had Quinn *caused* this tragedy? She'd long ago pushed this possibility out of her mind, but she wasn't sure she could any longer.

She sat in her car and fought an overwhelming urge to go back to her cabin, curl up on the bed, pull the covers over her head, and sleep. Sleep for days. She ruled that out. She needed to think this through. Right here. Right now. In the days and weeks after the accident, she'd had so many questions. Why had Jake driven out on the lake so late in the season when the ice might be unstable? Why had he taken his two best friends with him? Why had he been drinking that night when he never drank during training season? And why had he stopped his truck in the middle of the lake for several minutes, a decision that might have caused the ice to give way? Had what she'd said to him earlier that night had anything to do with it? And finally, why had he lied to her earlier in the day about why his truck was parked in front of that house on Scuttle Hole Road? It was this lie, after all, that had triggered their fight.

Yes, she'd had questions. But it was the tumultuous feelings she'd had that she thought about now. She'd felt shock, initially, that Jake had done something so . . . so *unlike* himself. So reckless. But the shock quickly gave way to grief, a feeling she'd never felt before that spring. And there was heartache, too, and sorrow, for the loss of him. Which brought her to guilt. At first, this promised to be the most damaging, the most paralyzing of all her emotions, especially since it came with an endless round of what-ifs. What if Quinn hadn't argued with Jake that night? What if she hadn't told him about losing her ring? What if she hadn't left him at the bonfire? And, most crippling of all, what if she hadn't left the bonfire *with* Gabriel? For guilt, and regret, were as much the result of having failed to act as they were the result of having acted.

The sheer hopelessness of the what-ifs, though, led her to another feeling. That had been harder to come by, and slower to take hold. But eventually, after the accident, when the days had turned into weeks and the weeks turned into months, she felt a flicker of resolve. She would keep going. She would go to college. She would rebuild her life, one way or another. If she was going to survive, though, and maybe, who knows, even *thrive*, she would have to stop thinking all these thoughts. Feeling all these feelings. She would have to put the past behind her. Either that, or it would drag her down.

There had been setbacks. Most memorably, during her junior year in college. And yet, for the most part, her life had continued to move forward. The guilt remained, but she'd pushed it under the surface. She'd kept it at bay, not realizing that in doing this she was compounding the problem by not confronting it.

But the guilt had always been about not stopping the accident. It had never been, at least not consciously, about *causing* the accident. Theresa had changed that. What had she said, exactly? Something about how Dominic had told her that Jake was looking for a ring, and that he wasn't leaving Shell Lake without it. Dominic was going to help him find it. Unbeknownst to Theresa, of course, was the fact that it was *Quinn's* ring that Dominic was talking about, the ring that Jake had given her. The ring that she'd lost earlier that day. Had Jake really gone out on the ice that night looking for it? *Think, Quinn. Think. Remember that day, that night. Remember it in all its details.*

CHAPTER 27

March 23–24, Senior Year,
Day and Night of the Accident

I think that might be it for the season," Gene said, as he and
Quinn trudged up from Shell Lake that evening, hauling
their gear with them.

"What? No ice fishing in May this year?" Quinn said, her
boots crunching on the snow. Her dad smiled, probably because
this wasn't impossible to imagine. Quinn was more circumspect. She'd never known any winters but northern Minnesota
winters, but they could still feel endless to her. On the first of
this month, for instance, when spring was almost within reach,
there'd been a blizzard; twenty inches of thick, wet snow had
blanketed the region, burying cars, closing schools, and even
forcing snowplows off the roads. Still, perhaps her dad was

right about the ice-fishing season being over. Most of the snow
from the storm had melted by now. And, when she and her dad
had arrived here, a couple of hours ago, the sky had been a brilliant blue, and the sun had glinted off the fine-as-sand dusting
of snow on the lake. Her dad, always cautious when it came to
ice fishing, had cut a test hole in the ice near the shore. He was
satisfied it was safe to fish; there were over four inches of clear,
solid ice. They'd found a spot to ice fish about fifteen feet from
the shore. Her dad had frowned, though, when he'd seen a couple of snowmobilers crisscrossing the lake later. "Just because
it's safe here . . ." he'd muttered, lowering his line into the water.

"I know," Quinn had said. As in *I know, I know, you've
drilled this into me by now, Dad.* Hunting, shooting, fishing,
whatever sport he taught her, Gene was a "safety first" kind of
a guy. And who could fault him for this? Certainly not Quinn.

Now she shifted the Styrofoam cooler in her arms—the ice
and the six walleyes in it were surprisingly heavy—and glanced
over at her dad as they crested the hill before the parking area.
"I'm sorry," she said.

"Sorry about what?"

"I wasn't very good company today," she said. It was true.
She'd been too preoccupied to say much of anything.

"Don't be silly. Of course you were," he said. But Quinn felt
unsure. This was the first, and now, probably, the last, time
they'd go ice fishing together this season. They'd meant to go
sooner, but between Gene working late at the timber company,
and Quinn's commitments at school, and, of course, her com-
mitment to Jake, they hadn't been able to find the time before

now. And what had Quinn done with that time, other than fish? She'd brooded.

"Hey," her dad said. "You don't have to entertain me. I have the walleyes for that."

Quinn smiled. As her departure for college approached, she found herself appreciating her father more than ever. Like now, for instance. He knew something was wrong. He'd known it since she'd come home from school that afternoon. He'd asked her, casually, on the drive out to the lake, "Is everything all right?" But when she'd responded with a noncommittal shrug, he hadn't pressed her. And he wouldn't. It wasn't his style.

Now, as they got back to their pickup truck, the sun was dipping below the pines and the light was emptying out of the sky. They loaded their gear—the cooler, an ice auger, two plastic buckets, and the fishing rods—into the back of the truck and climbed into the front. Gene turned on the engine, then blasted the heat and fiddled with the radio dial until he found a country music song he liked, Kenny Chesney's "Beer in Mexico."

"Do you think you can listen to this one more time?" he asked Quinn, as they snapped on their seat belts.

"It's fine, Dad," she said, with a half-hearted smile, of a song they'd been listening to since January. Ordinarily, she would have tried to sell him on the classic rock station, but as they pulled out of the parking lot and onto Birch Road, she was barely aware of the music. She was trying to decide if she wanted to talk to her dad about what was on her mind. He wasn't her first choice. Her first choice was Gabriel. But this was about Jake. And as much as she loved Gabriel, this was the one thing, the *only* thing, really, she couldn't talk to him about. On the rare occasions she'd been with Jake and Gabriel at the same time, she could tell the two of them had reached a truce, uneasy though it might be. Quinn knew, though, that even after nine months of dating Jake, Gabriel remained, at best, deeply skeptical of him. So that left her dad to talk to about it.

"Can I ask you something?" Quinn said, turning to him.

He turned down the radio. "Of course."

"Do you think Jake is a good person? An honest person?"

He looked surprised. "Jake? I think he's a good kid."

"But?" Quinn prompted. Because she'd heard a *but* in there.

"No. No *buts*," he said. "It's more . . . how do I say this . . . it's more of me recognizing something in Jake. One man to another. Do you know what I mean?"

Quinn didn't.

He hesitated, then started again. "He's good looking. He has a lot of charisma. And there's nothing wrong with either of those things, obviously. Except maybe, sometimes, he relies a little bit too much on those qualities. He gets away with things he might not otherwise get away with. He's what my parents' generation called a 'charmer.' You guys probably have a different word for it now."

"A player," Quinn said. "We call someone like that a 'player.'" She felt a little sick.

"Oh, I don't know if I'd use *that* word," her dad said quickly. "What's going on, though? Why do you want to know what I think of him?"

Quinn looked out the window, at the woods sliding by in the dusky twilight. "Jake lied to me today. And I don't think it's the first time he's lied to me either."

"Really?"

She hesitated. "I don't know," she said. "Early on, when we first started dating, I think there were times where he'd tell me he was going to be one place, and then he'd be in another place. Or he'd tell me he needed to do something after school or on a weekend, but when I asked him about it later . . ." She shook her head. "You know how, when you know someone, you can almost read them? You get a feeling when they say something that isn't true? But you *want* to believe it's true. Your heart wants to believe, even if your head doesn't. And Jake always had a way of explaining. He had a way of smoothing things over."

She frowned. There'd been other things, too, early in their relationship, things she hadn't questioned him about. Unexplained absences. Unanswered texts and phone calls. Quinn had chalked these up to how busy they both were, what with cross-country for him, the newspaper for her. And she'd been determined to not be *that* kind of girlfriend, the kind who always needed to know where her boyfriend was, who he was with, or what he was doing. She'd always been independent; why shouldn't Jake be too?

Her dad was quiet. Waiting, she knew, for her to say more. "Once, in December, I think I caught him in a lie," she said. She was remembering the night he'd given her the ring. "After that, though, I don't think there was any more lying." That night had changed something, she realized. He was different. More serious, more solicitous of her. And that warning voice inside of her, the one she'd tried to ignore before, had quieted. Until today.

"And then, this afternoon," she continued, watching her dad in profile, "I saw him before seventh period, and he said he'd pick me up tonight and we'd go to the teachers' basketball game, and then we'd drive out to the bonfire." (The teachers' basketball game was an annual high school fund-raiser.)

"Is the bonfire at Shell Lake?" he asked. She nodded. Juniors and seniors from her high school sometimes had bonfires there on Friday and Saturday nights. Her dad didn't mind her going to these things. He knew that Jake didn't drink. In fact, among Jake's friends, he was more or less the permanent designated driver.

"Anyway, Jake told me that first, after school, he had to drive to Ely and meet with a sports physiologist. I said that was fine, I was going ice fishing with you, and we could meet up later at our house. Anyway, after my last class, I went to Pearl's to pick up a hot chocolate, and then I realized I'd left my AP government textbook in my locker, so I drove back to school again, but this time I took the shortcut." Gene knew the shortcut she meant; it involved taking Scuttle Hole Road. "And then, right where Scuttle Hole comes into Winton, I saw Jake's truck, parked outside a house I didn't recognize."

"Are you sure it was Jake's truck?"

"I'd know it anywhere, Dad," she said, of Jake's medium blue Ford truck, with its GONE FISHING sticker, and its QFE 7654 license plate number that he swore stood for "Quinn Forever."

"What'd you do?"

"I kept driving. I was in a hurry. But I called him on my cell. He didn't answer. And I didn't leave a message. About five minutes later, after I got to my locker, he texted me. He said, *Stuck in Ely. I'll pick you up around 6:45 for the basketball game.* There was no way that Jake was on Scuttle Hole Road in Winton one minute and half an hour away in Ely the next."

Her dad slowed the pickup, going into a turn. He said nothing, but Quinn could feel his concern.

"I took the shortcut again on the way back," she said. She'd hated the way doing that had made her feel. Spying on her boyfriend? That wasn't her. She felt that same sick feeling now, remembering what she'd seen. "His truck was still there," she said. "I don't know whose house it was parked outside of," she added. "I couldn't see the number on the mailbox but the name said McGrath."

"Did you think about getting out and ringing the doorbell?"

"I did. I'm not that brave, though."

"You are plenty brave, Quinn."

"Besides, I had to get home. I was late meeting you. My mind was racing the whole drive back, though."

"Is there any way, Quinn, you think there might be a reasonable explanation for all this?"

"I don't know," she said, after a moment. But if she had to guess, she would guess it was an unreasonable explanation.

"Other than these incidents," her dad said, choosing his words carefully, "he's never mistreated you, has he? I don't mean physically, of course, but in any other way?"

"*No*, Dad," Quinn said, feeling protective of Jake for the first time. "He's been a good boyfriend. You know that." And he *had* been a good boyfriend. He'd been considerate, and tender and respectful. He was never harsh or unkind. She didn't tell her father these things now, of course. But it didn't matter. She could feel his judgment settling into place.

"Being a good boyfriend doesn't mean anything if he's not honest with you, Quinn."

"I know," she said.

Her dad was quiet. And then he asked gently, "Have you any idea why he'd lie to you?"

"I don't know for sure," Quinn said. And she didn't. But there were usually only a handful of reasons she could imagine that someone would lie about their whereabouts: cheating, drugs, something illegal, something that needed to be lied about. One of the boys on Jake's cross-country team had been expelled for using anabolic steroids. But Jake wouldn't do that. Anyway, none of it was good.

He took the next turn in the road carefully. "Are you sure you want to see him tonight?"

"Yes. But I don't want to go to the teachers' basketball game. I already texted him that and told him I would meet him at the bonfire." Quinn couldn't imagine sitting tonight in the bleachers in a sea of raucous students for two hours. "I'll drive myself or get a ride. I'm going to ask him at the bonfire, point-blank, where he was this afternoon. If he lies to me, I'll have another way to get home."

"That sounds like a sensible plan," he said. "Keep an open mind when you talk to him. Hear him out. But, Quinn, if you don't believe him, you can't stay in a relationship with someone who isn't truthful with you. You want someone who's honest. Whether they're a friend or a boyfriend. You know, someone like Gabriel."

She nodded, distractedly. She was glad she hadn't confided in Gabriel. He'd warned her about the conversation he'd over-heard between Jake and his then girlfriend, Ashlyn. She'd called Jake a liar. Gabriel would never say "I told you so." That didn't mean that he wouldn't *think* it.

It was warm in the truck now, and Quinn pulled off her gloves and looked down at her hands, pale in the lights from the dashboard. She flexed her fingers and frowned, then reached for her gloves and turned them inside out. "Oh, no," she said, groping around her on the seat.

"What is it?" her dad asked. They were entering the town now and they stopped at Butternut's only stoplight. "What's wrong?"

She turned on the light, checked the seat around her, un-fastened her seat belt, and checked the floor in front of her. "I lost my ring," she said, staring at her dad in disbelief. "The one Jake gave me."

"We'll find it when we get home," he said.

She shook her head. "It's not here." She checked her gloves again, the folds of her parka, the space between her seat and the door. Nothing. "I think I lost it fishing," she said. "That's the last time I took my gloves off. To bait the hooks." She turned to her dad. "We have to go back."

"Quinn, no. It's dark out now."

"We'll use flashlights."

"It's not safe, honey. And there's no guarantee we'll find it, anyway."

She looked at him beseechingly, but he was unmoved.

"How do you even know you lost it there?" he asked. "I mean, when was the last time you remember seeing it on?"

"I don't know. I had it on in eighth period. I know that." She knew because she'd gotten in the habit of twisting it around on her finger, and she remembered now that she was doing this in that class. "After that, I went to Pearl's, I went back to school to get my textbook, I came home, and then we went ice fishing. I know I lost it fishing, though. I would have noticed if I'd lost it before then."

"Not necessarily," he said. "There are other places it could be. We'll check the truck when we get back, and I'll help you check the house, too. You can go to Pearl's tomorrow, and school will be open Monday."

"Can we check the lake tomorrow?"

"Ice conditions permitting," he said. "It's going to be all right, though. You'll find it. *We'll* find it."

"Yeah, okay," she said.

After they got home, her dad, bless his heart, helped her look for the ring. They'd searched his truck, her car, their house, and his truck, again. Nothing. They'd retrace her steps tomorrow, he'd promised her. One way or another, they'd find it.

He'd insisted, then, that she have some dinner, and she had, but when he'd offered to find someone else to take the night shift at the timber company—he was covering for a worker who was sick—it was Quinn's turn to be firm. She'd reassured him that she'd be fine. He'd only agreed to leave her when she'd texted Gabriel and had asked him for a ride out to the bonfire. But between her anxiety over losing the ring and her dread over confronting Jake, the wait for Gabriel to pick her up had felt like an eternity.

"You're in a hurry," Gabriel commented, when Quinn scrambled into his dad's pickup later that night. Gabriel was in a good mood. She saw that immediately.

"I want to get going," she explained, tugging on her seat belt.

"All right then," he said, looking at her quizzically. But when she didn't offer any explanation, he put the truck in reverse.

Quinn leaned back against the seat, slightly breathless from her run out to the driveway. She'd been watching for him, at the front hall window, for the last fifteen minutes. He wasn't late; he said he'd come at nine thirty and he'd come at nine thirty, but by then Quinn didn't think she could endure being alone for one more second.

"Is everything okay?" he asked, as he backed out of her driveway and turned onto Webber Street. He looked over at her again.

"It's been a weird day," she said, not wanting to elaborate.

She didn't want to pretend there was nothing wrong now, but she didn't want to tell Gabriel what *was* wrong either.

"Did you spill some gas in here?" she asked, sniffing the air. "As in, *a lot* of gas?"

"Um . . . not that I know of," he said, looking surprised. "There's a can of it on the floor," he said, indicating the back-seat. "Maybe some of it splashed out or something. Do you want me to—?"

"It's fine," Quinn said, lowering her window a few inches.

They drove in silence through the town. "Thanks," Quinn said, when they turned onto Main Street.

"For what?"

"For the ride."

"Yeah. Of course. By the way, the teachers' basketball game was pretty funny. Mr. Raebeck was wearing sports goggles that kept falling off. Hilarity ensued." Gabriel was happy and re-laxed, Quinn saw, almost with annoyance. "I don't know how long I'll end up staying tonight. These bonfires aren't really my thing," he added.

"I don't know how long I'll stay either," she said. "But I have to talk to Jake." Her stomach wobbled. She hoped she was wrong about this. *About him.* But she didn't think she was.

"What's up with you and Jake?" Gabriel asked, as they headed out of town.

"There's something I have to ask him," she said, with unchar-acteristic evasiveness.

"You're being very mysterious," Gabriel said, brushing hair out of his eyes. "You sure he's even going to be there?"

"Jake? Yes. Why wouldn't he be?"

"I don't know." He fiddled with the radio, found "Same Girl" by R. Kelly and Usher, and turned it up.

"He told me he'd meet me there at ten," Quinn said, loudly, too loudly, over the music. It had never occurred to her that Jake might not be there.

"Okay, okay," Gabriel said. "Don't get mad at me. I was just wondering." He turned down the radio.

"Well, stop wondering. He'll be there," she snapped, and then immediately regretted it. "I'm sorry," she mumbled, more to the window than to him.

"Did you finish your government paper?" he asked, after they'd gotten onto Butternut Lake Drive. He obviously wanted to steer the conversation into neutral territory.

"I have to write the conclusion," Quinn said, staring at the woods out the window. They were much darker now than they had been three hours earlier when she and her dad had made this drive in reverse. "I'm not that worried about it, though," she added, chewing her lip. And she knew it was irrational, but she couldn't help but feel that if she hadn't forgotten the AP government textbook in her locker, she'd never have seen Jake's truck and she wouldn't have to confront him tonight.

"I have a couple pages left," Gabriel said. "I have to admit, though, that getting in early decision has kind of put a damper on my academic ambition."

"Don't forget, if your grades fall too much they can retract your acceptance," Quinn said.

He laughed. "They're not falling *that* much."

"You're in a good mood," she said.

"Anything wrong with that?" Gabriel asked.

"No." But she was too preoccupied, too tense to pursue the conversation any further. They lapsed into silence, and as they got closer to the lake, she tried, as best she could, to steel herself for seeing Jake. *Not much longer now*, she told herself, as they took the turnoff for Shell Lake. And, as if to spare her any more suspense, Jake's pickup was the first one she saw when they pulled into the parking area.

"See, he's here," she said, pointing.

"So he is," Gabriel said, slowing. He drove by Jake's truck, though, and parked at the other end of the lot. From her vantage point in the front seat, Quinn scanned the beach below. A couple of dozen students were already gathered around a big bonfire, its sparks drifting high into the blue-black sky. Beyond the narrow beach was the frozen lake: a dull grayish-white expanse that echoed the emptiness of the sky.

"It's strange," Quinn murmured of the scene. "They almost look like shipwreck survivors, don't they?" she said of the students huddled around the fire, as though at the edge of a frozen world.

"Maybe," Gabriel said, putting the truck in park and cutting the engine. "But if they're shipwreck survivors, they're drunk shipwreck survivors," he added, when one of the boys threw a wooden packing crate onto the fire, sending a shower of sparks, and a volley of raucous cheers, into the sky. Quinn smiled distractedly. Typically, she liked these bonfires. She'd never gone to them before she'd started dating Jake, and she could still do without their drunken rowdiness, but she liked the fire itself, liked feeling the heat of it on her face, hearing the roar of it in her ears. *Not tonight*, she thought, trying to pick Jake out of the crowd.

"I don't see him," Gabriel said.

"No. Maybe he's at the picnic tables," Quinn said, of the other place where people gathered to talk and drink but mostly to drink. "I'll find him, and then . . ." She trailed off. And then what? What would happen after she found him? After she talked to him? She didn't know. She hadn't gotten that far. If he was honest with her, she supposed she'd stay. If he wasn't, well, she'd get a ride home. To the extent that she had a plan, that was it. As she unfastened her seat belt, she realized her hands were clammy and slippery on the metal.

"Hey," Gabriel said, trying to get a smile out of her. "Are you sure you're okay?"

Quinn could only nod. They got out of the truck, and Gabriel headed down to the beach, while Quinn followed the footpath to the picnic area. As she walked, she pulled on her gloves, self-conscious about her ringless finger. Best to keep it under wraps for now. She pulled on her wool hat, too, though it wasn't as cold as it had been the last time she'd been here at night, a couple of weeks ago. *That* night was freezing, the icy air a stinging reproof to every inch of skin she'd left exposed. Tonight, it felt warmer. Cold, but clear, with no wind. This was good. She didn't know how much more frigid weather she could take in one winter.

As she reached the picnic grove she heard Jake's voice before she saw him. "Dom, what the hell?" he said. "Are you gonna finish the whole thing? *Christ!* Give it to me." Quinn frowned. He sounded different. She kept walking, until he and Dom and Griffin came into view. They were standing around a table wet with melted snow and passing a brown bottle between them. She watched as Jake took a long pull from it now.

"Jake," she said, though not loud enough for him to hear. But it didn't matter. Griffin saw her.

"Quinn," he called, and Jake turned and grinned at her as he handed off the bottle to Dom. He met her, halfway to the picnic table, and if she'd been nervous about seeing him, that nervousness dissolved, almost instantly, into disbelief. He was drunk.

"Hey, baby," he said, folding her into his arms, their down jackets swishing together. He kissed her before she could say anything to him. She smelled it on him and then tasted it on him. *Whiskey*, she thought, though she wasn't sure. Jack Daniel's, she found out later. She stopped kissing him, but Jake, undiscouraged, pulled off her hat and started kissing her hair. "I am so glad you're here."

"How much have you had to drink?" she asked, trying to extricate herself from him. She was completely blindsided. She hadn't seen him drink anything since that night in the Hoyers' cabin. And even then he hadn't finished his cup of wine. He was training hard now; he had back-to-back indoor track meets coming up.

"Only a little," he said, kissing her jaw, her chin, her neck.

She felt disarmed. She was familiar with the intensity of his affection, but this felt different.

"I think you've had more than a little," she said, self-conscious about the proximity of his friends. Not that they seemed to care. Not that they even seemed to notice. How long, she wondered, had they all been drinking here? "Can I talk to you?" she asked. "Somewhere private?"

"Yeah, somewhere private," he agreed, kissing her mouth again. "I want to be somewhere private with you."

"To talk," she emphasized, disentangling herself from him. "We can go down there." She pointed toward another clumping of picnic tables in the distance.

She started walking and Jake caught up to her and grabbed her hand. "We'll be back," he called over his shoulder to his friends, and then he smiled at her. It looked forced, devoid of Jake's easy charm. He stumbled, then, on a tree root, and Quinn thought he might fall, but he recovered, gracefully, and wrapped his arms around her instead.

Quinn stopped at another picnic table. "What are you doing?" she asked. "Seriously, Jake. I've never seen you *tipsy* before, let alone—"

"*I'm fine,*" he interrupted. He reached up and, clumsily but gently, touched her right ear. "Your earring is loose."

Quinn peeled her glove off and readjusted the gold hoop she'd put on earlier that night.

"*Hey,*" Jake said, and she realized, too late, her mistake. "What happened to your ring?"

Quinn looked down at her hand as if asking herself the same question. For once, she wanted to lie. *I took it off to clean the fish . . . wash the dishes . . . take a shower.* But the lie wouldn't come. "I lost it," she said.

"When?" Jake asked. Somehow, she had cut through the fog of alcohol.

"I don't know. I think it might have been when I was ice fishing with my dad here today," she said, gesturing at the lake.

He looked crestfallen, but only for a moment. "I'll find it," he said, confidently. "Where'd you go fishing?" he asked, already starting to head in the direction of the lake.

She caught his arm. "*Jake.* Wait. Don't be ridiculous. You can't go out there now. It's dark. My dad already said he'd help me look for it tomorrow."

"No, I need to find it. Where were you on the lake?" he said, trying to move again in the direction of the lake. She pulled him back.

"Jake, you can't look for it now. It's too dark. Besides, I was *way* out on the middle of the lake," Quinn said, gesturing out there. This time the lie came. She thought if she said she'd lost it out there, in the middle of the lake, instead of near the shore where she and her dad had been ice fishing, Jake wouldn't go looking for it. And this seemed to work, because he stopped, wavered, then appeared to reconsider his plan.

"Now listen to me, please," Quinn said. She put her hands on his shoulders and looked into his eyes. She needed him to focus on her. On what she was going to say. He leaned forward as if to kiss her. She put her hands on his jacket front to stop him.

"How was Ely?" she asked.

"That's what you want to talk about?" he asked. He concentrated on tucking a strand of her hair back into her hat. And something about the seriousness with which he did this made her want to cry.

"Yes, that's what I want to talk about."

"It was boring," he said.

"But, I mean, what happened? You drove there to meet with a sports physiologist and then what? Was that it?"

"Questions, questions," he teased. "You really are a journalist, aren't you?" This irritated Quinn. He was trying to distract her.

"Just answer me, okay?" she said. In the silence that followed, she could hear laughter down by the bonfire and a car starting somewhere in the parking lot.

"All right," he said, swaying a little. "I went to Ely and met with the physiologist. He was boring and boring and boring. And now I'm here with you." But he said this last part almost sadly, as he tried to pull her to him again. Quinn stiffened.

"Jake," she said. "You're lying. And you've lied to me before." She felt sick. She looked away from him. She didn't want to see him lie again. Something told her, though, that doing this was cowardly. She looked at him in time to see him try to smile. It didn't come out as a smile; it came out as a grimace. It was weak and watery.

"I didn't lie," he said, turning serious.

"You did. I saw your truck parked outside a house on Scuttle Hole Road. You didn't go to Ely." His face fell, for a moment. Then she could see him thinking, thinking of a way to get out of the corner she'd backed him into.

"I lent my truck to . . . this guy," he said, finally. "We switched. He wanted to see what my truck was like. I took his to Ely."

Quinn shook her head, vigorously. "What guy? And why would you trade trucks with him? I don't believe you. While you were parked at that house, you texted me you were in Ely. You lied to me." She heard her voice catch. "And I want to know why."

"It's not what you think."

"Then what is it?" she asked, relieved that she wasn't, after all, going to cry. He didn't answer her. "Just tell me, why were you there? Were you there with another girl?"

Jake moved closer to her. "Quinn, listen to me. Just . . . listen. There's no other girl. I promise. I don't love anyone else. I love you," he said, his gold eyes coming into focus. He dropped his voice. "I've never loved a girl like I love you."

Quinn was unmoved. She hated that even when she'd confronted him with his lie, he couldn't admit it.

"This isn't the first time you've lied to me, Jake. I can't be with you," she said. "I can't. I'm sorry. This won't work." Suddenly, she was on the verge of crying again.

"Quinn, wait. We'll work it out. I promise." He slid his arms around her, and she let him pull her close. She expected him to plead his case now, but instead, he said, with some of the same urgency he'd kissed her with when she'd first seen him, "Let's get out of here. Me and you. Let's get in my truck and drive. We'll go to California. I've never been there. We could live there. Get a place."

"You mean . . . stay there?"

"*Yes*," he said, tightening his arms around her.

"No. What about college, Jake? And your scholarship?"

He shrugged these away, as if they'd never been important to him. She stared at him, dumbfounded. She couldn't believe what he was saying. It was so out of character for him. He might be *romantic*, but he was not *a romantic*. He was grounded in the here and now. And why shouldn't he be? He already had everything he wanted.

He looked hurt. "Why don't you want to go?" he asked.

"Because you sound crazy, Jake," she said. "We can't leave here. We have to *graduate* from high school." She tried to push him gently away.

"Quinn. Don't go." He tried to hold her, but she didn't want to be held.

"I can't be with you, Jake," she said. "I don't trust you. And I'm not . . . I'm not your girlfriend anymore."

She spun around then and started walking, jogging almost, through the snow, soft and mushy beneath her boots, and under the low-hanging branches of the trees, one of which caught at her hat. She didn't stop. She retraced her steps and passed the table with Jake's friends at it. They called out something to her, but she ignored them. She thought Jake was calling out to her, too, but she tried not to listen. She sped up.

By the time she reached the parking area, she might have been running. She passed people arriving, walking toward the beach, carrying cases of beer and firewood. Some of them called out to her, but she kept moving. She had no idea why she was going this way, toward Gabriel's truck, when he would be down at the bonfire. Except that . . . he wasn't. She saw Gabriel sitting in his truck, engine running and lights on. She didn't know if Jake was following her or not. If he was, he didn't catch her. Miraculously, this one time she was faster than he was.

She reached the truck, yanked the passenger-side door open, and practically threw herself into the front seat. Gabriel, who was listening to music, was startled.

"Quinn," he said.

"Let's go. *Now*. Fast. Please." And Gabriel put the car in drive and took off, out of the parking lot. Quinn didn't look back. "It's over. I broke up with him," she said. She watched the truck's headlights slide over the ghostly white trunks of a stand of birch trees, and she shivered, inexplicably. She wasn't cold. But Gabriel turned up the heat. She nestled against the door and closed her eyes. She didn't want to think about Jake right now. Or the nine months she'd spent with him. She wanted to banish him, and it, from her mind.

CHAPTER 28

Quinn had no idea how long she'd been writing about the night of the accident, but when she finally looked up, the shadows of the bare tree branches had lengthened on the street in front of her. She put her laptop back in her computer bag. *Where am I?* she wondered, looking out the car window now at the tidy little houses. After fleeing Theresa in the IGA parking lot, she'd driven without paying attention to where she was going. She looked more closely at the house she was parked in front of now and then shook her head in disbelief. She was parked on *Webber Street*. Without even realizing it, she'd driven to the safest place in all of Butternut. This was *home*. Or had been once.

She'd parked three houses down from the yellow 1960s split-level house that she'd grown up in. It was the same house her parents had brought her home to after they'd left the hospital with her on an unseasonably warm May morning twenty-eight years ago, the same house she'd lived in with her mom and dad, and then just her dad, almost every day of her life for eighteen years.

She rubbed her eyes and studied the house through the windshield. It was the same. Well, not *exactly* the same. The blue mailbox with brown owls painted on its side had been replaced with an ordinary white one. She'd loved the owl mailbox as a child. Her dad had told her that it was her mom's first purchase for their house, bought at the hardware store on the day they moved in, and that she'd insisted that he pound the post in that night, before they went to bed. Gone, too, was a decorative birdbath, also her mother's idea, on the front lawn. There were a few new additions, too; a red plastic baby swing hung from one of the branches of the beech tree, a satellite dish was bolted to the roof above what had once been Quinn's bedroom window, and the house's trim had changed from white to dark green. Still, to have it look so much the same was comforting to Quinn.

She looked up and down the street. So many familiar houses and landmarks. So much unchanged. She wasn't surprised. Not really. Even in her childhood, this street had been caught in something of a time warp. It had been a place where people left their doors unlocked and had block parties and multifamily yard sales, and where children, in the summertime, gathered at backyard aboveground pools and played flashlight tag after dark. That's what it had been like in the 1990s, Quinn thought. *How lucky I was to have grown up here in this neighborhood, on this street, with my dad.* She missed him. He was the only person she could talk to about what Theresa had said.

She rummaged in her handbag for her cell phone. She found it, pressed *Dad* under her favorites, and listened to it ring.

"Quinny, my love," he answered, cheerfully. "You're back. How was Butternut?"

She didn't answer.

"Quinn?" he asked, concerned.

"Dad," she said, finally, her voice cracking. And the tears that she'd kept at bay while she was writing came now.

"Quinn, what is it?" he asked. "What's going on? Don't . . . don't cry, okay?" he said, quickly. "Please. Just . . . stop. And we'll talk." Quinn couldn't stop. She heard her father take a deep breath on the other end of the line, and when he spoke again, he sounded calm. Gentle. "Don't pay any attention to me. Of course you can cry," he said. "I'll wait. And when you're able to catch your breath, you can tell me what happened. Whatever it is, Quinn, we can fix it, okay?"

She nodded, even though she knew he couldn't see this. And she cried while he waited and, when the tempo of her crying slowed, he asked, "You've got some tissues there with you, don't you? Why don't you find them now. Just a big old handful of them. That ought to do the job." Quinn smiled. When she was a child and she cried, her father had always been out of his comfort zone. But the *rituals* of comforting, these he learned how to do, and do faithfully: bringing her the box of Kleenex; patting her on the back; repeating the sometimes meaningless, but always reassuring words and phrases he trotted out for the occasion. She searched in her handbag again, this time for Kleenex, and came out with a crumpled packet. She extracted a few pieces of tissue and dutifully mopped her face with them. Forced to focus on something other than how she was feeling, she calmed down.

"Quinn, what happened?"

"I saw Theresa, Dominic's mom, at the IGA."

"When was this?"

"I don't know. An hour ago?" she said.

"Wait a minute. You're *still* in Butternut? I thought you were staying for the weekend. Today is Wednesday."

"I know. But remember, I said I'd probably stay longer. And then I saw Gabriel and . . . I couldn't leave."

"Really? What's going on with him? Is he okay?"

"No, he's not," she said, crumpling up the tissue. "I mean, I don't know. He says he is. But he never left, Dad. He stayed here. He's been here all these years."

"And? What's wrong with that?"

"Nothing. He was supposed to study photography, though. Remember how talented he was?"

"I remember. But people change, Quinn. Things change. What's he doing?"

"He's working as a caretaker."

"Ah, well. Those jobs are hard to get. Good for him."

"No, Dad. It's not that. It's that he seems so different. So changed. I feel like there's something wrong. He seems stuck. Unhappy. And things aren't good between us. At first, he was angry at me for falling out of touch with him. Then he said he wasn't angry, he forgave me, but he didn't want to see me anymore," she said, slumping back against the seat. "I miss him," she added. "And I miss him . . . caring about me," she admitted.

"I can't imagine him *not* caring about you, sweetheart." His voice was gentle. Gruff, even. "The Gabriel I knew would have done anything for you. That's why he was my favorite." He was silent for a moment. "Quinn?" he asked then. "What about Theresa, hon? What happened with her?"

"Oh, her," Quinn groaned. She'd forgotten about her for a whole sixty seconds. "Dad, she said something to me. She told me—"

"You know she's got a drinking problem, right?" he interposed. "And I've heard, since the accident, that she's a little unstable, too."

"That's true," she murmured, thinking about the almost maniacal quality of Theresa's accusations. "She told me something, though, that I didn't know. She told me that the night of the accident, after I left the bonfire, Dominic called her from his cell phone and said that Jake was drunk and upset that he'd fought with me. And Theresa thinks it was my fault that Jake got drunk and then drove his truck out on the ice . . . and that's not all, Dad. Theresa said that Dominic told her that Jake had lost a ring, and he wasn't leaving Shell Lake until they found it." Quinn stopped to take a breath. "Dad, don't you see? That was *my* ring Dominic was talking about. And my ring that they drove out on the ice to find."

"Whoa, Quinn. Wait. What you're saying, it makes no sense."

"*It does,*" she insisted. "I never told you this, Dad. I never told *anyone.* But the night of the accident Jake noticed I wasn't wearing my ring. I told him I'd lost it ice fishing on Shell Lake. And he said he'd go look for it, right then. But to stop him, I told him we'd been out in the middle of the lake. If I'd have told him the truth, that we'd been fishing in the shallows, he'd have gone and tried to find it. So I lied to him. I never thought he'd go way out there to find it at night. But"—and here a sob escaped her—"he did go. Later that night. I think that's why he took his truck on the ice."

"My love, why didn't you tell me this ten years ago?"

"Because I tried not to think about it. It was too awful a possibility."

She heard her father take a deep breath. "Quinn," he said. "If you'd told me this before I would have said then what I'm going to say now. I'm sorry. But it's just not possible that a young man as smart as Jake would take his truck, *his truck,* out on the ice in search of a little bitty ring. At midnight. Even a drunk person wouldn't think they could find a ring with a truck. Sorry, love, it makes no sense. That's not why he drove on the ice."

She didn't say anything.

"Are you there, love?"

"Yes," she said, softly, following his logic.

"We'll never know why Jake did what he did," he said gently.

"But, Dad, even if he wasn't looking for the ring, he wasn't thinking straight. And if I hadn't fought with him that night, if I hadn't broken up with him that night, he might not have gotten so drunk. And then I left him there—"

"Quinn, you aren't to blame," he said. "It was an *accident*," he continued, calmly, but forcefully. "There was nothing intentional about anything that happened. You may feel regret or guilt about things you did that night. But you are still not to blame. You did not make it happen. Jake made a bad decision. We've been through this all before. Right?"

Quinn was silent. She had stopped crying. They'd had iterations of this conversation before—minus her recent revelation, of course—both right after the accident, and then later, when she'd withdrawn from college for part of her junior year. Right after the accident, she'd holed herself up in her bedroom and refused to see any of her friends, including Gabriel. After a couple of weeks of this, she'd gone back to school, but she'd still avoided her friends whenever possible. She'd gone to class, come home, and gone back into her room. What she remembered about this time, mostly, was her dad sitting on the end of her bed and explaining that what had happened that night was not her fault. Finally, whether because he'd worn her down, or because to believe she *was* at fault was simply too painful, she'd agreed with him.

"Yes, Dad, we've been through this all before," Quinn said now, a little wearily.

"Good. Now, when are you checking out of the Butternut Motel?"

"Oh. I'm not there anymore. I'm at Loon Bay. I couldn't stay at the motel. It was too depressing. I'm not sure yet when I'm leaving. But I'm okay, Dad. You set me straight." She smiled, tentatively. That was her dad's specialty.

"All right," he said. She knew he was probably against her staying. But she also knew he'd taken the measure of her stubbornness too often to object to it now. "I love you, Quinn. More than anything."

"I love you, too. I'll call you later."

As she slipped her phone back into her bag, Quinn wondered what she would do without her dad. He was a voice of reason, and, of course, of love. She looked over at their old house. The beech tree on the front lawn was as enticing as ever. As a child, she'd spent countless hours in it. It was the perfect climbing tree, with its reachable, horizontal branches. Now, she had to suppress the urge to get out of the car and go climb it again. She chuckled. If the house's current owners saw her up there, they'd think she was a nutcase. No, she'd go back to Loon Bay. There was someone else she needed to talk to.

CHAPTER 29

Later that afternoon, Quinn took the sandy path down to Loon Bay's waterfront. She felt curiously weightless, as if seeing Theresa, talking to her dad, and writing down her memories of that day and night had somehow hollowed her out. She was pressing her luck coming down here, she knew, when she should have been crawling into bed back at her cabin. But she'd gone to get a hot tea at the bar and grill, and her new friend, Gunner, had mentioned, a little too casually, that he'd just seen Tanner go down to the boathouse. *No point in putting this off,* she'd thought, taking her tea to go.

The sun was lowering and now only a few wispy clouds were blowing against a vivid blue sky. The resort's golden beach looked pretty, if a little lonely, when Quinn reached it. In another three months, of course, this stretch of sand would be lively. Every morning, the resort's guests and day visitors would establish a beachhead there and dig in with all their summer provisions. By then, the empty bay—whose dark blue water still looked cold and unforgiving—would be home to a flotilla of Sunfish sailboats, canoes, and kayaks, and the near silence that prevailed now would be replaced by the buzz of powerboats and the shouts of children being pulled behind them on water-skis or inner tubes that skimmed, at dizzying speeds, over the surface of the lake.

Quinn lingered for a moment on the beach and then walked over to the dock, following it out to the boathouse, a two-story gray-shingled building with several boat slips. "Tanner," she called, poking her head into the open door. It was shadowy inside, but she saw him hanging canoe paddles on the far wall.

He turned and smiled. "Quinn," he said. She felt relieved. She'd worried there would be tension between them, or, at the very least, awkwardness, but as he wiped his hands on his jeans and came over to her, she saw that this wasn't the case.

"Gunner told me you were down here," she said, as he gave her a friendly half hug and kiss on the cheek.

"I brought some new paddles down," he said. "It's that time of year. Annika needs to start thinking about gearing up for the season."

"She's lucky she has you to help her do it," Quinn commented.

"I try," he said. "I'm not as good as the handymen she uses, but, then again, I'm free. How are you doing?" he asked, leaning in the doorway.

"I'm doing okay," she said, sipping the tea she was still holding. Tanner looked unconvinced. "Long day," she added, by way of explanation.

"Do you want to talk about it?" he asked.

"Actually, I wanted to talk about the other night."

"Right. Yes. We need to talk about that," he agreed. He took a zip-up hoodie off a peg near the door and pulled it on. "I'm done for now," he said. "I just need to lock up the room upstairs."

"You mean the classroom?" Quinn said.

"Have you been up there before?" Tanner asked. He turned off the boathouse lights and locked the heavy padlock on its door.

"My dad signed me up for Sunfish sailing classes there when I was, I think, nine." The room above the boathouse was where they taught all the skills you could learn on dry land. She remembered her utter lack of aptitude at tying even basic knots. "Now that I think of it," she added, following Tanner up a flight of steps on the side of the boathouse, "I might not have actually made it onto a sailboat."

"They still teach those classes," Tanner said, opening the door. "I think it's more about giving parents free time than it is about teaching the kids to sail," he said, with a quick smile. He let Quinn into the large room and she saw it had hardly changed. One wall had a row of windows facing out over the lake; the other walls were strung with sailing pennants. In one corner of the room, a bookshelf was stuffed with nautical books, and, in the center of the room, a handful of small wooden tables had director's chairs grouped around them.

"Is it the same?" Tanner asked.

"Pretty much," Quinn said, thinking she had liked the room better than the class. Even now, the sunlight filling it turned the wooden walls and floors a warm, honey color and sent play-ful, watery shadows onto the ceiling. From inside the room, you could just barely hear the occasional, rhythmic slap of the water against the dock's pilings.

"Do you want to talk here?" Tanner asked, indicating a couple of the director's chairs.

"Why not?" Quinn said.

They sat down, Quinn still holding her tea. And before she could formulate what to say, Tanner pulled his chair closer and began, "About the other night. I feel bad about it." He quickly amended, "I mean, don't get me wrong, I loved hanging out with you, Quinn, and spending the night with you. Under any other circumstances, I'd want to see you again. But I feel like, I feel like Jake is just sort of hanging in the air between us."

She nodded. She knew what he meant. Quinn believed in ghosts. Not the kind on reality TV ghost-hunting shows. The other kind. The kind you couldn't see, or hear, but that you could feel. They were the ones who were always with you. The way Jake must always be with Tanner. And, in a way, with Quinn, though she'd been slower, perhaps, to understand this than Tanner. Sitting here, across from him, she was afraid she was going to cry again.

"Oh, God," Tanner said, seeing her expression. "I didn't mean to upset you. You're the last person in the world—"

"No," Quinn interrupted, realizing he'd misunderstood her expression. "It's not that, Tanner. I agree with you. That night was *so* fun. But I don't think it should happen again either. And I'm not upset about that, I just had a horrible day."

"What happened?"

"I had a run-in with Theresa Dobbs. In the bread aisle at the IGA, no less." She tried to smile, but she was too tired.

"*Ah*," Tanner said, "Theresa." She was reminded of how Gabriel and her dad had reacted when she'd first mentioned Theresa's name to them. "Was she drunk?" Tanner asked.

"She wasn't sober," Quinn said, not knowing how much to tell him about their confrontation.

"She rarely is," he said. "Except for the dedication ceremony. Someone—Jeffrey, I guess—got her sobered up for that. Honestly, though, sometimes I don't know that I blame her for her drinking. Dom was her only child. And Jake? She *loved* Jake. He was at her house almost every day of his life from the time he was five years old. She used to call him 'my other son.'"

"Did she?" Quinn murmured. Her chest tightened. She'd felt almost repulsed by Theresa that morning, but seeing the compassion in Tanner's expression now, and hearing it in his voice, she felt differently. After the accident, she realized, Theresa had had to bury not one son, but two.

"Yeah," Tanner said. "Ten years out, and she's still a wreck. She's the opposite of my mom, in some ways. Mom's hurting on the inside, but she doesn't want to be a burden to anyone else. Theresa, on the other hand . . ." His voice trailed off. He looked at Quinn closely. "Why? What did she say to you?" he asked.

"Um, do you really want to hear this?" she said, not knowing if she even had the energy to tell him.

"I do want to hear it," Tanner said. "So you're going to need to tell me. Without the benefit of one of those airplane bottles."

Quinn almost laughed. "That's all I need," she said. "Twelve more of those. No, I'll tell you what happened. But I'm going to give you the abbreviated version." Even *this* version, it turned out, was difficult for her to tell. Theresa, after all, had basically blamed Quinn, and her argument with Jake, for the accident. Quinn told Tanner this, but she was careful to leave out Theresa's mention of the ring. She figured Tanner wouldn't know anything about it and she couldn't bring herself to tell him what she'd only just recently told her dad.

"*Jesus,*" he said, when she was done. "That was inexcusable on her part. I hope you know, Quinn, that she's not thinking logically these days."

"Maybe. She's right about Jake and I getting in a fight, though. And we didn't just fight, either. We broke up. *I* broke up with him," she made herself say, never taking her eyes off Tanner.

He looked surprised. "I didn't know that."

"That's because I didn't want to tell your parents," she confessed. "I didn't want to add to their unhappiness." *Not then, and certainly not now.* "But I've often wondered, Tanner, whether I might have . . ."—she struggled with this next word— "*contributed* to the accident. He'd been drinking before I got to the lake, and, I don't know, I'm pretty sure he was drinking after I left it too. But if I hadn't broken up with him then, if I'd stayed with him at the bonfire—"

"Quinn, don't," Tanner said, though his tone was gentle. "Trust me. There's no point in doing what you're about to do. I've done it too. I've replayed that night in my mind a million times."

"You weren't there," Quinn pointed out. "You were, what, over four hundred miles away at college? I'm not sure there's anything you could have done to change things."

He got up and walked over to the row of windows. The late-afternoon sun had lowered, just since they'd started talking, and Quinn, watching him, lifted a hand to shield her eyes.

"I was there," he said, glancing over at her. "Not literally, but . . ." He started to lower the wooden-slatted blinds, easing the intensity of the sun and projecting their shadows onto the wall behind her. "Did Jake ever tell you how competitive we were?" he asked, when he was done, still looking out at the lake.

"Yes," she said. "He told me that the first time I ever talked to him. Well, ever *really* talked to him. I was writing a profile on him for the *Butternut Express*."

Tanner turned from the windows. "That's framed and hanging in his bedroom now," he said. "My mom's read it about a million times."

Quinn was silent. She was thinking, for some reason, of Mrs. Lightman putting on her lipstick in the morning. With great care, the way she must do everything now.

"So you know how it was between me and Jake," Tanner said, coming back and sitting down across from her again. "He was always trying to find a way to one-up me, and vice versa. Mostly it was a game. Sometimes . . . I think, it wasn't." He looked down at his hands and Quinn was struck, once again, by how similar this mannerism was to one of Jake's. *They were so much alike*, she thought, setting her now-empty cup down and tucking her legs up under her in the canvas chair.

"Jake knew that I'd driven out on Shell Lake my senior year," Tanner continued. "It was on April first. I did it on a dare. But it wasn't much of a dare. It had been a cold spring. They were predicting a late ice-out. So even my underdeveloped, risk-seeking teenage brain knew it wasn't that much of a risk. The ice was solid. Afterward, though, I bragged about it to Jake. How I'd done it so late in the season. How it was a record. I mean, how idiotic was that?" He looked up at Quinn for confirmation. She didn't give it to him. An only child, she'd long since stopped judging sibling relationships. "I was such a cocky son of a bitch," he went on. "And Jake had it in his head that he was going to do the same thing in the spring of his senior year. Wait as late in the season as possible and . . ." His voice trailed off.

Quinn shook her head. "What are you saying? That Jake did what he did because he was competing with you?"

"Yeah, I'm pretty sure. He texted me that night."

"When?"

"At 11:58 P.M., to be exact," he said. That was long after she'd left the beach, but not long before Jake drove out on the ice. She looked questioningly at Tanner. She wanted to know what the text had said, but she was afraid to ask.

He looked down at his hands again. "He texted me *I'm driving across Shell Lake tonight! Lightman brothers rule!*"

"Did you text him back?" she asked. It was so quiet in the

room she could hear the whir of a boat engine somewhere out on the lake.

"I was at a party," he said. "Doing shots of tequila. Flirting with some girl. It was noisy. And I remember being, you know, annoyed. Like, why is he texting me now? I read it, I guess, but I didn't give it a lot of thought. But I texted him back *Go for it*. That was it. I put my phone away and didn't give it another thought until the next morning when my dad called." He paused. "I could have stopped him, but instead I encouraged him."

"Oh, Tanner," Quinn murmured. She could barely breathe. "Did he . . . text anything back?"

"No. Nothing. That was it," he said. Tanner's face, though still young looking, was etched with grief. "As far as I know, that was the last time he talked to anyone other than Dom and Griffin. Other people were there, at the bonfire, but they didn't know Jake was going to drive out on the ice until they saw him doing it." Quinn felt the hair on the back of her neck prickle.

"I didn't know he texted you that night," Quinn said, almost in a whisper. "I've never heard anyone mention it before."

"Only a couple of people know about it. My parents, for one. And a few years later, I told someone else. And now you . . ." She tried, now, to imagine what it had been like for Tanner after the accident, but she couldn't. It was almost *un*imaginable. She asked him about it now.

"There were some bad years there," he admitted. "And my parents and I . . . we don't always get along. I'd told them about the text right after the accident. My mom didn't speak to me for months; she basically blamed me for the whole thing. My dad came around, though, and the summer after the accident, my mom finally called me. She broke down and cried. She said I was her only son now. And that I had to be careful. But even now, there's a strain between us.

"Anyway, after that summer, I finished college and moved to Minneapolis. I was working way too hard and probably drinking way too much. And, like I said, I replayed that night a thousand times. If I had been alone, if I had been sober, would I have texted him back: *Don't. It's too risky this time of year.*? Or would I have called him, and heard he was drunk, and talked him out of it? Or would I have asked to talk to Dom or Griff? I don't know. But then again, I can't understand why they decided to go with him. They must have been drunk too. And Dom would have followed Jake off a cliff. Still, I've imagined every possible scenario of how I could have stopped him."

"Could you have, though? Would he have listened to you?" Quinn asked.

"I don't know. He didn't always listen to me. I know because I tried to steer him away from some things in high school and I couldn't. But my mom, she thought I was the one person he would have listened to."

"But she's forgiven you, hasn't she?"

"As much as she can. And, in the meantime, I do what I can to make up for it. I take care of . . . things. The things that would have been important to Jake."

He looked down at his hands again.

"Have you forgiven *yourself*, though?" Quinn asked now,

knowing that this was much harder, in some ways, than forgiving someone else.

"I'm working on it," he said.

"Tanner," Quinn said, with a new urgency. He looked up. "You know it's not your fault, don't you? That there were other things happening that night too? Jake getting drunk, something he never did. Jake and I breaking up." *My telling Jake I'd lost my ring out on the middle of the lake.* "What I mean," she said, "is that there's no way to separate everything out. No way to know what was going through his head."

"Well, Jake had a lot on his mind that night. That much I know. But I share some of the responsibility for what happened."

Quinn nodded, slowly. She wouldn't argue with that. Not when she felt the same way.

Tanner smiled at her then, a sad smile. How a smile could be so sad, she didn't know.

After they'd finished talking, he walked her to her cabin, and they hugged before she went inside. Quinn skipped dinner and went to bed early. And her sleep that night was deep and dreamless. It left nothing in its wake, not even the ripple of a memory.

CHAPTER 30

The next morning, Quinn sat at one of the café tables on the deck outside the resort's bar and grill, drinking coffee and eating a poppy seed muffin. The morning sun was dazzling on the lake, and it was warmer today than it had been since she'd arrived in Butternut a week ago. True, she was the only guest who'd chosen to bring her breakfast outside, and she'd left her coat on, but she nonetheless felt optimistic about the arrival of spring. Gone now were the shrunken piles of old snow in the resort's driveway; gone, too, were the clumps of snow that, a few days ago, had still been visible in the woods. Before long, the earliest of the spring wildflowers—snow trillium, white trout lilies, and bloodroot—would sprout up on the edges of the woods, in thickets, and on the slopes of the lakeshore. And then, a little later, Quinn's favorite wildflower, the yellow lady's slipper, which did indeed look like a lady's slipper, like a puffy, rounded yellow silk shoe with long purple ribbons trailing behind it, would bloom.

She broke off a piece of her muffin and popped it into her mouth. It was delicious, as good as, if not better than, the muffins they sold at the fancy bakery in her neighborhood. It was funny, she hadn't missed her apartment for a couple of days. Evanston seemed very far away right now, she thought, noticing a solitary loon gliding past the dock below. She watched as it traced the shoreline of the swim area. When it reached a rocky outcropping, it ducked under the water and disappeared. Quinn squinted at the sunlit lake, watching for it to resurface.

She finished her muffin and brushed some crumbs off the tabletop and onto her plate. There was that loon, she noted with satisfaction, as it resurfaced on the other side of the dock. It was nice here, watching the water, but there was something she needed to do today.

When she'd woken up this morning, she knew she had to see Gabriel again. She needed to talk to him. *Really* talk to him this time. She'd been afraid, before, to push too hard, go too deep. She'd avoided being personal—she hadn't fully opened up to him, either.

Quinn gathered up her things and headed for the parking lot. Of course, this reticence with Gabriel was not new. Ten years ago, in the aftermath of the accident, she'd shied away from him and from talking to him about what had happened. And the way she'd done this was simple: she'd avoided him. The same way she'd avoided everyone else in those days. Everyone but her father, who wouldn't let himself be avoided.

As Quinn got into her car a few minutes later, she reflected on how narrow and self-focused her perceptions of Gabriel had been since she'd returned to Butternut. Initially, she'd thought that his life was diminished because it wasn't the life she'd imagined for him. *How judgmental,* she thought, as she drove down the resort's driveway. It was as though she, and she alone, could determine whether his life was fulfilling. When, in fact, only he could do that.

It was more than that, though. Her initial impulse with Gabriel was to try to recapture their high school friendship and their easy rapport. But as she navigated her way down twisty Butternut Lake Drive, she understood now that that was never going to happen. That friendship was gone. They were different people now; they'd changed, they'd grown. She should have understood that the moment he'd opened his door to her last Saturday. Instead, she'd kept comparing him to the "old" Gabriel, and she'd kept trying, absurdly, to find *him.* She had refused to look at the person he'd become. She'd had blinders on. And what about her need to understand why Gabriel had never left Butternut, why he'd given up on his high school dreams? Here, she'd treated him as a mystery to solve. But he wasn't a profile she was writing, a knotty story she was trying to untangle for readers. Whatever had kept Gabriel here all these years wasn't for her to uncover but for him to tell, if he chose to.

Something else occurred to her now. Since she'd returned to Butternut she'd fostered a belief that seeing Gabriel was important to understanding her past. As though spending

time with him would help her come to terms with her unre-
solved feelings about the accident. But this initial belief had
been stealthily replaced by something altogether unexpected.
Seeing him, spending time with him, had made her realize how
much she still cared about him. So even though he'd told her
not to come back, she still needed to talk to him. She needed to
apologize to him for not being there for him in the years after
high school. And she wanted to tell him how much she cared
about him. She knew she couldn't make up for lost time now.
But she wanted him to hear her out anyway. Even if it was years
late in coming, some things needed to be heard. And if, after
this, good-bye was what Gabriel wanted, then it needed to be a
proper good-bye, she thought, as she turned into his driveway.

WHEN QUINN PULLED up in front of Gabriel's cabin, his pickup
truck was parked out front. She got out of her car and headed
over to the front door, but she heard something that made
her pause and listen. *Thwack.* The sound was followed by silence, and then, a second later, another *thwack.* It was coming from behind the cabin, where she'd seen the woodshed
several days ago.

"Gabriel?" she called out, walking around the side of the
cabin. She saw him then, standing in the clearing, next to the
tree stump. He was positioning a log, and when he glanced
up at her and shook his head, she could have sworn that he
almost—*almost*—smiled. Then he straightened up and, in
the patch of sunlight he stood in, swung the ax in one fluid,
graceful motion, splitting the log in half.

"I guess I wasn't clear the last time you were here," he said, tossing the logs he'd just split onto the woodpile.

"Clear about . . . ?" Quinn said, stalling.

"About you not needing to come here."

"No, you were clear." She looked for a place to sit down but couldn't find one. "But I'm not here now because I think I 'need' to be," she said. "I'm here because I want to be here. There are some things I want to tell you, before I, you know, say good-bye."

"Shoot," he said, setting up another log to split. "Let's hear what you've got to say, Quinn." He didn't say this unkindly, but she got the distinct impression he wanted her to get it over with as quickly as possible.

"Would it be possible for us to talk without you holding an ax?" she asked, after he'd split the log.

Gabriel flashed her a quick smile as he set the ax down and chucked the logs he'd split over onto the woodpile. His smile transformed his face, for a moment, and she was struck again by how handsome he was.

"Can we, maybe, sit down somewhere?" Quinn asked, when he came over to her, wiping the perspiration off his brow with his flannel-shirted sleeve. He didn't smile again, but he indicated the cabin's back steps. Quinn sat down on one of them but was disappointed when he chose to stand and lean against the step railing instead. She took a deep breath, preparing her words, but for some reason she saw an image of the photographs she'd seen hanging in his bedroom. Would she ever get a closer look at them? *Focus, Quinn.*

"The first thing I want to say is that I'm sorry," she began. "I'm sorry I wasn't there for you our senior year, or after I went away to college."

"Quinn." He shook his head. "I told you the other day, that was my fault too. Our losing touch. When you came over here, that first day, I shouldn't have put all the blame on you. That was wrong of me."

"Well, then I want to apologize for my half of it," she said. "But the truth is, Gabriel, that when I got to college, I missed you. I missed you so much." She kept her voice and her gaze level, trying to control her emotions. "And the few times I *did* talk to you on the phone that fall, afterward, I would cry. Just . . . *cry*. So when you didn't call me back after the last time we talked, a part of me felt relieved. I mean, don't get me wrong, it hurt, Gabriel. But I didn't know what to do with you. With *us*." She paused, caught her breath, and pushed on. "I told myself I had to stay focused. I threw myself into my classes. I had a campus job. *And* I volunteered for an after-school literacy program. I did everything I could to stay busy. It's not like I *wanted* to fall out of touch with you. I *wanted* to hold myself together. The best way to do that, I thought, was to stay in motion. All the time."

"Did it work?" he asked.

"For a while," she said. The wind blew, shaking the branches of the pine trees and moving Gabriel in and out of the shadows. "It worked until it didn't work anymore," she said. She picked at a loose thread on the knee of her blue jeans.

"Quinn?" he said. She looked up. "Keep going," he said, and

for some reason Quinn didn't understand, these words made her heart beat faster.

"I was okay, sort of okay, until I had some kind of a . . . break-down," she said, stumbling a little over this word. "It was the fall of my junior year."

"What happened?" he asked. He held himself still now, as still as he used to ask her to hold herself when they were having one of their photo sessions and he wanted to get the right shot.

"Well, that fall, I was taking five classes," she explained. "Against the advice of my adviser. I was working, volunteering, all of it. And one afternoon, in the library, after I'd pulled an all-nighter, it all caught up with me. I collapsed."

"What do you mean, 'collapsed'?"

"I don't know. I don't remember. I fainted, I guess. Someone helped me back to my dorm room. I got into bed. My room-mate, Isabelle, thought I was sick or something. She and my other friends kept bringing me stuff. You know, food, maga-zines, lecture notes. What have you. They'd never seen me like that before. At first, I think, they were waiting for me to pop back up again, and then, when I didn't, they made me go to the student health center. When they couldn't find anything wrong with me, and I didn't get better, my friends got scared." They weren't alone. Quinn was scared too. The trouble was, she didn't have the energy to do anything about it.

"Did they call your dad?" Gabriel asked.

"Not right away," Quinn said. Some hair had worked its way loose from her ponytail and was blowing in her face. She tucked it back behind her ear. "That took a couple of weeks. By then, I'd stopped going to class. Stopped leaving my room. Stopped leaving my *bed*," she said. Those days were still a blur to her. She'd spent most of her time sleeping. "I was barely eating," she continued. "I think that was the last straw for Isabelle. I'd begged her not to call my dad, so she called the dean instead. *He* called my dad." This memory was painful, painful because she could still remember how afraid her father had been when he'd arrived at school to pick her up and how ashamed she'd been to realize she was the source of his fear.

"What happened?" Gabriel asked.

"I withdrew from school. I went to live with my dad and Johanna in Winona," she said, thinking of those first difficult days at their house. But she was still grateful to Johanna for that time. It was Johanna who'd best understood what Quinn needed. Not what she'd *wanted*—which was to be left alone— but what she'd *needed*. Johanna hadn't addressed what Gene referred to as Quinn's "problem"; she seemed to take it for granted that Quinn would be all right. Instead, she'd insisted, gently but firmly, that Quinn "pitch in" around the house and, before Quinn knew it, she was helping Johanna cut quilt squares, or bake bread, or make apple butter. And Quinn, the least domestic of people, had found first distraction and then comfort in these chores.

"How long did you stay with them?" Gabriel asked.

"About three and a half months," she said. "Just long enough, I suppose, to put myself back together again." She smiled at him, but he didn't smile back.

"Did you get help, Quinn? Professional help?"

She rolled her eyes. "Yes, Gabriel. I got help. I'm not a Neanderthal. Well, that and Dad and Johanna said that was the deal. I needed to see a therapist. So they found me a therapist, Mrs. Wasser, a friend of a friend of theirs, or someone from their church, I forget which." Quinn remembered what she'd looked like, though. She'd favored dangling earrings and floaty skirts and fringed ponchos, and she'd sometimes seemed to Quinn as if she might simply float away. Her office, too, was odd. It was full of shapeless, primitive-looking ceramic sculptures Mrs. Wasser made in her free time. She had been kind, though, at a time when Quinn had needed kindness. "I don't know if she was a *brilliant* therapist," she finished. "I don't think I dealt with *everything*."

"I don't see how you could have, in three and a half months," he pointed out.

"Maybe not," she agreed, wrapping her arms around her calves and pulling her knees up under her chin. "Just talking to her, though, was good. Just telling her, you know, how sad I felt about Jake's death." She rested her chin on her knee. "How much I cared about him." She frowned, remembering something. "But I realized in talking to her that my feelings for Jake might have been more of an infatuation, a physical attraction that at that age may have felt like love, but maybe . . . wasn't love. I was only seventeen," she said. Quinn looked at Gabriel as she said this, but his expression gave nothing away. "And, let's see, what else did Mrs. Wasser and I talk about . . . We talked about the fact that I felt guilty that I'd fought with Jake that night, that I'd broken up with him, and that I'd left the bonfire without him." *That I'd left the bonfire with you.*

But even as she told Gabriel these things, about her "break-down," about her talks with Mrs. Wasser, there were, even after all these years, things that happened the night of the accident she still wasn't ready to talk about. She'd *never* told Gabriel that she'd lost her ring the day of the accident. And she'd never told him about how she'd fought at the bonfire with Jake about why his truck had been parked outside the house on Scuttle Hole Road. And, of course, she'd never told Gabriel what she finally revealed to her dad yesterday, that she'd lied to Jake about having lost her ring out on the middle of the lake.

"Did you talk to your therapist about me?" Gabriel asked, breaking into her thoughts.

"Yes," she said, surprised by his directness. "I did. I talked to her about how you were my best friend. About how much you meant to me. And how you were a part of the guilt I felt about leaving Jake that night." She resisted the urge to look away from him now as she said this next thing. If it was hard for her, she figured, so much the better. "I talked about us, and about how much I loved being with you that night, after the bonfire. But that it couldn't work. Not after Jake died."

Gabriel shook his head when she said this, and Quinn, her face heated, hurried on. "Gabriel, you *have* to understand, if I hadn't left the bonfire with you that night, they'd all still be alive."

"And if you'd stayed at the bonfire, Quinn, you might have been in that truck too. Did you ever think of that?" he asked, with a flash of anger that was as pure and as fleeting as lightning, gone almost before she could register it.

"No," she said, her voice rising. "That would never, *ever* have happened, Gabriel. I would never have driven out on the lake with Jake. And I wouldn't have let Jake get in that truck either. Not when he was that drunk."

"So, after you stayed with your dad and Johanna for three and a half months, you went back to Northwestern, didn't you?" Gabriel asked. Quinn couldn't help but feel he was steering the conversation onto safer ground.

She nodded, feeling somewhat deflated. "That next semester, spring semester, I went back. I took a light course load, including ceramics, if you can believe it." This had been Mrs. Wasser's suggestion, and it got an almost smile from Gabriel. He knew that Quinn, who loved art, had no talent for it herself. "I stopped working and volunteering. I just tried to, you know, take care of myself." It was then that she'd started running—so out of shape, at first, that she had trouble jogging a mile. By the end of the semester, though, she was running in 5K races.

"Did you keep seeing someone? A therapist, I mean."

"I did. I talked to Mrs. Wasser on the phone for a while. But at some point, I decided I just needed to move on." A gust of wind blew, flapping the edges of the canvas tarp that was covering one of the woodpiles.

Gabriel's gray-blue eyes looked dark in the bright morning light. "And did you?"

"I tried to. But recently, I started having trouble again." She told him then about the aftermath of the accident she'd

witnessed this past winter and how she'd worried it was trigger-
ing the beginnings of another breakdown.

"I'm sorry, Quinn," Gabriel said, quietly, when she'd finished.
And his voice had real warmth in it.

"That's the reason I came back here."

"What do you mean?"

"If I could fall apart after seeing an accident on the highway,
then I obviously hadn't dealt with Jake's death. And I thought if
I came back here, I'd be forced to deal with it."

"Yeah, I can see that," Gabriel said. He kicked at a tree root
and she noticed the dried mud flaking off his work boots.

"All right, I've talked about myself enough," she said. "Now
it's your turn." When he didn't respond right away, she said,
"Come on, Gabriel. Talk to me. What's going on with you?"

"Nothing's going on, Quinn. Nothing I want to talk about,"
he said, zipping up his jacket. "I'm glad you talked, though." He
looked over at her. "And I'm sorry about your breakdown. I wish
I'd known about it at the time."

"That's okay," she said, but she couldn't hide her disappointment. Gabriel was willing to listen, nothing more. Still,
she wasn't done yet. "There's one more thing I have to say," she
told him.

"What's that?"

"I care about you," she said, simply. The words caught in her
throat. *No. No crying now. Get this out first.* "I love you," she
said, steadying her voice. "I want you to know that. I've never
stopped caring about you. And I don't know why you never left
Butternut, or why you seem like you might be unhappy, but if it's

somehow my fault, even a little bit, I'm sorry." Her eyes burned with tears, but she tried to smile at him.

"Quinn," he said, and for a moment, he looked stricken. "Thank you," he said. "Thank you for saying that."

Quinn wiped at the corner of her eye. She stood up and dusted off her blue jeans.

"Come on," he said then. "I'll walk you to your car." And Quinn came down the two steps on the porch and they walked together to the front of the cabin. He stopped beside her car. Quinn came up close to him, close enough to feel the almost gravitational pull he exerted on her. He reached for her then and hugged her for what seemed like a long time. Quinn hugged him back. She savored the feel of his hands, firm on her back, and the softness of his flannel shirt against her cheek.

"Is this good-bye?" she said.

"I think so."

CHAPTER 31

Quinn picked up the glass animal, a caramel-colored doe with tiny white spots on it, and turned it over in her fingers. She'd owned one almost exactly like this when she was a child. She put it back on the mirrored shelf, with the rest of the glass animals on display, and looked around Butternut Drugs. Why, exactly, had she come here? She wasn't sure. But after she'd left Gabriel's cabin, this was the place she'd wanted to be. And she'd thought, *Why not?* It wasn't as if she was in a hurry; she'd decided she would leave Butternut tomorrow morning. Now she had the whole rest of the day to fill.

The drive into town had been interminable. She'd cried, silently, the whole way, letting the tears drip down her cheeks. She picked up another glass animal now, this one a blue jay, and then gently put it back down. There was a little dust on her fingertip, and she blew it off and wandered over to another display, this one a selection of North Woods–themed shot glasses. She wanted to be with Gabriel. *How* exactly she wanted to be with him, she wasn't sure. But the knowledge that he didn't want to be with her brought with it a fresh wave of pain. She picked up a shot glass with a loon on it, thinking that she might give it to her dad and Johanna, who, for some reason, collected shot glasses, but when she went to the register to pay for it the man behind the counter was giving directions to an older couple.

"You know how I'd get there?" he was saying to them. "I'd take Scuttle Hole Road. It's not well traveled, but it's fast. Mostly, it's just locals who use it. You go down Main Street, take a right, and . . ." Quinn didn't hear the rest. She returned the shot glass to its shelf and headed for the door. She'd thought all she had left to do before tomorrow morning was to pack, tell Annika she was checking out, and say good-bye to Tanner. But it turned out there was one more thing she needed to do. She was going to the house on Scuttle Hole Road, the house where Jake was parked on the day of the accident. If possible, she was going to find out why he'd been there that day. And if she couldn't find that out, she'd at least find out whose house it had been then.

QUINN SAT IN her car, parked on the shoulder of Scuttle Hole Road, and looked out at the house's desolate front yard. She was nervous. This place looked even worse than she'd remembered it looking ten years ago. Then it had been a small gray ranch house with peeling paint, a junk-strewn yard, and a mailbox with the name *McGrath* painted on it. And although those features were still evident, at this distance she also noticed the grayish bedsheets tacked up in the front windows in place of curtains, and, in the side yard, a disemboweled washing machine that someone had left open, as if they'd recently tried to put a load of laundry in it. *Why didn't I come here after the accident?* she asked herself. But, in truth, the thought had never even occurred to her. Somehow the reason for Jake being here that day had become unimportant after his death. And besides, in the aftermath of the accident, Jake's and Dom's and Griffin's deaths made the lie Jake had told her seem almost trivial. How could it possibly compete with what had happened next? No, all she could think about back then was keeping herself pulled together long enough to graduate from high school and leave Butternut.

She got out of the car now and started up the front walk, careful to step over some broken glass. When she pressed the doorbell, she heard it ring inside the house, barely audible over the blare of a television set. But someone heard it. A moment later, a corner of one of the bedsheets in the window moved, and then the front door swung open. A woman whose age Quinn couldn't determine—forty? forty-five?—stood in front of her. She was thin and dressed in a dirty sweatshirt and blue jeans. Her long blond hair was lank, her blue eyes bloodshot, and her eyelids were heavily lined with black liner. She had the complexion of someone who'd spent too many days in the sun, and too many nights drinking. Still, there was a kind of ruined beauty about her, and an odd familiarity, too, that Quinn found so disorienting she wasn't even aware of the woman's hostility until she spoke.

"What do you want?" she asked Quinn, and then she stuck her head out of the house and looked around, as though Quinn might have brought company with her. "If you're here to sell me something or talk about God, I'm not interested," she added, closing the door a few inches.

"No, wait," Quinn said quickly. "I'm not here to do either of those things. I know this is going to sound a little strange," she said—and she smiled, hoping to put this woman at ease, but she only looked blankly at Quinn. "Do you know who lived here ten years ago?"

"Yeah. I lived here," the woman said. "I've been here for eleven years now. Why?" She sounded defensive, suspicious even.

"I'm from Butternut," Quinn explained, backtracking. "I went to Northern Superior High School and—" But the woman's implacable hostility stopped her midsentence. "Did you know Jake Lightman?" Quinn blurted out.

"Who?"

"Jake Lightman."

"I don't know anyone by that name," the woman said. "And, like I said, I'm busy." She gestured back into the house, where Quinn could hear *Judge Judy* on TV. The woman closed the door a few more inches, but then paused and watched, eyes narrowed, as a car came around the bend and drove past the house. "Huh," she said, as if something about this car or its driver confirmed a suspicion she'd already had. She looked back at Quinn now and started a little.

"What do you want again?" she asked Quinn now, with slightly more interest, and slightly less unfriendliness than before.

"I'm sorry. I won't take up much more of your time," Quinn said. "My name is Quinn LaPointe and ten years ago, on March twenty-third, my boyfriend, Jake Lightman, came here and I was wondering why."

The woman tilted her head. "What? Hell if I know why. Ten years ago? March? I can't remember two weeks ago. A lot of people came and went back then," she added, searching in her back pocket for something.

"But Jake would have been in high school, his last year. You don't remember him?" Quinn persisted.

"I told you, I don't know who that is," the woman said. She extracted a crumpled pack of Pall Malls from her back pocket and jiggled the contents, pulling out one slightly bent-looking cigarette. "Maybe he was a friend of my sister," she conceded. "She stayed here sometimes then. Before she moved." She put the cigarette between her lips but didn't light it.

"Your sister?" Quinn repeated. But even as she said this it dawned on Quinn who her sister was. *Of course. That's why she looks so familiar.*

"Annika Bergstrom. She's my sister," the woman said, leaning on the doorframe. "She lived here with me for a while once. Maybe it was around ten years ago. Now she lives at Loon Bay. I think. I don't know. We don't talk much. Are we done here?" she asked, the unlit cigarette still between her lips.

But before Quinn could say anything, the woman slammed the door shut. Quinn heard her retreating footsteps, and the television set being turned up louder. She backed away, then, trying to make sense of what she'd just learned.

So, that was Hedda, the sister whom Annika had mentioned a couple of nights ago. Had Jake been here to see Annika? Had he been cheating on her with Annika? No, she couldn't picture this. He'd never even mentioned her before. Or had he, for some reason, been here to see Hedda, and she couldn't remember him? Or was Jake here to see someone else, one of the people who "came and went back then"? Quinn went down the front steps and almost tripped on some debris as she crossed the ragged yard to her car. She had to talk to Annika. She might shed some light on this.

CHAPTER 32

One day. Two sisters. Three houses, Quinn thought, as she walked from the parking lot at Loon Bay to Annika and Jesse's cabin. She paused on their front steps. Theirs was a larger version of the guest cabins scattered around the resort, but it boasted some individual touches that set it apart. It had, for instance, window boxes that Quinn imagined would soon be planted with geraniums, and a brass pinecone door knocker that someone kept polished, and floral-print curtains hanging in the windows. *This is a home,* everything about it seemed to say. As opposed to a house. And, picturing Hedda's house, still so fresh in her memory, Quinn knew that whoever had taught Annika how to make a house a home, it hadn't been her sister.

She used the pinecone door knocker, and, almost before she'd let go of it, Annika opened the door.

"Quinn," she said, her blue eyes widening.

"I need to speak to you," Quinn said, dispensing with formalities. And, if Annika had begun to let her guard down the last time she and Quinn were together at the bar, it went right back up now.

"It's not about your cabin, is it?" she asked.

"No," Quinn said.

Annika hesitated, making some internal calculation Quinn wasn't privy to. "Okay," she said. "Why don't you come in. Jesse's home sick so . . ."

"Do you need me to come back?" Quinn asked. She'd assumed Jesse would be in school.

"No, he's fine. Just a sore throat. He's in his room. We can talk in the kitchen." She gestured Quinn inside and, closing the door behind them, led her through the living room and dining room and into the kitchen. The interior of the cabin, like the interior of the guest cabins—which Quinn now knew Annika must have had a hand in decorating—was devoid of clutter, or cuteness or decorative objects. Instead, like its smaller counterparts, it had a utilitarian feel that nonetheless managed to be both appealing and comfortable.

"Why don't you wait here," Annika said, gesturing at the kitchen table. "I'll be right back. I want to check on Jesse." Quinn sat down and looked out the window. The view from here, of the resort's basketball court, was unremarkable.

"Sorry about that," Annika said, reappearing. "Jesse's good on apple juice. What about you?" she asked. "Can I get you anything? Coffee?" Her hand hovered over a coffeepot on the counter.

"No, thank you," Quinn said.

Annika seemed at a loss. "Well, I think I'll have some," she said, bustling about. Annika was nervous, Quinn realized, with surprise. And, what was more, she was stalling. "Okay, let's see," she said, bringing a mug of coffee over to the table. "What else? Oh, I forgot." She left and came back again with an egg timer, which she wound up and set down on the table between them. "For Jesse," she explained. "For playing his video games. He gets half an hour. If I set this, he can't argue with me."

Annika pulled out a chair and sat down across from her, and Quinn was struck by the resemblance between her and her sister. Indeed, Hedda was Annika's doppelgänger, she realized. Her *ruined* doppelgänger, but her doppelgänger nonetheless. If you could subtract years from Hedda's age, and a lifetime of hard living—of *living hard*—from her, you would arrive back at Annika. Annika with her blond hair pulled back in a ponytail, her unblemished skin devoid of makeup, and her clothes, though casual, effortlessly neat and, somehow, *ironed* looking. Did Annika, with everything else she had to do, take the trouble to iron the button-down shirts she seemed to favor? Quinn wondered. She had a feeling that she did. Right after she polished the brass door knocker.

The egg timer sounded loud in the silent room. But now it was Quinn's turn to stall as she searched for the right words. "Look, I'm sorry," she said, finally. "I don't know how to ask you this, so I'm just going to do it as directly as possible. I should tell you, first, that I came here from your sister Hedda's house, in Winton. I went there to ask her why Jake was at her house the day he died. I know he was there," she added. "I saw his truck parked outside that afternoon."

Whatever Annika had thought she might say, it was obviously not this, and she pushed her chair back a few inches, its feet scraping against the linoleum floor, as if to get farther away from Quinn.

"I need to get something," Annika said, standing up. "I'll be right back." Quinn stared after her, bewildered, and, for some reason, an image of Annika came floating back to her. It was of her stopping to talk to Tanner at the dedication. Odd that she should think of that now. But then Annika returned to the kitchen and set something—a little twist of tissue paper—down on the table. Was that for Quinn? She had no idea. She felt a flicker of annoyance, though, as Annika sat down across from her again. Whatever had sent her out of the room was a mystery. But, for the first time since she'd opened the door, Annika had regained her customary composure.

"Annika," Quinn said, ignoring the tissue paper on the table. "Do you know why Jake was at your sister's house that day? Hedda was no help."

"She never is," Annika said. When Quinn didn't respond to this, though, Annika folded her hands, pale and smooth, and placed them on the table in front of her. She looked down at them before she spoke. "He was seeing me. I asked him to meet me there after school," she said, softly. "I was pregnant with Jesse." She looked up at Quinn now, as though these words would explain everything, but she must have seen from Quinn's expression that they didn't.

"Jake was the father," she added. "I was four months pregnant, and I needed to tell him."

At first, Quinn was only aware of the ticking of the egg timer.
It sounded, now, obscenely loud. Annika's voice, on the other
hand, as she continued to talk, sounded as if it were coming
from far away. Either that or it was muffled, a cottony whisper
spoken through layers of fabric. Or maybe snow.

"Jake was the father?" Quinn asked, when Annika stopped
talking. She rephrased it. "Jake is Jesse's father?" Annika nodded. And for the second time since she'd sat down at this table
a recent memory came back to Quinn. In this one, Annika
was standing on the sidewalk outside of Pearl's, two days after
Quinn had gotten to Butternut, and she was telling Quinn that
Jesse would be ten in August. Her mind was working unusually
slowly. Sluggishly. But, yes. It added up. Jake's death. Jesse's
age. It was possible. And, for some reason, knowing this was
like putting her finger on a jigsaw puzzle piece and moving it
into place.

"I was right," she said, almost to herself. "Jake *was* cheating
on me. He denied it, that night at the bonfire, but that's what
the lying was about . . ." It hurt now, she realized. A decade after
it had happened, the knowledge of his lying and cheating still
hurt. But not like it once might have. It wasn't a sharp pain, but
a dull, amorphous ache, a slow spilling, spreading through her.

"But, Quinn? Jake was cheating on me, too."

"What do you mean?" Quinn asked, startled.

"I started seeing Jake a year before you did. We were still
together the summer he started seeing you."

"*What?*" Quinn asked, incredulous. She was almost indignant. She remembered that summer now. The things she and Jake had done together—swimming in the lake at sunset after he'd picked her up from the newspaper, lying on a blanket in a meadow on a stolen Sunday afternoon, pretending to watch a movie in his family's rec room—but also the way Jake had made her feel while they were doing them. He'd made her feel like she was the only girl in the world. Boy, had she been wrong.

And despite feeling disoriented, Quinn's curiosity got the better of her. "When . . . I mean *how*, did you start seeing him?" she asked now, wanting but at the same time not wanting to know.

"I went to school with him and Tanner my whole life. But I never paid attention to Jake. He was two years younger than me. The summer after I graduated from high school, things changed," she said, tracing the rim of the coffee cup with her finger. "One afternoon, I was driving on one of the county roads, and I passed Jake. He'd been running but he'd gotten a cramp and he was walking home. I stopped, and I offered him a ride. He didn't want to go back to his house, though. It was a beautiful day. He said he wanted to go to Butternut Lake. I said . . . okay. I could drop him off there. On the way, we talked. He asked me out. I said no, he was too young for me. But he asked me again . . ."

Quinn nodded. Jake's powers of persuasion, or seduction, were not at issue here. That didn't mean Quinn wanted to *hear* about them, though, and, to her relief, Annika said no more about that day. But she kept talking. She *needed* to talk. Quinn could see that. In fact, it was as though Quinn had opened the floodgates. And whether she wanted to hear everything Annika had to say or not, she was going to listen to it anyway. *You need to know this*, she told herself. *You've wanted to know for years why Jake lied to you. Now you're finding out.*

"No one knew about us," Annika continued. She went on to tell Quinn that her and Jake's relationship had unfolded, almost entirely, in secret. There was no question of Annika's father finding out about them. As long as his daughters were living under "his" roof, they were not allowed to have boyfriends. Once, Annika told Quinn, when Britta was still living at home, her boyfriend made the mistake of dropping her off at their house—not in front of it, but down the road from it—and her dad had seen him and had run after his car with a rifle. He'd managed to get a few shots off before Britta's boyfriend sped away.

So the first summer that Annika and Jake started going out, they met at Hedda's house on Scuttle Hole Road, or if no one was home, at Jake's house. Sometimes, they'd go to Ely to a movie or a restaurant, but they didn't do that very often, and finally they didn't do it at all. When summer ended, things got even harder. Annika got a job, working the night shift at a hospital cafeteria in Duluth. Jake went back to high school, and to the cross-country team, which he was captaining as a junior. They still tried, when they could, to see each other, but it was never enough. For Annika, at least. And she suspected, too, that there were other girls Jake saw, other girls before Quinn. Annika had a faraway expression on her face as she talked. She seemed almost unaware of Quinn's presence. And the pain that Quinn had felt earlier subsided, a little, in the shadow of Annika's story.

"If you thought he was cheating, why didn't you break up with him?" Quinn asked, remembering how Jake had been dating a girl named Ashlyn in the fall of their junior year. But she felt a surprising protectiveness for Annika now, almost as if she were forgetting her own connection to all this.

"I couldn't break up with him," Annika said, lifting her shoulders, as though, even after all these years, she was still defenseless in the face of Jake's unfaithfulness. "I fought with him about it. About him cheating. And I tried to end it with him. I did. But I couldn't let go. I loved him." Her cheeks pinkened now with some memory of that love. "I know it must be hard for someone like you to understand," she said. "Someone from a normal family. When I met Jake, though, I thought I was . . . *nothing*. He told me I was beautiful. And smart. He made me feel good about myself. He told me he loved me. No one had ever said that to me before. Not even my mom. Not even when I was little. I mean, not that I could remember." She looked away, struggling to control the feelings this memory brought with it.

How could Jake have been so duplicitous? Quinn thought now. He'd been willing to have a relationship with two women at the same time. Wooing them both, making them both feel special, and desired, and loved. And yet he'd been lying to them both about his feelings. Or he hadn't—an even stranger possibility. Of course, it was hardly unusual; infidelity was the oldest crime in the relationship book. But Quinn, not knowing she was being deceived at the time, had been spared the pain that came with that knowledge. Annika, on the other hand, had not. And Quinn's initial feelings of hurt and indignation underwent a kind of reversal. Annika had suffered from the same transgressions as she had. The surprise was that Quinn herself was one of the unwitting agents of this. Faced with this now, she felt an unexpected empathy for Annika.

It was quiet in the kitchen again, but for the ticking of the egg timer, until Annika, in a fit of pique, snatched it up off the table and turned it off. "I need more coffee," she said, getting up. "I think I'll switch to decaf, though."

"Decaf sounds good," Quinn said. And sitting at the breakfast table, watching Annika make a new pot of coffee, she realized she had more questions to ask. "So . . . the whole time I was with Jake, he was with you, too?"

"No, not the whole time. He broke up with me in mid-December," Annika said, sitting back down at the table. Yes, it made sense, Quinn thought. Those last three months with Jake, she hadn't sensed he was lying to her. Not in the way she had in the early months of their relationship.

"Is that when you found out about me? In December?" Quinn asked.

Annika shook her head. "No, I knew about you from the beginning. Since I started working at Pearl's the summer you started seeing him. I was standing in the window one afternoon, when business was slow, and I saw you two drive by in his pickup. I recognized you," Annika added. "From high

school and from Pearl's, too. You used to come in there with
your friend who had the camera. I asked Jake about you and
he said you were friends. I wanted to believe him. And part
of me did, but part of me didn't. When he broke up with me
in December, he told me he was in love with you. He admitted
he'd been seeing you since July. I knew then that he'd been
lying all along," Annika said. She paused for a moment and
looked at Quinn before continuing. "He told me he was giving
you a promise ring. He showed it to me the day he broke up
with me. He told me he was giving you the ring that night."

"He showed you the ring?" Quinn was stunned. "Why would
he do that?" she asked.

"So I would believe him, I guess," Annika said.

"But wait a minute. When did you find out you were pregnant?" Quinn asked.

"About two weeks after he broke up with me. At first, I pre-
tended it wasn't happening . . . Oh, God, I was so scared about
my dad finding out. When I was three and a half months pregnant, though, Hedda said I could move in with her. About a
week later, I started to show." Quinn closed her eyes, for a moment. It was hard to think about.

Annika got up now to pour two cups of coffee and brought
one over to Quinn.

"What did Jake do when you told him?" Quinn asked.

"He was so upset," Annika said. "He was pacing up and
down my sister's kitchen. He kept saying he was in love with
you. He said he'd already planned everything out. He was going to go to the University of Wisconsin, and then he was going

to marry you. He didn't really say all that to me. He was more thinking out loud." Her cheeks flushed with something. Anger, maybe. "And I said, 'Well, I can't do this alone, Jake. It's your baby too. And you're going to have to help me.' Finally, I think, it sank in. He stopped pacing. He got quiet. He sat down and he put his head in his hands. I thought he was going to cry. But he didn't. He was like that for a long time. Then he said you'd break up with him. He said everything was over. His *life* was over. Then he got up and said he was going to get drunk. Then he left. I never saw him again."

"Oh my God," Quinn said, staring at Annika.

"Yeah. It was pretty terrible. But Caroline helped me through it," Annika said with a wistful smile. The first smile Quinn had seen since they sat down. "She was the only person then who knew about me and Jake. Even now, not that many people know. It's not a secret. Jesse knows his dad's name. He knows he drowned. But I haven't told him how. I should, probably. He's getting older. I should tell him before someone else does . . ." She trailed off.

"Tanner knows all this, doesn't he?" Quinn said, wondering at how much he'd withheld from her.

"Yes, I told him the summer before Jesse was born. He helped me too. A lot. He helps *us* a lot," Annika said. Quinn looked, reflexively, out the window at the basketball court. She'd watched Tanner and Jesse shoot baskets there. And remembering her own misguided night with Tanner, Quinn hoped, no, prayed, that Annika and Tanner had only ever had a platonic relationship. The possibility of her and Annika sharing not one, but two brothers filled her with dread. But she didn't have the courage to ask Annika this now. Instead, another question came to her.

"Annika, you weren't going to tell me any of this, were you?" Quinn asked now. "I mean, if I hadn't come here today, I'd have gone home without ever knowing about you and Jake and Jesse." And Quinn couldn't help but feel stung by the realization that if she hadn't stumbled upon Hedda she might never have known any of this.

"I wanted to tell you," she said, looking abashed. "I really did. That's why I sent you the clipping about the dedication. I was hoping you would come."

"*You* sent that?" Quinn shook her head. "So . . . you wanted me to come, but when I did, you avoided me," she said, remembering running into a reluctant Annika outside of Pearl's.

"I know. Weird. Right? But as soon as I saw you, first at the dedication and then in front of Pearl's, I couldn't tell you. I was scared. I didn't know how you would react. Each time I thought about telling you, I just couldn't do it." Quinn was silent.

"There's something I want to give you," Annika said now. She seemed nervous. She untwisted the piece of tissue paper in front of her and took something small and gold out of it. Quinn leaned closer and instinctively held out her hand. Annika placed it in her palm. It was the ring with the aquamarine stone. It felt cool, and light, almost insubstantial. She stared at it. And all this time she'd thought it was on the bottom of Shell Lake.

"Where did you find it?" Quinn murmured, looking up at Annika.

"The day of the accident, you dropped it in Pearl's. When you paid for hot chocolate. I saw it fall to the floor, and after you left I picked it up. Once I saw what it was, I should have given it back to you. But I didn't want to. I was angry at you. Later, after Jake died, I just put it away. I was a mess. I felt like the accident was my fault. I know that Jake got drunk because I told him I was pregnant. Then, when Jesse was born, I had to stop thinking about it. I thought about sending it to you. But I couldn't. And then I thought that if you came back here, I'd tell you about Jake and then I'd give it to you. But I didn't have the guts. I was afraid you'd get angry . . . And I liked you," she added, with some of her old reserve. "I didn't know that I would."

"I'm not angry," Quinn said, closing her hand over the ring. And it was true. She felt many things, but anger at Annika was not one of them.

"Mom?" Jesse said, as he pushed open the kitchen door. Quinn and Annika both looked at him at the same time. "I need more apple juice," he said.

Annika got up, and Quinn took in his pajamas, his messy hair, and his sleepy eyes. He was a cute kid, she thought. More Annika than Jake. He smiled at Quinn. And that was the first time she saw it. If he'd smiled at her sooner, she might have known he was Jake's son.

CHAPTER 33

Quinn slipped her tattered cashmere sweater off the hanger, folded it, and placed it on top of her already full suitcase. *There.* She was packed. All she needed to do was take one last look around the cabin for those things that seemed to delight in being left behind: the forlorn sock under the bed, or the lipstick tube that had rolled under the sink. She opened the top bathroom sink drawer and glanced inside it. It was empty, but for an extra bar of the lavender-scented hotel soap. And the smell of it, oddly enough, reminded her of a trip she'd once taken with her dad.

By the time Quinn was seven, her maternal and paternal grandparents had all died. But before that, right after she'd turned six, her dad had taken her to visit his mother, Estelle LaPointe, in Green Bay, Wisconsin, where he'd grown up. For the two nights they stayed there, Quinn slept in her father's childhood bedroom.

She'd been disappointed it no longer looked like a "boy's" room, but instead had been turned into a "guest room," a new concept for Quinn. Still, as a consolation prize, she found a few Happy Hollisters mysteries in its bookshelf that had once belonged to her dad.

Almost all her memories had to do with her grandmother's house. There'd been a glass paperweight with a butterfly inside it on Estelle's coffee table, white lace doilies on the arms of the armchairs, a lamp with a shepherd girl statue attached to it in the dark master bedroom, and the smell of lavender, always lavender, in the front hallway. Estelle was almost eighty by then, and to a little Quinn she seemed *ancient*. She'd spent most of her time in a big armchair in the living room with a TV tray next to her, watching game shows or listening to a ball game on an old-fashioned transistor radio, nibbling on shortbread cookies. During the day, her dad took Quinn around the city to show her the sights. At night, they sat at the white Formica-topped table in the kitchen and had dinner with Estelle. After her grandmother said grace, these meals were largely silent, and Quinn, swinging her feet beneath the table as she balanced peas on her fork, kept looking back and forth from her dad to her grandmother. Why didn't they *say* anything to each other? she'd wondered.

When Quinn and her dad were on the train back to Minneapolis—the train ride had been Gene's idea of an adventure for Quinn—she'd asked him if he would miss his "old home." And he'd explained to her that *home* wasn't always a house, or even necessarily the place you'd grown up. "Home is the place you *choose*," he told her. "The place you want to be. It's where love grows." A home, he said, could be anywhere. It could be in the middle of the wilderness or in the heart of a big city, or even on Webber Street in Butternut. He'd kissed her on the forehead then. "Right now, Quinn," he'd said, "home for me is wherever you are." She'd spent the rest of the train ride eating the shortbread cookies her grandmother had packed for her and looking out the window at the towns and the backyards and the cornfields speeding by.

Quinn turned off the light in the bathroom and went to look out one of the cabin's windows. It was a gray day. A fretful day. Where was home for her? She wasn't sure she knew anymore. One week in Butternut and her whole center of gravity had shifted. She loved this town, and this lake, with all her heart, but it was no longer home. There was Evanston, the place she'd lived for the last ten years. But she no longer felt the pull of that, either. Of course, she had an apartment there. And a bicycle and clothes and books and houseplants and friends. Friends she could meet for coffee or a drink or, like Katrina, for a run, or, like Annie, to hear an indie band play. So, yes, she had friends. Good friends. But not *great* friends. Not *close* friends. In the six years since she'd graduated from college, she hadn't made any of those kinds of friends, nor had she had any lasting romantic relationships. She'd liked men, dated them, and even, in a few instances, graduated beyond the "dinner and a movie" to a weekend trip (or a Thanksgiving dinner with her dad and Johanna), but on the emotional level, she'd tried to keep her relationships uncomplicated. Mostly what she'd done since college, she realized, was to work hard at her writing. She'd had a routine there, a schedule, an orderly life. But Evanston? It wasn't home, not in the deepest sense of the word.

Quinn noticed now, from the window, the resort's swing set. It was right beyond the basketball court and a couple of its slatted swings were stirring in the wind. Annika had made her home here, at Loon Bay, she thought. And despite all the difficulties of her life in Winton, she'd chosen to settle—for now—only ten miles away from there, on Butternut Lake. She hadn't had to run far to find a life. *A home.* After all, she'd had Jesse here with her. And Quinn remembered that yesterday, after Jesse had gone back to his video game, Annika had apologized for taking the ring. Quinn, feeling so many disparate emotions, not only about the ring but everything else, too, had said nothing. She'd hugged Annika instead.

After she'd left their cabin, Quinn had stopped by Tanner's. She didn't stay long; she didn't have the energy to. But she wanted him to know that Annika had told her about Jake and Jesse. She scolded him, then, for not telling her sooner. Tanner had apologized. He'd felt that, on this point, he'd needed to defer to Annika, and she hadn't been ready to tell Quinn yet. Quinn had asked him about his parents then. She assumed that they knew Jake was Jesse's dad, and she was hurt that they hadn't told her either. Had they, like Tanner, been willing to let her leave Butternut without knowing the truth? "Quinn, my mom didn't think any good would ever come of telling you," Tanner had said. "They thought it would only upset you. And truthfully, my mom has never fully accepted Annika, anyway." He'd explained to her that when Annika first came to his parents, after Jesse was born, his mom didn't believe that Jake was Jesse's dad. And when Tanner had interceded, and his mom finally *did* believe it, she'd blamed Annika for the accident, and for making Jake behave irrationally that night. It had taken months for her to come around, months for her to apologize to Annika. Eventually, his parents had worked out an arrangement where Jesse came over to their house one Sunday a month. They'd also set up a savings account for him, and a college account. But they weren't close to Annika.

Tanner, on the other hand, was. He'd done everything he could, short of moving here, to support both her and Jesse. He talked to them each by phone a couple of times a week, came up once a month, sometimes more, and spent his holidays and long weekends here. It was being with Jesse, not being at Loon Bay, that made him feel close to Jake.

And Quinn told him something she'd wanted to tell him at the boathouse the day before. She told him about the lie she'd told Jake that night, about the ring being lost out on the lake. She wanted Tanner to know, for his own sake, that the accident was probably caused by a convergence of many things, instead of any one thing. He'd acknowledged this might be true, but it didn't change his conviction that he bore some responsibility for the accident. All he could do now, he said, was to make sure that he watched out for Jesse and Annika. Quinn had one final question for him as she was leaving his cabin. Had he and Annika ever been romantically involved? He'd shaken his head. "No, never," he'd said. "We've never been more than friends."

Quinn left the window now and went to zip up her suitcase, but before she could finish even this simple task, someone knocked on the cabin's door. Annika, Tanner, or housekeeping, she decided, going to open it. Gabriel was not on her list. But it was Gabriel who was standing on the other side of it now.

"Hey," she said, not bothering to hide her amazement. This time, he had come to her, she thought. He looked strange, though. No, *not* strange, different. Even in this chilly weather, he was wearing only a white T-shirt and blue jeans, and, maybe it was the day's gray light, or maybe it was Quinn's ruminations on the concept of *home*, but it seemed to her that his skin had a pale nobility to it, the bluish circles under his eyes an undeniable romanticism.

"Can I come in?" he asked, looking over her shoulder into the cabin.

"Of course," she said, stepping aside. She felt suddenly, irrationally, happy. Gabriel walked past her and looked briefly at Quinn's half-zipped suitcase, sitting on the bed.

"You're leaving?" he asked, turning to her.

"I am," she said. "But I don't know where I'm going," she added, surprising herself.

"You're not going back to Evanston?"

"Eventually, I'll have to. I have an apartment there. I'm not sure I'll stay, though. I don't know if it's the right place for me anymore." She caught sight of herself in the mirror above the dresser and looked quickly away. She looked different too. Her eyes were shining, and her cheeks were flushed. "Maybe I'll travel," she said. "It's been years since I've taken a real vacation. Maybe I'll take a road trip."

"A road trip?" Gabriel repeated. He tilted his head a little and smiled at her. *Why is he here?* Quinn wondered, happiness spilling through her.

"Come with me," she said, impulsively. Gabriel looked surprised. He shook his head.

"Why not?"

"Quinn, there's something I need to tell you," he said. He walked over to the sitting area and chose one of the red leather armchairs. "It's about the accident."

"Okay," she said and sat down in the armchair opposite his. She assumed by *the accident* he meant *the night of* the accident, as opposed to the accident itself. But the question he asked her next surprised her.

"Do you remember the teachers' basketball game at the high school that night?"

"Of course. I didn't go to it, though."

"I know. But I did. For the first hour. Jake was there, you know that, right?" She nodded. "He and Dominic and Griffin were sitting in front of me in the bleachers. They'd been drinking, obviously, and they were being loud. And obnoxious. Just yelling things that weren't funny, but that were borderline mean. Anyway, it bothered me. I can't explain it. I wouldn't have cared if . . ." *If Jake hadn't been my boyfriend,* Quinn thought. "Anyway," he said, "I was watching the game and wondering where you were and then, just like that, you texted me. You asked me if I'd give you a ride to the bonfire."

"You texted me right back," Quinn said. "I remember because I was upset that night. It made me feel better, I think, to know I was going to see you."

"I felt the same way," Gabriel said, "though maybe with a little more . . . *intensity* than you did. I was all about the intensity in those days. But I'm getting off track. I left the game after that. Once I realized you weren't coming, I didn't see any point in staying." He paused and rubbed his eyes. "I went out to the parking lot," he continued. "I'd driven my dad's truck, and it was parked in back. When I got to it, I saw Jake had parked his truck right behind it."

He stopped and looked up at the ceiling, as though he'd find some kind of guidance up there.

"Go on," Quinn said.

He cut his gray-blue eyes back to her. "I don't know what I was thinking. No, wait, that's not true. I *do*. I was thinking if I drove you to the bonfire and Jake never made it there, I'd get to hang out with you that night."

Quinn cocked her head. "I don't understand."

"I siphoned the gas out of his tank, Quinn. Right there in the parking lot. I had the tube and a gas can in my dad's truck. I'd used them earlier in the day." He ran his fingers through his hair. "It was one of those stupid ideas you have when you're seventeen. I was full of them in those days. They'd just pop into my head. I mean, I didn't always *act* on them. This time, though, I did. My plan wasn't very well formed, but I thought if I siphoned the gas out of his truck, he'd get out of the game and he'd be stuck. He'd get a ride to a gas station eventually, or get someone to bring him a can of gas, or whatever, but by then, it'd be late. Maybe he wouldn't even come out to the bonfire."

"Wait," she said. "You did that in the parking lot? With all those people around?"

"No, that's just it. There weren't any people around. And I'm fast at stuff like that. You know that."

"Jake didn't say anything to me about running out of gas," she said.

"Because he didn't. Not then. That's the killer, Quinn. *Literally*, the killer. I didn't have time to get all the gas out. A bunch of people came out of the game early. They were getting close, and I didn't want them to see me, so I stopped."

"So . . . it was a stupid prank," Quinn said. "Why didn't you tell me about it back then?"

"Quinn," Gabriel said, leaning forward, a sense of urgency animating him. "You're not getting it. I left Jake just enough gas to get to the bonfire and drive out to the middle of the lake." Quinn wrapped her arms, instinctively, around her. "That's why he stopped on the middle of the lake. He was out of gas. Otherwise, he would have kept driving to the boat launch on the other side. That's what everyone does when they drive across. That's what his brother did. No one stops in the middle of the lake. Not in late March."

"*Stop.*" Quinn held up her hand. "Gabriel, just . . . stop. *You don't know that.* You don't know that's why he stopped. For all you know, he still had a little gas in his tank."

"No, he didn't," he said. He rubbed his eyes again, as if to clear them, and in the light from the window, he looked tired, *so tired.* He kept going. "When they finally towed the truck out of the lake, the police inspected it. My dad knows their guy. Their mechanic. And he told my dad that, as far as he could tell, there was nothing wrong with the truck. Nothing that might have made it break down. But the gas tank was empty." Gabriel leaned back in the armchair, and watching her, he opened his hands, palms up, in a gesture that suggested he'd given her everything. Everything he had. And now he was empty. He was waiting for her to say something, she thought, waiting for her to confirm everything he'd said.

"But, the truck was underwater. Maybe the gas leaked out of the tank. And that's why the tank was empty."

"No, Quinn. The mechanic said the tank was sealed and there were no leaks. I don't know, maybe he was wrong. But that's what he told my dad."

"Gabriel," she said, choosing her words carefully, "for that night, there are so many variables to consider. Maybe, maybe when Jake drove out on the lake, he was running on fumes. Or maybe it was still enough to get him to the other side, and he stopped for another reason. Or maybe, even if they *hadn't* stopped, they would *still* have gone through the ice." She looked hard at Gabriel, hoping, through sheer force of will, to impress all this upon him. He looked skeptical, as if he'd already gone through each of these arguments in his own defense, summarily discarding every one of them. "Besides," she said. "There were other things happening that night, Gabriel, that you couldn't have known about. Things like . . ." She stopped. "Jake's life was . . . *complicated*," she said, searching for a better word and settling on this one. "And whatever you did, when you siphoned off his gas, you did *not* put him on that lake. Only Jake did that. You have to understand that," she said, emphatically. She couldn't let him go on thinking he was solely responsible for this tragedy.

"What do you mean, 'other things'?" Gabriel asked, his eyes narrowing.

"I mean . . ." And Quinn told Gabriel everything she now knew about that night. Absolutely everything.

Gabriel listened in silence. He looked surprised to hear about Tanner's text and troubled to hear about Quinn's lost ring. But he nodded, a little, when she told him about Jake being Jesse's dad, as though he had suspected as much himself.

"You didn't kill them, Gabriel," Quinn said, when she was done. "And, if you did, then I could say the same thing about myself. So could Annika. Or Tanner. So many things converged that night . . . don't you see? There was alcohol, and sibling rivalry, and mistakes, and pranks, and a theft, and texts, and lies and secrets . . . In the end, though, it was Jake. He made a fatal decision." She got up and came over to him, sitting on the arm of his chair. Except for their hellos and good-byes, it was the closest she'd been to him yet. She took his hands in hers. She held them tightly, and an emotion she couldn't quite read passed over his face.

"Have you ever talked to anyone else about siphoning the gas?" she asked him.

He shook his head. "Only you," he said.

"Gabriel, you cannot carry this whole thing on your shoulders anymore. *It was a prank.* I *know* you; you don't have a malicious bone in your body. And your siphoning gas had nothing to do with Jake's decision to drive on the lake. Nothing."

"I don't know, Quinn. It's terrible to think you might have caused an accident that killed three people."

"I know. I've felt guilty too. For ten years. We all have. Maybe we always will. But feeling guilty doesn't mean you *are* guilty. No one committed a crime. No one did anything, intentionally, to harm Jake, or Dominic, or Griffin. We've all felt remorse. But we, *you*, still have to move on. You have to live your life." Her voice was soft. She was still holding his hands in hers.

He gently pulled his hands away. She let hers drop back into her lap.

"I'm glad we talked about this," he said, sinking back into his chair. And maybe she imagined it, but he looked lighter, younger even.

"So am I," Quinn said. *I only wish we'd talked about it sooner.* But this was not the time for *more* regret. "Will you come with me? I don't want to leave here without you," she said.

"Quinn," he said, with a slight smile, and then he shook his head. "I can't think straight right now. I haven't slept much lately. I can't make a rational decision."

"Sleep first, then, and think later," she said. "But stay here." She didn't want him to leave. Not after what he'd just told her. She got up from the arm of his chair and moved her suitcase off the bed. "Here," she said, patting the bed. "You can sleep here."

And when he looked doubtful, she went over to him and took him by the arm and brought him over to the bed. "You are too tired to drive. You'll have to sleep here. After you sleep, we'll talk."

"But what will you do?" Gabriel asked, standing next to the bed, and looking for all the world like the only thing he wanted to do was lie down on it.

"I have some writing to do," Quinn said.

CHAPTER 34

March 24, Senior Year,
Gabriel's House, After the Bonfire

After Quinn's fight with Jake at the bonfire, Gabriel drove her back to Butternut. He was careful to avoid the subject of Jake. He talked to Quinn, instead, about a road trip he wanted to take that summer. He'd spent his whole life east of the Mississippi River, he explained. After graduation, he wanted to go west. As in *far* west. All the way to the Pacific Ocean. And he was full of ideas about the best routes to take, the best places to camp, the best landscapes to photograph. And Quinn, unused to this prolific, one-sided conversational style from Gabriel, was nonetheless grateful. It required only that she listen, which was all she felt capable of doing. *Don't think about Jake*, she told herself. *Not right now.* Tomorrow, she would think about him. About them. And how what they'd had together was over.

As they approached Butternut's lone traffic light, Gabriel slowed. "Do you want to come over? We can watch a movie," he asked.

"Aiden and Brody are probably playing hockey with the remote," Quinn pointed out.

"Nope. I liberated the DVD player. It's in my room now. It was the only way to keep Colin from watching *Any Given Sunday* again. I mean, even I was starting to memorize the dialogue."

"Isn't it mostly grunts?" she asked, but the light had changed and Gabriel was still idling there. She checked her watch. Her dad wouldn't be home until morning when he got off the night shift. "You know what?" she said. "A movie sounds good."

When they got to his house, it was surprisingly, no, *shockingly* quiet. His parents, he said, were visiting family in southern Minnesota, Brody and Colin were "in the wind," and Aiden was in his room, trying to write rap music, which, according to Gabriel, who'd heard some of his finished product, was a complete waste of time. He mixed them drinks from his parents' liquor cabinet and raided his family's junk food stash for some popcorn. Then they'd retreated to his bedroom, where Gabriel locked his door (this was second nature to him), set their drinks down, and turned on the bedside table lamp. As he riffled through his extensive DVD collection, Quinn glanced around his room. She hadn't been here since he'd been accepted to RISD back in December. She remembered that afternoon, and the photographs he'd shown her from his college portfolio. How beautiful they'd been, she thought. They were like visualized memories, moments between the two of them that were now frozen in time. She looked around for the portfolio. There was no sign of it. She wondered what he had done with it.

"How about this?" Gabriel asked, holding up *Butch Cassidy and the Sundance Kid*. Quinn nodded. She'd never seen it before but she knew enough about it to know there were chase scenes, gunfight scenes, jumping-off-cliff scenes— enough action scenes, in short, to distract her from thinking. *From feeling.*

"Why don't you take the bed?" Gabriel said, sliding the DVD into the player. "I'll take the floor."

"Gabriel, there's more than enough room for both of us," Quinn pointed out, of his queen-sized bed. She pulled off her boots and sat down, sliding over to make room for him. He came and sat beside her.

"Are you cold?" he asked, handing her a drink.

"A little."

"I'll get you something," he said, leaving the room. He came back and tossed her the macramé throw from the living room couch, which his mother had woven in purple and gold, Minnesota Vikings colors. "You know, you really should take up macramé," he said.

"I think I will," she said, settling it over her. "I think it's what's been missing in my life." She offered him some of the blanket and he slid under it with her.

"What is this, by the way?" she asked of the drinks he'd mixed for them.

"Um, I tried to make a mai tai. But I didn't have all the ingredients. I think it might be more mai than tai."

"Or more tai than mai?"

"Could be." He smiled. The light from the bedside table lamp lit up his slightly messy light brown hair. His bedroom windowpanes rattled in the wind, and, as Quinn snuggled under the throw, a ragged little sigh escaped her.

Gabriel looked over at her. "You're going to love this," he said as the movie started. And she did. For the next couple of hours, she watched with rapt attention.

"That was perfect," Quinn said, draining the last of her syrupy-sweet cocktail from its plastic cup as the credits rolled. "It definitely belongs in our top ten."

"Ten? I was going to say top *three*," Gabriel objected.

"Okay, three," she said, handing him her empty cup.

"You know," Quinn said, turning onto her side and facing him. He was lying on his back, looking up at the ceiling. "I think we should take that road trip together. We can drive through the Bighorn Mountains," she said, of the area where Butch Cassidy and the Sundance Kid had their hideout.

"Definitely. But, just so you know, the movie wasn't filmed in Wyoming." He told her then about the filming of the movie and about some of the theories of what had happened to the real Butch and Sundance. It was unlikely, he said, that they'd gone down in "a blaze of glory" as they had in the movie. At the very least, he pointed out, the director's note at the beginning of the movie— ". . . most of what follows is true"—was a creative interpretation of the word *most*.

Quinn listened to him, surprisingly happy. And maybe it was the movie, or the cocktail, or Gabriel's voice, but she felt relaxed. She hadn't been alone with Gabriel like this, in his room, to watch a movie or hang out and talk, for a long time. She'd forgotten how much she loved being alone with him.

"What's that sound?" she asked now, raising herself up on one elbow and listening.

"That's Aiden. Trying to rap," he said, of the "music" coming from the room next door.

"Gabriel, *that's awful*," Quinn said. "He's not serious, is he?"

"Uh, if by serious you mean he thinks he's going to get a recording contract, then yes."

Quinn started laughing, and Gabriel did too. But then, watching him, she turned suddenly serious. She reached out and touched his face, without even thinking about it. He was still for a moment, so still, and then he leaned over and kissed her. Softly at first. And the kiss was more of a revelation than a kiss. As though it suddenly revealed to her something that she'd kept hidden from herself. He put his arms around her then and pulled her gently to him. And she slid her hands under his T-shirt and felt his smooth, warm back. The kiss deepened. *Our lips fit together perfectly*, she thought. *As though we are supposed to be kissing. As though we are supposed to be together.*

They woke the next morning to someone pounding on Gabriel's bedroom door.

"Gabriel, wake up! *Open the door!*" Aiden shouted. They'd been asleep in each other's arms, but now Gabriel scrambled out of the bed and pulled on a pair of blue jeans. Quinn sat up, the covers slipping off her. She shivered in the early-morning chill. Gabriel brought Quinn her clothes, which were draped over the desk chair, where he'd put them last night. As she started getting dressed, Gabriel called out to Aiden, "I'll be there in a minute." Aiden pounded again.

"*Aiden, calm down,*" Gabriel called, as he pulled on his shirt. "I'm coming."

He opened his closet door and motioned for Quinn to stand behind it, so Aiden wouldn't see her. Then he smiled at her and, holding her face, kissed her on the forehead. "He's probably looking for the Froot Loops," he said, as he went to open the door.

QUINN SET HER computer down on the end table beside her. She wasn't satisfied with what she'd written. She'd need to work on it some more. She'd stopped writing before she'd gotten to the part where Gabriel had opened the door and Aiden had told him that Jake and Dominic and Griffin had drowned in Shell Lake. *Before* she'd gotten to the part where she jumped out Gabriel's window and ran all the way back to her house on Webber Street. *Before* her life had changed forever. *Before* whatever it was she and Gabriel had begun, had embarked on, was cut short.

Still, she had one thing to show for writing this scene. Self-knowledge. She understood now, sitting here in the cabin at

Loon Bay, that the night she'd spent with Gabriel had become tangled up in her mind with Jake's death. At the time, she could not untie the two. There had been no way forward with Gabriel. It was as though there'd been some invisible causation at work, as though the intimacy between her and Gabriel had mysteriously compelled Jake and his friends to get into that truck and drive out onto the ice. Yes. This was what she'd feared in the days and weeks after the accident. Was it irrational? Superstitious? Magical thinking? Perhaps. But, in the face of tragedy, the mind had its own way of explaining the inexplicable. Unfortunately, she'd never talked to Gabriel about any of this. Unconsciously, she'd ruled out the possibility of a romantic relationship between them the moment she'd heard that Jake had died. But then, instead of talking to Gabriel about the accident and about their night together and giving the two of them a chance to heal, she'd shut down and shut him out. And then she'd left Butternut. And during that time, and the time since then, Gabriel had been wrestling, alone, with his own guilt—a guilt that in many ways must have eclipsed her own.

Quinn looked at her watch now. It was almost noon. Her suitcase was on the floor. Gabriel, lying on his back, one arm thrown over his head, was on the bed. She got up and tiptoed over to him. His face, in sleep, with the guardedness and reserve fallen away, was beautiful. She studied him. She could do this all day, she thought, and never get tired of it. But she didn't want him to wake up with her staring down at him, so she moved away, back to the armchair she'd been sitting in. She leaned over and closed her laptop, still on the end table.

"Quinn?"

She looked over at Gabriel. He was half sitting, propped up on his elbows behind him.

"How long did I sleep for?"

"A little over an hour," she said.

He sat up and put his feet on the floor. "I don't think I could have driven home," he admitted. "I was so tired. Have I delayed your departure?" he asked, gesturing at her suitcase.

Quinn came and sat down, gingerly, on the bed beside him. "No. I told you, I want you to come with me."

"What makes you think I can just pack up and leave?" he asked.

"Because you *can*," she said. "You're renting your cabin on a month-by-month lease. And the caretaking business? That won't heat up until closer to Memorial Day. I was going to leave this morning, but I can leave tomorrow. That will give you time to do whatever you need to do." He stood up and stretched, then looked at her quizzically.

"Gabriel, you haven't left this area in ten years. The open road is calling." She smiled. "It's time to go. Time to move. Time to mend," she added. And she felt something like exhilaration saying these words.

He smiled and leaned against the cabin wall. "First you come to Butternut and never seem to leave, and now you're leaving but you're insisting that I go with you."

"Well, why not?" she said. "What have you got to lose? Ten years ago, we were planning a road trip. Remember? The Grand Canyon, the Badlands, the Bighorn Mountains, the Mojave

Desert, Monument Valley Tribal Park, Yellowstone . . . One week, Gabriel. I'm asking you for one week."

He laughed. "That's a lot to see in one week," he said, before turning serious. "I don't know."

"It's not about knowing," she said. Her heart was beating hard. He leaned toward her, fractionally, and even this subtle movement filled her with happiness. "It's about living."

"Let me think about it, Quinn," he said, as he walked to the door. "Can I call you in the morning?" He turned to look at her, his hand on the doorknob.

She nodded. She was afraid that if he walked out that door, she'd never see him again. But she couldn't stop him. She'd asked him to come with her; the rest was up to him.

CHAPTER 35

The sky was a deep cloudless blue, and the morning sun was shining on the water, on the stately pines, and on the granite dedication stone that only a week ago had been unveiled here in a clearing on the shore of Shell Lake. It was only in the low sixties outside, but the day felt balmy to Quinn. And she noticed, now, at the base of one of the nearby birch trees a patch of snowdrops, their little white flowers bowed in the sun. At last, it was April.

As Quinn reached out and touched one of the smooth gray lake stones that someone had placed on top of the dedication stone, she saw Annika and Tanner approaching through the trees. She'd asked them earlier that morning, after putting her suitcase in her car, to meet her here. She'd wanted to say goodbye to both of them, but also to Jake. And it had struck her that a small informal gathering here might be the best way to do that.

"Hey, Quinn," Tanner said, coming up to her and giving her a hug. "This was a good idea."

Annika, standing beside him, smiled. "I'm glad you thought of it," she said to Quinn. She unbuttoned her jacket and loosened her scarf. "I know you said that we could each say something, if we wanted to. I've written something down, if that's okay," she added, looking from Quinn to Tanner.

"That'd be great," Tanner said. And the three of them, as if on cue, arranged themselves in front of the dedication stone.

"I'm not usually good at things like this," Annika said, a little self-consciously. "You know, making speeches." She hesitated, and then she took a folded slip of paper out of her pocket and opened it, squinting at it in the bright sunlight. "Jake, I wish you could be here," she began, not looking up. "I wish you could meet Jesse. You'd love him. You'd be proud of him. I know you would. He's . . ." Her voice caught here. "He's a really good kid. Smart, like you. And athletic, too. He plays pee-wee basketball, and he's the best one on his team. And that's not just me being his mom." She looked up, quickly, at Tanner, and he nodded his encouragement. "And, um, what else?" She studied the paper again. "I miss you," she said. She reached up and caught a tear, at the corner of one eye, with her fingers. "And I forgive you." There was silence, and Quinn thought she was done, but then Annika glanced at Quinn and smiled, a shy smile, before glancing away again. "By the way, Jake, I finally met Quinn. I like her. And I gave her back her ring." She folded up the piece of paper and slipped it back into her pocket.

"That was beautiful, Annika," Tanner said.

"It really was," Quinn agreed. "Tanner, why don't you go next," she suggested.

He placed his hand on the dedication stone. "Hey, buddy," he said, after a moment. "I think about you all the time. The other night, I was having a beer and looking out over the lake, and I thought, 'Jake should be here for this. He'd appreciate it.' Needless to say, you being gone has left a big hole in my life." He paused and seemed to collect himself. "I'm sorry, Jake, that I didn't stop you that night. I wasn't there for you when you needed me. But I'm watching out for Annika and Jesse. And for Mom and Dad. And I love you. I love you, little brother. Okay, that's it," he said, and he took his hand off the stone and looked at Quinn.

Quinn was already crying. She'd started when Annika had said she wished Jake could meet Jesse, and she had cried all the way through Tanner's simple but heartfelt words. She took a deep breath, though, to steady herself, before she began to say the words she'd thought of over a solitary coffee that morning. "Jake, I'm so sorry about what happened to you, and of course to Dominic and Griffin, too. I've missed you, for many years, and I've struggled with my role in all of this. It's taken me a long time to come to terms with. But now, I want to remember you. And I want to remember you the way you were that summer afternoon when I interviewed you in the bleachers. You were serious, and thoughtful, and interesting. And you were interested, too. You asked me about me, and my mom and my dad. You talked about loving—and hating—to run. You talked about Tanner. You were your best self then, I think. That's the Jake I'll remember. I love and I miss you. Good-bye."

Tanner, who was standing between Quinn and Annika, put his arms around them now. They were silent for a moment. A breeze off the lake stirred the pine boughs.

"Do you still want to do this, Quinn?" Tanner asked.

"Yes, I do," she said. She and Annika, both crying quietly, watched as Tanner took the spade she'd asked him to bring and dug a small hole in front of the dedication stone.

"Is that good?" he asked Quinn, when it was about four inches deep.

"That's perfect," she said, taking the ring out of her pocket. She knelt and placed it carefully in the dirt. She stepped back and Tanner filled the hole and tamped it down carefully.

"You know someone might find that one day," he said gently, standing up.

"I know," Quinn said. "I don't mind. It'll be here for a while, anyway."

"You need to get going. Don't you?" Tanner asked. He was tapping dirt off the spade.

"I do. I have a long drive ahead today," Quinn said.

There were hugs and good-byes now. And Quinn left Annika and Tanner talking in the clearing.

WHEN SHE APPROACHED the parking lot, she saw Gabriel leaning against the side of her car.

"How'd it go?" he asked.

"You were right," she said. "It *was* a good idea." After leaving Quinn's cabin yesterday, Gabriel had come here to pay his respects. This morning when he called her to say he was coming with her, he'd suggested she might want to go back to Shell Lake too.

"How are Annika and Tanner?"

"They're okay," Quinn said, thinking of their beautiful words. "We're going to stay in touch. Here, you drive first." She tossed him the car keys.

He caught them and opened the passenger-side door for her. As she got in, she noticed once again Gabriel's Nikon camera, sitting on the backseat next to his duffel bag. She smiled.

Gabriel got in, started the car, and rolled down the windows. Once they were on Butternut Lake Drive, the air was sweet and the sunlight dappled on the road. *Good-bye, Butternut,* Quinn thought. *Loveliest place on earth.*

"So where are we going?" Gabriel asked, when they stopped at the traffic light in town.

"West. We're heading west," Quinn said. As the light changed to green, he took her hand.

Insights,
Interviews
& More . . .

Meet Mary McNear

Amelia Kennedy

MARY MCNEAR, *New York Times* and *USA Today* bestselling author of the Butternut Lake series, writes in a local doughnut shop, where she sips Diet Pepsi, observes the hubbub of neighborhood life, and tries to resist the constant temptation of freshly made doughnuts. Mary bases her novels on a lifetime of summers spent in a small town on a lake in the northern Midwest. ᴄᴠ

Discussion Questions

1. In chapter 6, Quinn makes a distinction between feeling guilty about the accident and feeling responsible for it. Do you agree with this distinction? And is it possible to be both responsible for *and* guilty about something you have or have not done?

2. In the beginning and at the end of the book, Quinn contemplates the meaning of *home.* In the beginning of the book she describes Butternut as her home, the place she was born and grew up. Her dad says that home is the place where love is. Does she find a "home" at the end of the novel? What does *home* mean to you?

3. Quinn has three dreams in the novel. They all take place on Shell Lake. The first two are primarily about Quinn's guilt. But the last dream, the one where Gabriel pulls the ring out of the lake, is different. Why? What do you think it means?

4. Do you think that the burden of guilt Gabriel carries with him is greater than his actions warranted? Quinn thinks that guilt is often proportional to one's own moral compass. Is this the case with Gabriel? If so, what does it tell you about Gabriel? ▶

Discussion Questions *(continued)*

5. Quinn returns to Butternut and the scene of the accident in order to "confront" her past. She believes that if she does this she won't have another breakdown. What do you think caused her first breakdown in college?

6. The book depicts two mothers who have lost children: Maggie Lightman and Theresa Dobbs. They've both handled tragedy very differently. Of course, there are as many different ways to handle tragedy as there are different kinds of people. Do you empathize with both women? How have you handled tragedies in your life?

7. Tanner sends a three-word text to Jake that he can never get out of his head or take back. Have you ever sent a simple, maybe even an innocuous, text to someone that you have regretted?

8. Why do you think Jake drove his truck out on Shell Lake that night? Do you think there was one reason, or several?

9. Do you think Annika bears any responsibility for the accident? Why? Or why not?

10. Why do you think Annika and Jake kept their relationship a secret? Annika didn't want her crazy father to know. But why didn't Jake tell his parents and his friends?

11. After Annika's revelation, Quinn wonders if it is possible to romantically love two people at the same time. What do you think? And is it possible to really love someone you are cheating on?

12. Quinn's mother died before Quinn can even remember her. How do you think her mother's absence affected Quinn's development and character? ∽

The World of Butternut Lake

Welcome to the world of Butternut Lake . . . and to the unforgettable people who call it home.

Butternut Lake, a fictional lake in northern Minnesota, is based on the many childhood summers I spent on a beautiful lake in the Midwest. I saw Butternut as a setting where I could explore real-world issues of love and loss, family ties and friendships, tragedy and comedy. It is a place where my characters can wrestle with the ghosts of the past and step forward— sometimes boldly—into the future. All six of the Butternut Lake novels focus on different characters: a young widow coming to terms with her husband's death in Afghanistan; a lovely café owner whose long-gone charming ex-husband returns to town; a home health aide on the run from her past; two very different sisters, one with a long-buried secret; a single mother and Butternut's main librarian grappling with a decision she made as a teenager; and a young reporter struggling with the guilt and loss over her boyfriend's tragic death. All of these characters find both themselves and love on the shores of Butternut Lake.

It's summer, and after ten years away, Allie Beckett has returned to her family's cabin beside tranquil Butternut Lake, where as a teenager she spent so many carefree days. She's promised her five-year-old son, Wyatt, they will be happy there. She's promised herself this is a place where she can start over after her husband's death in Afghanistan. The cabin holds so many wonderful memories, but from the moment she crosses its threshold Allie is seized with doubts. Has she done the right thing in uprooting her little boy from the only home he's ever known?

Allie and her son are embraced by the townsfolk, and her reunions with old friends are joyous. And then there are newcomers like Walker Ford, who mostly keeps to himself—until he takes a shine to Allie . . . ▸

The World of Butternut Lake *(continued)*

BUTTERNUT SUMMER

Every summer on Butternut Lake the tourists arrive, the shops open, and the waves lap its tree-lined shores. But this summer Caroline Keegan's life is turned upside down the moment Jack, her ex-husband, strides through the door of her coffee shop. He seems so changed—stronger, steadier, and determined to make amends with Caroline and their daughter, Daisy. But is he really any different, or is he the same irresistibly charming but irresponsible man he was when he left Butternut Lake eighteen years ago? For Caroline's daughter, Daisy, the summer is filled with surprises. Home from college, she's reunited with the father she adores—but hardly knows— and swept away by her first true love. But Will isn't what her mother wants for her—all she can see is that he's the kind of sexy "bad boy" Daisy should stay away from. And when Daisy discovers Will's secret, she wonders if her mother might be right . . .

Mila Jones has fled the big city seeking a safe haven on the serene shores of Butternut Lake. She's taken a position as a home health aide looking after Reid Ford, a handsome but embittered man who is recovering from a terrible car accident. Reid doesn't want to be looked after and he does everything he can to make Mila quit. But Mila has secrets of her own; she needs this job and she's determined to make it work. Against all odds, Mila slowly draws Reid out. Soon they form a tentative, yet increasingly deep, bond with each other. But the world has a way of intruding, even in such a serene place, especially when Mila's past catches up with her. ▶

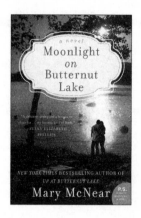

The World of Butternut Lake *(continued)*

THE SPACE BETWEEN SISTERS

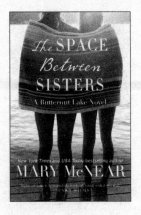

They are two sisters who couldn't be more different. Win, a schoolteacher, is organized and responsible and plans her life with care. Poppy, who is once again out of a job, is impulsive and undependable and leaves others to pick up the pieces. But despite their differences, they share memories of the idyllic childhood summers they spent together on the shores of Butternut Lake. Now, thirteen years later, Win, recovering from a personal tragedy, has taken refuge on Butternut Lake, where she's settled into a tranquil routine—until Poppy unexpectedly shows up on her sister's doorstep with her suitcases, an aging cat named Sasquatch, and a mysterious man in tow. Although Win loves her beautiful sister, she wasn't expecting her to move in for the summer. At first, they relive the joys of Butternut Lake. But their blissful nostalgia soon gives way to conflict, and painful memories and buried secrets threaten to tear the sisters apart.

For the lovely Billy Harper, Butternut Lake is the place she feels most at home, even though lately she feels the only one listening to her is Murphy, her faithful Labrador retriever. Her teenage son, Luke, has gone from precious to precocious practically overnight. Her friends are wrapped up in their own lives, and Luke's father, Wesley, disappeared before his son was even born. No wonder she prefers to spend time with a good book, especially Jane Austen's books, where everything ends in perfection. But Billy, the town's librarian, is about to learn that anything is possible during the heady days of summer. Coming to terms with her past, the death of her father, the arrival of Cal Cooper— a complicated man with a definite interest in Billy—and even the return of Wesley will force her to have a little bit of faith in herself and others . . . and realize that happiness doesn't always mean perfection. ᗡ